The Secret of Breathing Deeply

by

Lance Hawvermale

The Secret of Breathing Deeply

COPYRIGHT © 2019 by Lance Hawvermale

Cover Art by *Diana Carlile*

The Wild Rose Press, Inc.
PO Box 708
Adams Basin, NY 14410-0708
Visit us at www.thewildrosepress.com

Publishing History
First Mainstream General Edition, 2019
Print ISBN 978-1-5092-2545-3
Digital ISBN 978-1-5092-2444-9

Published in the United States of America

Her father's casket emerged from the dark hollows of the plane. Pushed from behind, it glided along the cold steel rollers of the cargo ramp, a simple gray box without adornment. A few airline workers in matching jumpsuits became unintentional pall bearers as they lifted it from the ramp and transferred it to a wheeled gurney.

Jessie Alomar watched it all with her thumbs hooked in her jeans pockets. Her father had taught her to stand like that, like an Arizona tomboy, a woman just as likely to throw you a baseball as ask to borrow your mascara. She should've worn a skirt. A black skirt. She should've worn a black skirt and some respectful shoes instead of coming here dressed just like the man who occupied that coffin on this Flagstaff airport tarmac. But she knew the greatest way to honor him was to show him how much of his spirit survived in his only child.

The impromptu funeral procession approached, stopping a few feet away from her. One of the men said something, but Jessie was too intent on her memories. He moved his feet uncomfortably, shifting his weight, and only then did she look up.

He repeated himself: "Are you Mrs. Alomar?"

Reading lips was like painting glass. At times the brush strokes stood out clearly, if the light was right and properly angled. But then things got muddy, the paints smearing into one another due to any number of reasons. This time it was easy. Dusk was an hour away, the tarmac still bright on this midsummer afternoon. Jessie had no trouble seeing his words.

"I'm not a *Mrs.*," she replied in her foggy-voiced way, "but yeah, that's me."

Dedication

To Lindsey
and the miracle we witnessed on the beach

Chapter One

Her father's casket emerged from the dark hollows of the plane. Pushed from behind, it glided along the cold steel rollers of the cargo ramp, a simple gray box without adornment. A few airline workers in matching jumpsuits became unintentional pall bearers as they lifted it from the ramp and transferred it to a wheeled gurney.

Jessie Alomar watched it all with her thumbs hooked in her jeans pockets. Her father had taught her to stand like that, like an Arizona tomboy, a woman just as likely to throw you a baseball as ask to borrow your mascara. She should've worn a skirt. A black skirt. She should've worn a black skirt and some respectful shoes instead of coming here dressed just like the man who occupied that coffin on this Flagstaff airport tarmac. But she knew the greatest way to honor him was to show him how much of his spirit survived in his only child.

The impromptu funeral procession approached, stopping a few feet away from her. One of the men said something, but Jessie was too intent on her memories. He moved his feet uncomfortably, shifting his weight, and only then did she look up.

He repeated himself: "Are you Mrs. Alomar?"

Reading lips was like painting glass. At times the brush strokes stood out clearly, if the light was right and properly angled. But then things got muddy, the paints smearing into one another due to any number of reasons. This time it was easy. Dusk was an hour away, the tarmac still bright on this midsummer afternoon. Jessie had no trouble seeing his words.

"I'm not a *Mrs.*," she replied in her foggy-voiced way, "but yeah, that's me."

"My name's Derek. I've been instructed to assist you in the repatriation of the remains."

Jessie absorbed that. What an odd phrase. *Repatriation of the remains.* Was that the standard euphemism for shipping a dead body back home? "Thank you. What…what do I need to do?"

"We have some paperwork, if you don't mind. It'll take only a few minutes." By now he'd slowed his speech like they always did. After realizing she was deaf—or *hearing impaired*, if you wanted to be PC, which Jessie rarely was—he over-shaped his words and spoke with noticeable slowness. He didn't know any better. And Jessie was too depleted by grief to care.

"That will be fine," she said, though nothing in the world was fine anymore.

Her dad had raised her by himself and was probably her best friend, if you wanted to get real about it. Jessie had always thought of him as a combination of Moses and Indiana Jones, full of wisdom and ready to lead humanity to salvation if only he could keep himself from being distracted by rumors of treasures on far-flung shores. This time those shores were Costa Rica. And Archie Alomar hadn't even had the decency to come back to Arizona alive.

She blinked several times and told the tears to hold their fire.

"While you're taking care of that," Derek said, "we'll transfer the remains to the car sent by the funeral service."

This time she only nodded. Derek motioned toward an office inside the nearest hangar. Jessie followed him. Behind her, the others resumed their march, rolling the casket across the concrete.

Jessie turned to watch it go. She wondered what the wheels sounded like as they carried her father away.

****

Will his insurance pay 4 burial?

Jessie looked from her phone to the woman across from her in the back of the limousine that carried them through the city of Flagstaff. "You're the only person I know who texts from five feet away."

After a few seconds, the phone vibrated in her hand.

2 dark in this damn car 4 U 2 C my lovely lips.

Rolling her eyes at her silly friend, Jessie explored the limo's electronics console until she found the button that activated the dome-light. "Better?" she asked.

Li smiled and leaned forward. "Much." She dropped her phone on the seat and took Jessie's hands, entwining their fingers together in some kind of sisterly love-knot that Jessie appreciated even though her heart wasn't currently in it. "You're really holding up, aren't you?"

Holding up? Yesterday she'd overseen the return of her father. Last night she hadn't slept so much as floated, lying on her back and drifting from one island of memory to the next, finding her father hip-deep in a different activity each time she stopped to say hello. He was a medicine man. He'd obtained his doctorate in osteopathic medicine from a university in Glendale and spent most of his time and money trying to heal the poor and mend the soft bones of children off the street. He vacationed in outrageous places. When Jessie was seventeen, she'd spent the summer at his side in an aluminum-walled clinic in Bali and had made out once or twice with a nice Hindu boy. Ten years later, she couldn't remember his name.

"Does that mean you're *not* holding up?" Li asked.

"Holding up is overrated."

"Maybe so. But it beats a nervous breakdown. Believe me, I've tried one or two of those on for size. Holding up is the lesser of the two evils."

Jessie appreciated what her friend was trying to do, but there was a time for permitting yourself to be distracted by banter and a time for folding in half and letting go. Her chest still faintly ached from the power of her sobs last night, the juvenile thrashing she'd given the bed, the muddled shouts of *no fair* she'd hurled at God or whoever was listening. Archie Alomar was twenty years her senior, which meant that Jessie should've been at least seventy years old before she was forced to ride in this black car behind the hearse that carried him. Or fifty at the very least. Twenty-seven was still too young to be an orphan.

Li squeezed once to get her attention again. "You're really worrying me here."

"I'm really worrying *me*."

Li let it go, unable to find the magic words.

The car slowed as it neared the cemetery gate.

Jessie stared through the window at the marble stones and asked herself what she'd do without him.

Chapter Two

How anyone could eat after a funeral was a riddle beyond Jessie's ability to solve. Yet normal people did it all the time. After they'd put her father in the ground and said their words and cried their tears, they came to her house with the enthusiasm of Mormon settlers at a barn-raising. Casseroles arrived in insulated carriers, desserts in Tupperware containers. Now, nearly three hours later, they'd returned to their post-funeral lives with the leftovers Jessie insisted they not leave behind.

"You going to be okay?" Li asked, standing in the doorway.

"Probably not."

"That's not what I want to hear."

"Then close your eyes."

Li frowned. "I don't get it."

"That's what I do when I don't want to hear what someone has to say," Jessie explained. "I just close my eyes."

"Ah, right. One of the perks of being deaf, huh?"

"The only one. Come here." She pulled her friend into what was probably her thirty-seventh hug of the day. She was getting good at them.

"I'll text you," Li promised.

"I have no doubt you will."

"Are you saying I text too much? I'm worse than a junior-high schoolgirl, aren't I?"

"Goodbye, Li."

"All right, all right, I'm going. Take it easy, kiddo."

Jessie closed the door.

What followed was only silence.

Standing there with her hand flat against the door, she no longer felt the vibration of dozens of feet or the gentle way their voices moved the air. Though she hadn't been able to hear the metallic tinkle of silverware against their plates, she'd felt the noises around her. When they opened her oven door too quickly, when they flushed her upstairs toilet—these things spoke to her not in sound but in subtle tremors no one else recognized. She was happy they were gone.

Not really happy, of course, but *relieved.* Happiness was still a few time zones away.

So now what? Upstairs to die another death on her bed? Into a bathtub of water hot enough to make her sweat? Onto the roof to jump?

She smiled sadly to herself. She wasn't quite that desperate yet.

Instead, she settled in with the envelope they'd sent with her father's body. There was no use putting it off. Taking a seat on the couch, she dispelled her uncomfortable, closed-toe shoes and curled her legs beneath her. Her living room smelled of strangers. She still detected at least two different types of perfume lying under that peculiar scent of too many people occupying a too-small space. Apparently her sense of smell was better than that of the typical woman off the street. Not that it did her a lot of good. She also had excellent eyesight and a memory for fine detail, all of which she would have traded for a single afternoon of hearing at a Mozart festival.

The envelope contained documents from the government agencies responsible for that celebrated phrase, the repatriation of Archie's remains. A few were copies of things she'd signed when she took possession of the casket, but one bore the ominous header YOUR RESPONSIBILITIES.

She read it quickly. Add speed-reading to her list of gifts that currently didn't matter.

Evidently when someone died overseas, whatever assets they owned in the foreign country were subject to that country's laws, but ultimately it was the duty of the next of kin to saddle up and stake their claim to that property if they didn't want it forfeited to the court.

The last page was an inventory of everything her father owned in Costa Rica, the country where he'd lived for the last eleven months. A note reminded her that the items listed here were only those subject to taxation and did not include personal effects and other non-taxable goods, such as home furnishings, artwork, clothing, and pets. The major entry in the taxable category, of course, was the clinic. Archie held a fifty percent interest in *dispensario médico*, a three-room medical service in some impoverished Costa Rican village as close to the proverbial middle of nowhere you could get without actually being, well, nowhere.

"Damn."

Jessie hadn't thought about this until now. But part of dealing with a parent's death was going through their attic and finding something to do with all the stuff they'd accumulated. Except Archie had no attic, no basement, no library full of old phonographs and stacks of the *Saturday Evening Post*. Instead, he had a raggedy business in Central America and no one to claim it but his kid.

"Lucky me."

He'd invested thousands in it and probably lost more than he earned. But he saved lives. He joyfully served a community where no one had insurance, which meant his karma was probably good enough to either get him through the express lane at the pearly gates or reincarnated as the next Dalai Lama, depending on how you leaned religiously.

Jessie, whose own karma hovered somewhere between room temperature and lukewarm, doubted her chances of ever accomplishing anything half as noble. She worked as a freelance grant writer, specializing in obtaining state and federal funding for higher education and other branches of academia. As a freshman English major she'd fantasized about editing glossy fashion magazines in cities where they drove electric cars and smoked purely for looks, but instead she turned her writing skills to safer albeit less romantic work. The big plus was doing it all from home. Sometimes she put in ten-hour days, but at least she got to wear her pajamas. And since her interactions with clients were all handled online, she didn't have to worry about all that *Sorry, but I'm deaf* crap that being among co-workers would've required.

But Costa Rica?

Because she was self-employed, Jessie didn't have vacation days lying around, so any break she took would be on her own dime. She'd taken a week off at Christmas, but that was seven months ago. This was July, and the universities that employed her were prepping for the coming fall semester, so work was abundant.

She knew nothing of Costa Rica. Was it safe there? Was it covered in dangerous jungles full of those snakes they talked about on Animal Planet? Was it ruled by a dictator who censored the media and wore designer suits? More importantly, did they have a Starbucks?

Her phone buzzed against her leg.

She checked the screen: *U know I'm here if u need me.*

She typed back, *Thanks.*

I know it sux, but this 2 shall pass, right?

We'll see.

Ever since the advent of text-messaging, Jessie's world had opened a bit wider. Friends who'd been terrified of using the clunky old telecommunications device for the deaf, or TDD, were more than happy to chat the day away through texts and instant messages; suddenly old acquaintances were coming out of the wireless woodwork. And Li, bless her heart, was the Queen of the Qwerty Keyboard.

U still there?

Think I'm going to take a nap, Jessie told her, though it probably wasn't true.

Sounds good. Luv u.

Jessie dropped the phone in her lap, and immediately her eyes went back to the legal documents. Her father had been killed in a fall. He'd been out in the wilderness near the village where he worked, and he'd slipped. That was all she knew.

She wanted more. The last time she'd spoken with him—four days before he died—their call had been cut off. Cell service was spotty out there. And then Archie himself had been cut off. The abruptness of it offended her. Wasn't she owed more than that?

She doubled over.

The pain moved from the emotional to the physical with startling speed. With her mouth open, she waited to vomit all over her living-room carpet, but the sensation was not yet ready to leave. It held on, cramping her to the point of tears. Staring straight at the floor, wondering if she should get up and stumble to the bathroom, she tried to distract herself by placing her phone flat on the carpet and tapping the internet icon on its screen.

She spent the next seven minutes reading of Costa Rica, land of coffee beans and environmentalism. From its mysterious shores, her father's ghost beckoned.

Chapter Three

Rubio Mora ducked just as the gun appeared.

"No fair!" Alberto shouted.

Rubio laughed from behind the young pineapple tree's clay pot. "No fair? You're the one with the water pistol, sir. Talk about no fair. The question is, are you brave enough to charge my tree?"

Accepting the challenge, Alberto leaped around the pot, the dimples deep in his cheeks as he pulled the trigger of the red plastic gun.

A needle of water hit Rubio in the middle of the chin. "Hey, you!" He reached out to grab the boy, but Alberto skipped backward, as quick as a forest sprite, working the trigger as he retreated.

"I'm a ninja!" Alberto announced. "You can't catch ninjas!"

"I can sure give it a try." Rubio pounced, growling dramatically, sending Alberto running barefoot around the corner of the clinic and into the sun, squealing in make-believe fear.

Rubio pulled up and let him go. "That'll teach you to mess with me and my kung fu! And be careful, okay? One skinned knee per week is your limit. You're going to run us out of Band-Aids."

From a distance, Alberto yelled something that sounded like a promise to be safe, more or less.

Rubio wiped the water from his face. He never

tired of the village kids, no matter how many times they asked him to play goal-tender or how often they left him weary at the end of the afternoon. Maybe one day he'd even amaze his mother and have some boys of his own.

He smiled at himself because he could hear her clucking her tongue at him. Catholic men so close to thirty years of age were supposed to be bouncing at least their second baby on their knee, or perhaps their third.

You know what you're doing to me? his mother would ask when she was really laying into him. *You're going to turn me into an elderly grandma. I want to be young enough to enjoy my grandbabies. Rubio, are you even listening to me?*

"Even when you're not here, Mama," he said, then turned and walked back up the gravel path to the clinic.

He'd worked here for nearly a year now, the only paramedic in the village of Cerro Viejo. Though he came from the working-class Desamparados district of San Jose and graduated from the university in San Pedro, he'd ended up here in the hinterland because he had one of those hearts. It led him off to a place surrounded by water and teeming with snakes and venomous frogs. It brought him here on an internship but didn't let him leave when his studies were complete. They needed someone out here, someone to help them construct a better life. And for want of someone more qualified, they got Rubio Mora.

He let himself in through the crooked screen door.

"Welcome very!" Greta greeted him from behind the receptionist's desk.

"Hello, Greta." The middle-aged German woman

had worked here for six months, and her shaky command of the Spanish language still amused him. Rubio had offered to speak to her in English, a common tongue between them, but Greta usually refused. She was as determined in this as she was in everything else. Continuing in her rough-hewn Spanish, she said, "Elena and daughters is here to see. Waited in the examination room."

"Thank you."

He stopped at Greta's counter—immaculate as always—and checked the clipboard where his patients signed in for their appointments. They'd listed their symptoms: upset stomachs, skin rashes, swollen ankles, spider bites. So far it wasn't anything that Rubio couldn't handle. But sooner or later, one of them would show up with a condition beyond his skill level, and there would be no Dr. Alomar to make them well...

"What is your matter?" Greta asked, sensing the change in him.

"Nothing."

"Nothing is lying. *Something* is your matter."

"It just seems like an uphill battle, that's all."

Greta's blond eyebrows narrowed into a sharp V. "This phrase I do not know."

"I mean that there's only so much I can do for these people. I'm a medic. That's as far as my training goes. I'm great for splinting a broken finger and getting fishhooks out of somebody's arm, but—"

"The hospital is send another doctor." She frowned, unsure of her Spanish. "Did I say that right?"

"Almost. The hospital *will* send another doctor. Except they won't."

"They must. Hospital owning clinic, no?"

13

"Well, they've been funding about half of our operating expenses, but getting a new doctor in here is probably way more of an investment than they're willing to make."

"But why?" Greta got that look on her face that Rubio imagined to be in the repertoire of all women from her country, a bristling grimace that said she was about to smite you like one of the old Germanic gods. "This their responsibility!"

"Maybe so. Or maybe they'll just pack up their toys and go home."

"But what happening to us then without clinic?"

Rubio shrugged. He had no answer for her. He returned the clipboard to the counter and headed for the exam room, wondering what he'd do when he was unemployed—and asking himself where these people would go when they needed a doctor. "Until they pull the plug, I guess I'll just keep bailing out the boat and try to keep us from sinking."

"I missing Dr. Alomar."

"Me, too," Rubio said. "More than you know."

Chapter Four

Like a woman in an antique diving bell who hoped slowly to ascend to the surface, over the next four days Jessie waited for the pressure to ease. But the loss remained, exerting so many pounds per square inch that she marveled at her own ability to function.

In desperation she booked a last-minute flight to San Jose, the capital of Costa Rica.

Yes, her savings account took a hit. The airlines really tarred and feathered you when you didn't buy in advance, as if in a warning to others. She consoled herself with the hope of selling her father's half of the business for whatever little it might be worth.

"No thoughts of keeping it open?" Li had asked when Jessie explained her intentions.

"I can't. I'd have to hire a physician. My father was a doctor, so he didn't have to spend any money to pay someone's salary."

"Think it's worth much?"

"You don't see me holding my breath, do you?"

And now here she was, returning to the very airport in Flagstaff where she'd claimed the casket, although now she dragged a wheeled carryon and asked herself again if this was the only way to settle her father's accounts. She'd emailed various government entities and posted her questions on a discussion forum, and the consensus was a fairly definite yes. If she wasn't there in person to take care of things, eventually the system would take care of them for her, and though she was no expert on Costa Rican property law, she was certain that the system wasn't acting in her best interests. It never was.

"I'm leaving on a jet plane," she said to herself, quoting a song she'd never heard. At least she never had to worry about getting stuck on a long flight with a crying baby or someone who snored too loudly in the seat beside her. "Don't know when I'll be back again."

She checked in at the automated kiosk and headed for her gate, while around her hundreds of mouths opened and closed, feet went up and down, and bags darted right and left, a chaotic, soundless jumble that was probably aggravating as hell for those who had to listen to it. Some travelers evidently chose to hide from the racket, the cords of their earbuds disappearing in their pockets. What music was playing in those pockets? Though she'd never heard the songs, Jessie had read a thousand lyrics, most of which were ditzy or horny or obnoxious or all three. Very little of it was poetic, regardless of the genre. Her favorites were those with the most bass. Say what you would about the social value of gangsta rap, but that stuff pulsed in a way she could feel in her bones.

When she reached the security checkpoint, she passed through without difficulty, as she'd carefully ensured that everything was stowed in its proper see-through container. Despite the fact that her bottle of perfume was 3.4 ounces, they blurry-eyed TSA personnel didn't hassle her for being four-tenths over the legal limit; sometimes reason prevailed even at the Department of Homeland Security. After a thirty-minute wait, she boarded her plane, pleased to have a window seat.

She considered texting someone. Anyone, really. The art of waiting patiently was dead. Nobody did it anymore. If you had time to kill at a bus stop or in the back of a cab, you surfed silly websites or chatted with your Aunt Evangeline. The deaf were no different. Jessie used to carry a paperback with her for such occasions, but that was Dark Ages stuff. Ever since the people of the developed world had gone Internet mad, Jessie had gone right along with them.

But now she had nothing to say.

Her return flight was five days away. That was five days without income, five days in a country where English was not the predominant language, five days of being unable to read Spanish-speaking lips. She'd learned that nearly everyone in the tourism and hospitality industry spoke good old American slang, but if their accents were pronounced, she'd have to resort to body language or perhaps ESP.

Someone sat down beside her.

Jessie didn't turn around. Not yet. Instead, she closed her eyes and let herself imagine that a hunky movie star was slumming it in coach and had, by a freakish alignment of the stars, been assigned a seat next to hers. Or maybe that smooth-cheeked quarterback she saw last night on TV. Without a doubt, he'd fall for her the moment he saw her face, just like they did in the plots of practically every novel on the bestseller list. He'd fall for her, and by chance he also happened to be an expert in American Sign Language and a sucker for women who worked in worn but comfy PJs.

She turned around.

"Hello," the man said.

****

White hairs curled out from beneath his plaid duckbill hat, and the lenses of his glasses were so thick that they distorted his eyes from certain angles, reminding Jessie of when she dipped her foot in the pool and saw it displaced by refraction. She guessed his age at seventy-five.

"I always get stuck in the middle seat," he said.

Jessie wasn't sure how to respond. She opted for just smiling.

"The name's Percy," he said, "and if I talk too much it's only because I'm nervous."

So much for movie stars. Jessie exhaled and said, "I'm Jessie."

He nodded as if he wasn't at all surprised by either her name or the way she spoke. She'd been told that her voice sounded as if it were coming through a wall of sand. Certain kids used to call her Cotton Mouth when she was young.

"Had a dog named Jessie once," Percy told her, still nodding. "Of course, that was long before you were born…unless you actually happen to be fifty years old but really good at hiding it."

She smiled. "Feels that way sometimes."

"Doesn't it, though? For me, that's a good thing. Some mornings I get up and I swear I'm thirty years younger. You know what I was doing when I was fifty?"

She shook her head.

"Playing guitar in honky-tonks and letting women half my age buy me beer." He waved a liver-spotted hand. "Mid-life crisis. Thought I was the second coming of Bob Dylan. That lasted about six months till I came to my senses and bought a set of custom golf clubs." He frowned. "Did I mention that I talk too much when I'm nervous?"

"It's okay."

"Polite of you to say so." He searched around for his lap belt and snapped it in place.

Jessie did the same, though what good a seatbelt would do you in a plane crash, she'd never really figured out.

Eventually the flight attendants got the overheads locked down, and minutes later the plane rumbled toward the runway at a pace that Jessie figured was barely above walking speed. The flight from Flagstaff to the layover in Dallas was scheduled for a little over four hours, with a stop at Phoenix in between. From there, Costa Rica's capital city of San Jose was a mere three hours through the air, even though on the map it looked much farther. Costa Rica was almost in South America, with only Panama in between. The Pacific ocean caressed its western coast, while on the east lay the fabled Caribbean Sea. The name itself meant *rich coast*, a place of cloud forests, environmentalism, semi-active volcanoes, and—according to the New Economics Foundation—the happiest people in the world.

"We'll see," she said.

Percy said something on her periphery, so she turned away from the window. "I'm sorry?"

"Oh, I just said that you're whispering to yourself like a silly old man. And I should know."

She offered him a grin that said, *Don't mind the*

19

silly woman who's talking to herself because she does it all the time. "I guess I'm a little nervous, too."

"You don't fly often, either, huh?"

"I've seen too many airline disaster movies."

"Damn Hollywood is wrecking our lives."

With Percy's company, the time waiting for takeoff was made a bit more bearable. He made a joke about flying to an old-folks' home in Dallas, and she played along by remarking on how the nurses' assistants were supposed to be very young and very good-looking at places like that. Percy said he hoped to God to avoid finding out for several more years. Though Jessie had dug out an airline magazine to pass the time while she waited for the captain's go-ahead to use electronic devices, Percy proved far more entertaining—and shortly after the plane was in the air, Jessie realized that not once had he given any indication that he cared she was deaf. No elaborate slowing of his speech, no over-emphasizing his words—the deaf community called that *monkey lips*—just a nice, gentlemanly senior citizen who understood how to tell an interesting tale.

And like a gentlemen, he knew when to take his leave. When they taxied to a stop at DFW, he unbuckled his lap belt and extended his hand. "It was a joy speaking with you, Jessie."

She shook, appreciating the honesty in his eyes. "My pleasure."

"Actually, I *know* that's untrue. You sat there for two hours talking to a dirty roadmap of a man in clothes twenty years out of style. I, on the other hand, sat here for two hours talking to a comely young maid who reminded me of a time long before she was born. It was *my* pleasure, and that's a fact." He stood, and after retrieving his scarred leather bag from the compartment above the seat, he fished a business card from one of its pockets and handed it to her. "Just in case you're ever in Dallas and in desperate need of a cup of coffee, with or without a dram of whiskey to give it a bite."

"Thank you."

And then he was gone, melding into the line of travelers disembarking at the front of the plane.

Jessie looked at his card.

PERCY J. RAMSHEN, Ph. D.
PROFESSOR EMERITUS, ANTHROPOLOGY
UNIVERSITY OF TEXAS AT DALLAS

She lifted her eyes from the card, but Percy had already disappeared.

****

A hand touched her shoulder.

Jessie looked up from her book.

"The pilot has turned on the seat belt sign," the attendant said with a smile as practiced as any Jessie had ever seen. "We'll be landing in about twenty minutes."

Jessie stowed her tablet, but only after finishing the last page of the chapter. Stories were important to her, regardless of the genre. The written word brought her the sounds of the world that she otherwise never would've known. For example, microwaves made annoying beeps when your food was finished. Who knew?

The San Jose airport was not as large as she'd expected, but what it lacked in size it made up for in anarchy. As soon as she cleared the gate, she encountered a floor-to-ceiling window on her left, behind which a hundred hands and faces pressed against the glass as family members tried to get their first glimpse of loved ones coming home. Because the country was built on the tourist trade, shuttle drivers of all colors and creeds waited for visitors from afar, holding signs bearing their names. The signs ran the budgetary gamut from cardboard to custom-printed placards, but it was difficult to see them all through the push and pull of the crowd.

Jessie had booked a driver in advance, as she had no desire to try and read the lips of an excited, Spanish-accented cabbie. But she quickly realized that spotting her name in the chaos would be more a matter of luck than anything else.

Before she went any farther, she veered away from the crowd behind the window and found the ladies' room; she never used an airplane lavatory unless her bladder was about to take matters into its own hands. In the stall, she texted Li to let her know she'd arrived okay, and—unsurprisingly—Li fired one back at her almost immediately. Did that woman *live* on her phone?

Everything kewl? Li asked.

Still in airport. Will let you know when I get to the hotel.

Hot Latino men ratio?

Jessie shook her head. Li had changed little since high school. *None in sight.*

2 bad.

Jessie left the restroom, dragging her bag behind her and wondering again if she'd packed enough clothes. She didn't plan on staying more than a few days—but only one bag? One *carryon-sized* bag? Since when had she become so practical?

"Since Daddy died," she said to herself, and that ruined everything. She'd gone the last three hours without thinking of him.

She stepped through the glass doors and into the human carnival outside the airport. Young women waited for their crushes, and aging mothers welcomed their sons. Taxi drivers smiled at her and offered their services, but she only gave them a closed-mouth smile and shook her head. The smell intrigued her. Her father had hauled her off on various jaunts about the planet in his personal quest to save it, and one thing she noticed was that every foreign city exuded its own scent, a blend of its people, its industry, and its way of life. She breathed in something that reminded her of cinnamon, only rougher, as if the warm afternoon were heating up a spice rack when Jessie had happened along.

J. ALOMAR

Her quick eyes noticed the sign, and she headed that way automatically. The man who held it wore khaki pants and an avocado-green polo shirt bearing a company logo. Through her travel agent, Jessie had requested a fluent English-speaker, not because she was in any way biased against those whose native language was something else, but simply because she didn't have time to play the role of stranger in a strange land. Clear communication was essential.

"I'm Jessie Alomar," she said as she approached the man.

His sudden smile was like torchlight. "Wonderful! I am Manuel, your driver."

Before Jessie could say anything else, Manuel swooped into action like a super-hero's sidekick, whisking her bag into the back of a minivan bearing the same insignia as his shirt—a pineapple with a smile and comically large eyes.

She realized he was talking as he closed the door.

"I'm sorry," she said, interrupting him. She pointed to her ear, as she'd done so many times before. "I can't hear you. Would you mind repeating that?"

Manuel sort of froze for a moment, then it occurred to him what was happening. It wasn't so much the gesture to her ear that helped him figure it out so much as the somewhat muffled way she pronounced her words. Jessie watched it all play through his face before his smile returned, just as bright as before. "Welcome to Blue Vista Eco-Tours. We hope you had a pleasant flight."

"It was fine, thanks."

"Excellent." He opened her door for her and made a point of looking right at her when he said, "We will now go to your hotel unless you have another destination you would prefer."

"The hotel is fine." She climbed into the minivan, which was spotless. Why couldn't she keep her own car in this condition? Her Impala looked a combination of her bathroom on a Sunday morning and a rush-hour 7-Eleven.

As Manuel got them going, it quickly became apparent that he was vexed. Jessie guessed why. Normally he would've spent the trip to the hotel extolling the wonders of his city, relating its history and bits of local lore. But her deafness robbed him of that. Occasionally he looked over and smiled somewhat uncertainly.

Jessie didn't mind missing the guided tour. It gave her the chance to absorb things on her own, her eyes playing across the skyline to the wild hills beyond. So far San Jose looked much the same as any other overpopulated capital, though most of the billboards were in Spanish, and the sports stars pitching cell phones on the bus advertisements were soccer players instead of the quarterback of the Seattle Seahawks.

What places had her father frequented here? The city library was a solid bet, but from there? If she could follow the trail of his spirit, where would it lead?

The van slowed to a stop.

Jessie looked up to see they'd reached the hotel, the Grano de Oro. The room rates were way above average, but so too were the accommodations—or at least they'd looked that way in the pictures. Jessie had instinctively wanted something frugal, but at the last second she'd changed her mind. When you were retracing the footsteps of your favorite man in the world, you went all out.

Manuel opened the door for her, and she stepped onto the sidewalk in front of the hotel, still wondering why she hadn't been given the chance to say goodbye.

Chapter Five

Rubio Mora was known in Cerro Viejo not only for his first-aid skills but also for his expertise at giving piggyback rides. Liza leaped onto his shoulders, arms around his neck, legs cradled in his arm. "Go!" she shouted.

"We'll be right back," Rubio told Liza's mother as she finished her paperwork at Greta's counter. "If we have your permission, of course."

Liza's mother, Hanna, smiled with the long-suffering grace that only pregnant women could muster. She was better than eight months along. "Please, take this monster child somewhere else."

"*MONster?*" Liza said dramatically.

"Hold on!" Rubio warned.

They dashed out the door, where the sun waited for them.

"Have you ever heard of Alaska?" Rubio asked her as they wove between the plants on either side of the path.

"I've heard of California," Liza said.

"No, it's a bit farther north. It's snows up there."

"I wish I could see snow."

"Me, too."

"It looks neat on TV. And I could wear mittens!"

"Yes, I suppose you could. But in Alaska, dogs pull sleds through the snow."

"What's *sleds*?"

"A sled is a wagon. It slides on the snow."

"And dogs pull it? Like Simi?"

Simi was one of the many local mutts that roamed Cerro Viejo, gentle and usually hungry. "Yes, just like Simi. And do you know what they men say when they want the dogs to pull the wagons faster and faster?"

"They said, 'Go, doggie!'"

"Well, that's certainly a good thing to say, but they have a special word they use, a very interesting word."

"What is it?"

Rubio shifted his arms, gaining a better grip and alleviating some of the load from his back. He was fairly fit and had built up his stamina by swimming nearly every day since he was a boy, but toting a six-year-old would eventually tire the ablest of men.

"What's the magic word, Rubio?"

"The word is *mush*."

"Mosh?"

"Mush." There was no Spanish translation. If you were racing in the Iditarod, the dogs didn't care about your nationality; they just wanted to run and know the cold wind against their noses. "So when we're playing piggyback after your appointment, if you want to go really fast, then you should probably be like those sled-racers and say—"

"Mush!"

Rubio ran. He stayed on the trails, zigzagging between the bright orange orchids that bloomed wildly around the clinic. Forests surrounded the village on all sides, and Rubio had come to know them well, along with the animals that inhabited them. His morning walk to the ocean took him through two hundred meters of dark wetland, the shadows cool and deep against the exposed roots of mangroves older than the village itself. He took Liza on a quick tour, ducking under a low-hanging branch, and then returned her to her mother as she was shouting, "Mush! Mush!"

After he lowered her to the ground and said goodbye to her mother, he waved until they were out of sight, then fetched a bottle of water from the small refrigerator behind the counter.

"Do not taking my Slimfast," Greta warned.

"Don't worry about that. I'd rather drink goat's milk."

"I see goat in village, so if you are not careful being, I will make you drink your words!"

Rubio laughed. "Will you marry me, Greta?"

She showed him her fist, her white knuckles wrinkled by a lifetime of beating up smartasses.

Rubio held up both hands. "Warning received."

Greta looked back at the stack of papers in front of her, but not fast enough to conceal her grin. "I have working to do now, please."

"Yeah, so do I. Supplies are running low. I need to take inventory and place an order."

"Ah, reminding me. Here." She handed him a call-back slip.

Rubio glanced at the name. "Gavina Herrera."

"Yes."

Rubio bit down on his teeth so as not to say something that would get him a broken-Spanish tongue-lashing from Greta. She hated cursing in any language. "I thought we had until the end of summer."

"Summer not lasting forever."

"No. Unfortunately it doesn't." He wanted to hold

on to the feeling of Liza on his back and the sun warming his face, but reality could no longer be ignored. Gavina was not only a hospital administrator who held the clinic's fate in her hands, but she also happened to be an old flame—or a not-so-old flame, as the case may be. They'd met when Rubio accompanied Archie on a fund-raising trip to San Jose. Educated in Los Angeles, she was successful and coldly beautiful. Their relationship had been mercurial; like all burning things, it had flared hotly but eventually lost its fire.

With Gavina's note pinched between his fingers, Rubio headed for the supply room. Along the way he passed Dr. Alomar's door. No one had been inside his office since he died. More than anything, Rubio wanted the bearded, blue-eyed American to tug the door open suddenly and let his rambling spirit refill the slowly evaporating clinic. He even slowed his steps, foolishly hopeful.

Nothing happened.

Rubio continued to the supply room, wishing he had someone to blame.

Chapter Six

Jessie ate breakfast as she'd eaten it for most of her life: alone.

Oh, there was Patrick two years ago, a high school debate coach with a sense of style plagiarized from *GQ*, but his idea of breakfast was a protein shake and maybe—if he felt especially bold—a third of a cantaloupe. Archie Alomar had raised a lumberjack in pigtails. Jessie could put away the pancakes and coffee with embarrassing ease. In recent years she'd forced herself to dial back the calories, because power walks in the evening went only so far.

"How is everything this morning, *señorita*?"

"It's wonderful, thank you."

"And what do you think of our *gallo pinto*?"

"Just as good as you promised." She'd accepted his suggestion of rice and black beans, flavored with cilantro and peppers. Accompanied by three squares of fried cheese, it was the best meal she'd had in weeks.

"I will be nearby if you need anything more." The gentleman waiter in the button-down collar smiled, gave her a half bow, and glided away, stopping to attend to a bouquet of white azaleas that crackled like fireworks near a window. The dining room combined classic pillars and scrollwork with the open-air feeling of a European piazza. No one in the place wore jeans.

Her phone vibrated softly in her pocket.

Hey, grl. U up yet?

Jessie considered not replying. Part of her wanted a distinct division between her life back home in complacent suburbia and her excursion here to the unknown. Li blurred the edges between the two, reminding Jessie that her routine would eventually resume, regardless of what happened here in Central America.

For no particular reason she thought of Patrick the debate coach again. What had Li said about him? *Any man who wears cufflinks on a Thursday has never scrubbed a toilet in his life.*

She put her thumb to the little keyboard: *Currently being ravaged by a stranger I met on a train.*

Liar.

Bodices are being ripped, Jessie typed.

Pants on fire.

Jessie smiled at her friend. Li's hobbies included reality TV and shoe stores, and the day wouldn't be complete without at least one conversation about sex, pectoral muscles, or old Antonio Banderas movies. Jessie was glad to have gotten this one out of the way early. She needed to spend the rest of her day concentrating on settling her father's affairs.

She signed for a tip larger than she would've left in the States, still wrangling with the conversion between *colones* and dollars, then met her driver in front of the hotel. The humidity wasn't as oppressive as she'd anticipated. Manuel wore the same user-friendly smile as yesterday. He had thick brown arms that contrasted with his white polo and equally white teeth. "How are you doing this fine summer day, ma'am?"

"As right as rain."

"I'm sorry?"

She shook her head. "I'm fine, thanks."

Manuel kept smiling as he grabbed her bag and placed it carefully in the back of the minivan, caring for it as if it were a baby in a car seat. "The drive to Tortuguero is about three hours, but I assure you the ride is very beautiful!"

"I'm looking forward to it." From San Jose, she would travel overland through the Costa Rican countryside to the border of the Tortuguero National Park. Once there, she'd board what they called a water taxi. The village of Cerro Viejo was located on a narrow strip of land between a series of canals near the Caribbean Sea. The brochures said it was accessible only by watercraft. Jessie had never been on a boat in her life.

"You are here on vacation, yes?" he asked as he held the door for her.

"More or less."

"More? Less?"

"Part vacation and part…other stuff."

"Ah, that sounds like a very interesting trip. As a matter of fact—"

Jessie settled into the passenger's seat and missed whatever else he was saying. She didn't mean to be rude. She simply wanted to unload her father's business interests, pay off whatever debts he might have, and aim herself like an arrow at a day in the future when she didn't think about him every hour.

She remembered one of their many talks about boys. Like any father, Archie distrusted all of them. "When I want to see if a boy is right for you," he'd said, "I'll take him fishing. You can learn a lot about a person when it's just the two of you, a small boat, and nowhere to hide."

Manuel got behind the wheel. He was still talking as he drew the shoulder harness across his chest, but he seemed to have forgotten that she couldn't understand him without seeing his mouth.

Jessie didn't bother to explain.

****

A goat wearing a silver bell ambled across the road. Manuel slowed the minivan and gestured to the shirtless boy running down the hill in pursuit of the animal. Jessie didn't mind the delay. She'd spent the last three hours cataloging the country's multi-colored heart, and the sight of this wayward goat was one more token she'd take back home. Though her cell service often disappeared, she sent occasional updates to Li, if only to keep the woman from asking *R U still OK?* every half-hour.

Little clusters of small houses, she typed. *They have flat roofs.*

Most of the communities along their route were comprised of small but brightly painted homes. Their yards were packed earth or unchecked vegetation, with nary a lawnmower in sight, but the rampant wildflowers made even the most modest of them look inviting.

Passing a banana plantation.

Workers leaned over water-filled troughs and moved clusters of green bananas to men with machetes who lopped off bunches of a suitable size. Asian tourists had disembarked a bright red bus and were observing the operation, pointing their slender phones at people they didn't know.

Just realized I haven't taken a single picture.

Y not?

Mind is elsewhere, I guess.

Focus, luv.

Focus is overrated. She watched the boy catch up with his runaway goat and lead the animal back across the road. He waved at Manuel and said something that Jessie couldn't make out.

Manuel turned to her. "Do you have goats in America?"

"Not in my neighborhood."

"That is one more reason we do not drive quickly on these roads. You probably go much faster on your highways."

"Faster than we should. I could get used to slow and easy for a while."

"Then you, *señorita*, have come to the right place."

As they continued on the road that curved through ribbons of shadows cast by the massive *Guanacaste* trees, the land flattened out, reminding Jessie of the coastal areas not far from her home. She considered telling Li about the strange blue vines and the remarkable number of hummingbirds, but if she weren't careful, her phone's battery would sputter out long before she reached the coast.

Manuel made a point of turning directly toward her. "Only two more kilometers to go. You brought sunglasses?"

"Yes." They were cheapies she'd bought for five bucks, but with her habit of losing them or sitting on them, she didn't want to invest in a name brand. "Why do you ask?"

"Oh, my brother-in-law, he works here at the dock. He sells sunglasses, Oakleys, Ray-Bans..."

"Real Ray-Bans?"

Manuel kept his face turned toward her, which was slightly disconcerting, considering he was also trying to drive. "They have the brand name on them."

"Does that make them real?"

A philosophical look came over him. "What *is* real these days, *señorita*?"

"You may have a point."

Manuel laughed. He kept talking, but having turned his attention back to the road, his words were lost in profile.

The minivan surged through one last pothole the size of a crater on the moon, then rolled through an open gate to what looked to be a marina. Dozens of small boats were moored along a pier crowded with backpackers, groups of students, neo-hippies, and couples on their honeymoon—one of which wore matching hats and track suits emblazoned with the Canadian flag.

"The whole world comes here," Manuel said, pulling into a slot between two bright yellow tour trucks.

Jessie, feeling like a very small part of the whole world, got out of the van and put her feet somewhere in the vicinity of where her father had put his. As this was the only civilized launching point for Tortuguero National Park, this is where he would have come, gathering with these eco-tourists, probably carrying the same sagging leather satchel he'd bought as a Peace Corps worker in India. Where was that bag now?

Manuel got her attention by touching her arm. "You can board your water taxi there, under the red awning. Your guide will have your name."

She thanked him and shook his hand, giving him a good grip because that's how she'd been taught. Then she slid the strap of her carryon over her shoulder and drifted between the crowds of waiting passengers. She played her eyes over their lips and determined that many of them were speaking languages other than English. They'd traveled from around the globe to visit what was reportedly the most biodiverse country on earth. But Jessie doubted that any of them had come for a reason like hers.

On her way to the motorboat Manuel indicated, she saw a man hawking sunglasses from a card table near the gift shop. Though her five-dollar specials were riding her head and waiting to be called to action, she said to hell with it. Maybe a pair of knock-off shades was just what she needed to survive in this tropical land. She would buy the ones with the darkest lenses, not only because the sun seemed brighter here this close to the equator, but also because they would give her something that no woman could be without—a decent place to hide.

Chapter Seven

Rubio Mora ran.

He ducked low-hanging palm fronds and jumped the muddy places along the trail. His steps came down harder than they should have; anger fueled him. He'd just concluded the most frustrating phone conversation of his life. The woman in charge of financial matters at the sprawling and modern *Hospital de La Negrita*, Gavina Herrera, had informed him that she wouldn't be funding the clinic beyond the end of the month. She invited him to meet with her in two days to take care of the final documents. All of Rubio's arguments, from the emotional to the intellectual, had failed to move her. And so now Rubio moved himself.

Sweat formed along his hairline and cooled the back of his neck. He sprinted through alternating pools of light and shadow as the sunlight worked its way through the leaf cover. Rubio left the village farther behind, heeding the call of the sea.

Their history together made it even worse. And because their conversation had been conducted on Skype, Gavina had looked him in the eyes when she explained the fiscal infeasibility of sustaining Cerro Viejo's medical facility. She was a thirtysomething ladder-climber with an MBA from Stanford, and her designer eyeglasses gave her a look of both sexy professionalism and—when necessary—calculated contempt. She played racquetball and collected art, while Rubio collected children with ear infections and old men with gout.

Rubio leaped a mangrove's rolling roots and landed on the sand. Having reached the beach, he increased his speed.

The Caribbean waited for him.

Gavina had flirted. That's how their dialogue had begun, with her saying that Rubio was looking as good as ever. Her goodwill had rapidly eroded, though, when she started reading off numbers and using them as excuses.

Rubio slowed to a walk, his chest rising and falling from the exertion of his run. He stripped his shirt over his head and let it drop to the sand.

He'd fallen for her shortly after their first meeting. She was as driven as she was unpredictable. She said she wanted to fly away with him to a place called Telluride to teach him to ski. Rubio wasn't sure where Telluride was, but it sounded mysterious and certainly expensive

"Rubio!"

One step away from where the water swept up the shore, he turned around.

"You must hurry!"

Rubio squinted against the sun. "Alberto? What are you doing out here?"

"Greta sent me!" Alberto yelled. "It's an emergency!"

Rubio sighed. Emergencies in Cerro Viejo usually consisted of an ingrown toenail or food poisoning from eating spoiled fish. Such was the life of a rural medic. He returned to where he'd dropped his shirt and scooped it up forcefully enough to fling sand like a slingshot. So much for the calming embrace of the ocean. "So what's the matter this time? Did old man Enrique's hen stop laying eggs again? I'm not a veterinarian, you know."

"Hanna is about to have her baby!"

Rubio stopped. Liza's mother wasn't due for another week, at least. She was scheduled to be taken to a proper hospital in the next two days. But if she were about to give birth right now, right here, then Rubio was going to have to do whatever he could to help, simply because there was no one else that could. Was he prepared for that?

"Rubio, come on!"

It didn't matter if he was prepared or not. Clutching his shirt in his fist, he ran.

Chapter Eight

Jessie sat near the prow of a twelve-foot boat as it carved a line through the flooded trees. Dense foliage flanked the inlets that comprised the national park, so that anyone who wanted to reach Cerro Viejo had to navigate a series of winding causeways that made Jessie think of every movie she'd seen where hapless jungle explorers met a bad end on a piranha-filled river. Except this wasn't Brazil, and there were no flesh-eating fish.

There were, however, crocodiles.

Okay, so they were actually called caimans, according to the guide, who sat backward on his bench seat at the front of the boat and explained to his six passengers the difference between the two species, but it was still a formidable creature despite being somewhat smaller than its cousin. They'd spotted the toothy reptile basking on a moist log. The driver at the back of the boat, manning a small outboard motor, guided them within thirty feet of the beast and let them work their cameras.

One lounging lizard, she typed, but then she realized she had no cell signal out here, so instead of trying to send the message, she left it open and used it as an impromptu journal.

Other passengers: two kids and single dad, a couple from Spain.

Spain was her best guess. They'd introduced themselves in English, but Jessie had been able to see only a few words through their accents.

The tour continued. The vibration of the motor buzzed against the bottom of Jessie's feet. When she put her hand on the side of the boat, she felt the knock of the water as the craft skimmed across it. She looked to the treetops, hoping to see a monkey, but there were only birds, most of which she couldn't identify. Behind her new aviator-style sunglasses, her eyes searched the layers of the leaves. She'd never seen so many shades of green.

She missed most of the guide's spiel. He constantly turned to point out an amphibian or a butterfly, so tracking his mouth was pointless. Jessie kept her own log. *Guide looks like Hispanic Pavarotti.*

Twenty minutes later, the dock appeared.

The causeway broadened considerably. On its west bank were the private jetties of bungalow hotels, each offering a handful of rooms to honeymooners and others looking for refuge off the proverbial beaten path. To the east was a series of docks made of wood and old tires, beyond it the village of Cerro Viejo.

Jessie was the only one disembarking. Apparently the others were either continuing the excursion or waiting to be dropped off at one of the exclusive inns across the way. The guide helped her from the boat and fetched her carryon, and after she went through the motions of saying thanks and handing over a tip, she turned and breathed in the scent of the soil-packed streets. These aluminum buildings represented her father's home away from—no, scratch that. Archie never really had a home, at least not for very long.

Cerro Viejo was his town as much as any other.

She walked.

The vegetation had been cleared to create a small nook for this hodgepodge assembly of houses, all of them fairly small, most of them a little worse for wear. Their roofs were not peaked, but flat and often made of plywood planks. A few of the buildings leaned to one side or the other. All of their windows were open wide. Chimes moved in the faint breeze, making noises that Jessie had been told sounded like spoons tinkling together. Of course, no one could sufficiently explain to her what two tinkling spoons sounded like, so there you had it.

People smiled at her. The residents were not only familiar with tourists, in many ways they depended on them—even if those tourists were sometimes insufferable, which was probably often the case. Front porches doubled as merchant stalls. Jessie could have spent an hour collecting handmade necklaces, hats, and woodcarvings of sea turtles. And maybe she would later, because Li would murder her if she didn't return with the requisite number of silly trinkets. But right now just wasn't the time.

She glanced down at the sketch her boat pilot had rendered for her. He'd marked the dock and a few obvious landmarks, such as the nearby cluster of fire-red orchids spewing like lava from an earthenware enclosure. From there, a trail of two tire tracks led north. At the end of that path was supposedly her father's clinic.

Here we go, she typed. *Come what may.*

She situated the strap of her bag more comfortably on her shoulder. Had they loved her father here? Or was he just another outsider like her?

She took a few steps along the trail just as a man burst from the trees.

Shirtless and shoeless, he ran across the village toward the very path that Jessie was following. His skin was the color of clay baked to a dark luster under the sun. Jessie thought again of the Amazon movies she'd seen, where native warriors with bodies like athletes soared through the jungle as they pursued their prey, their muscles like those of a jaguar. But the look on this man's face wasn't that of a hunter but of someone hurtling toward trouble.

Jessie took several steps to the side to get out his way.

He threw his dark eyes at her briefly as he neared. For a moment it was almost as if he recognized her, then he looked away as he soared by, a black-haired spirit warrior who made no sound as he ran.

Others followed him.

Jessie saw it in their faces. Drawn by the urgency left in the man's wake, a few of the villagers trotted after him. Jessie wondered what they were saying. What was going on?

It didn't matter. She was caught up in it and soon found herself picking up speed. The villagers' energy grabbed her, bundled her up, and pushed her along the trail toward whatever problems her father had evidently left behind.

****

As Rubio closed in on the clinic, Greta held the door open for him, waving him inside. "Faster running! Faster running!"

He caught himself on the door jamb. "Is

she…okay?"

"Do I look like midwife to you? Inside!"

Rubio entered the clinic, wiping the sweat from his eyes. The commotion came from the building's single examination room. Six women were jammed inside, various generations of Hanna's extended family, with Hanna herself lying on her back on the paper-covered cushion. The women talked as loudly and rapidly as gunfire.

"Ladies! Ladies, please, excuse me."

As soon as they noticed him, they turned their howitzers on him, bombarding him with questions and commands, forcing him to wave his hands to calm them down. "Please, one of you at a time!"

Normally in Cerro Viejo, the men made the decisions and put fish on the table; it was a provincial way of thinking and one of which Rubio wasn't particular fond. But in matters of pregnancy, the matriarchy asserted itself, and any man unwise enough to stand at ground zero during childbirth deserved his fate. Rubio, still trying to catch his breath, quickly realized that his presence was only further inciting them.

So he shouted: "*Everyone stop!*"

The women fell silent.

Meanwhile, the clinic lobby continued to fill with spectators. The local rumor was that Finn Vargas, a Bribri Indian and local beach guide, was selling time slots for Hanna's big day. For five hundred *colones* or one American dollar, you could bet on the particular hour, with the winner taking half the pot and wily Finn taking the rest. So everyone was inordinately interested in Hanna's delivery.

In the quiet moment the women gave him, Rubio assessed the situation. Hanna lay on her back, biting her bottom lip, but she didn't appear to be in undo pain or distress. A woman on either side of her held her hands, the lines etched into their dusky faces saying they'd been through these things before and no young bachelor was going to help them, despite his medical training and college degree. Greta had muscled her way to the front of the onlookers and blocked them from the exam room. She, too, had the look of a woman who doubted the situational usefulness of men, especially those under the age of forty. Rubio felt suddenly outnumbered.

"Hanna," he said with a calm that surprised even him, "tell me how you feel."

Immediately the burly woman on Hanna's right opened her mouth to explain, but Rubio cut her off with a wag of his finger that would have been comical under other circumstances. He tried again. "Hanna, talk to me."

"There was pain," she said.

"Pain right now?"

"Not so much anymore."

Another woman—Hanna's mother-in-law—actually got a few words out before Rubio shook his head at her. She quieted at once.

Interesting. Was he actually getting good at this? Or were they just biding their time?

"What kind of pain?"

Hanna spoke at length. Rubio had always enjoyed hearing her speak, as she annunciated the Spanish language better than anyone in the village; the rest of them spoke with a disregard for crispness that was common to country people of all nations. ". . . but the feeling passed," she concluded, "and it has not come again since we arrived here."

Rubio extracted a pair of latex gloves from a cardboard dispenser. "Do you mind if I take a look?"

The mother-in-law scowled. If by *take a look* he meant ogle the private parts of her son's wife, then maybe he was about to get his arm broken just below the elbow.

"Listen," he said, sensing their shared unease, "I know I'm not Dr. Alomar. I don't have his level of training or his experience. And if I had my way, he'd be the one standing here right now and I'd be hanging out in the corner, hoping to pick up a bit of whatever it was that made him so damn cool. But he's gone. And we all miss him. But until the hospital sends us another doctor"—he glanced at Greta in case she was about to tell everyone that the hospital had no intention of doing that—"then I'm sorry but you're going to have to be satisfied with me. Now is that going to be okay with everyone?"

He checked their faces, finally settling on that of Hanna's younger sister, Pilar, who was raising a plucked eyebrow at him.

"Do you have a question?" he asked her.

"Yes. Why are you standing here wearing only your trousers and gloves?"

Giggles rippled throughout the room and adjacent lobby.

Feeling the warmth spread through his face, Rubio became aware of his half-naked body.

"Show off," Pilar said.

Rubio waved it away but couldn't resist a grin, which everyone noticed but pretended they didn't.

Married or not, Pilar had always been an insatiable tease.

Rubio tried to ignore them by grabbing the stethoscope and bending over Hanna's bed. A few seconds later, he marshaled his concentration, and the world consisted of nothing but the two of them.

"You're doing fine," she said softly.

"Glad someone thinks so."

"Dr. Alomar would be very proud of you, holding your own with all these old geese."

"The day's not over yet. The geese may get the better of me yet. Now hush for a moment while I hear what your baby has to say."

This was his favorite part. With the stethoscope's earpieces adjusted comfortably, he moved the metal diaphragm over Hanna's distended belly, closed his eyes, and listened.

Chapter Nine

Half-dressed runner is a doc, Jessie typed.

This time she pressed SEND.

What had looked like an emergency turned out to be just a bunch of people eager to welcome a new member to the human race. But now, ten minutes later, it seemed as if that little person wasn't quite ready to join the mayhem.

Jessie could barely see the doctor over the shoulders of those in front of her. His cheeks were as smooth as a teenager's, but faint lines around the corners of his eyes revealed his age. Here was a man who lived under the sun his ancestors had worshipped. His black hair was thick, curling where it brushed his ears.

She caught only one word of what he was saying: *Alomar*.

Was he talking to these women about her father? Everything else was in Spanish, so Jessie couldn't say if the man was invoking Archie's spirit or condemning it. It was a question she would certainly ask.

When it became apparent that the pregnant woman wasn't going into labor, the bodies in the lobby began to disperse, heading back outside and returning their hats to their heads. As they went, Jessie took the opportunity to get a look around. She turned a full circle and surveyed her father's clinic.

In typical Archie fashion, he'd taken a three-room concrete bunker and turned it into an ode to the Grateful Dead. The playful bears and skeletons that served as the band's mascots danced across a paper border fixed to the walls near the ceiling. The curtains on the open windows were tie-dyed. Jessie recalled with perfect clarity the day he'd explained to her, wearing his most serious expression, that history's greatest-sounding music was universally acknowledged to be that of Beethoven, the Grateful Dead, and the theme song to *Rocky*.

She closed her eyes, holding the image of his face as long as she could.

When she opened them again, it was clear that she'd missed something. A broad-shouldered caucasian woman of indeterminate age stood in front of her, speaking in what must have been an alien tongue. Jessie couldn't understand a syllable of it.

She held up a hand. "Please. Could you slow down?"

The woman frowned. She wore the expression of a fry cook working a double shift and forced to put up with complaining customers.

"*¿Habla inglés?*" Jessie asked.

"Oh, I speak English, all right." She crossed her arms. "Now are you lost or what?"

"I'm not lost. I'm just..." Well, now that she thought about it, she *did* feel a bit lost, but not in the way the woman implied. "I was just wondering if you could tell me—"

"Wait a minute." The frown deepened. It now bordered on suspicion. "Why do you look familiar? Have I seen you before?"

49

"If you'll let me explain—"

"You're not a fugitive, are you? Has your face been on a poster at the market?"

Jessie shut her mouth and considered the woman. She was a fierce gatekeeper, exactly the kind of administrative assistant her father would have recruited. The pretty secretaries never charmed him, but those who looked like card-carrying Teamsters made him melt. Like a mafia don, Archie liked having muscle at the door.

The woman's eyes moved to a point just beyond Jessie's shoulder, indicating that someone else had spoken. Jessie turned to see the doctor pulling on a blue scrub top, which was actually too bad, because his tile-like abdominals certainly weren't doing any harm being exposed. He held the door while the expectant mother and her escorts slowly departed. He spoke Spanish and smiled in a way that was meant to be reassuring; Jessie had seen smiles like that before and didn't necessarily trust them.

Then the awkwardness started. Jessie looked back and forth as the doctor and surly secretary traded information, all of it meaningless. She stood there with her bag over her shoulder and her dockside sunglasses clutched between her fingers, picking up clues from their postures and waiting to be included in the conversation. As one of the world's handicapped, that's what she wanted most of all—inclusion.

The secretary switched to English midway through her sentence: "...but I think she's American, so be on your best behavior."

The doctor approached. He was still barefoot, the cuffs of his khakis lined with sand. He offered her a hand and gave her a replay of his smile of seconds before. "I know exactly who you are, Ms. Alomar."

Mystified, she hooked her sunglasses onto the corner of her pocket and shook his hand. "You do?"

The smile changed, turning more genuine. "When you were twelve years old, you skipped school for half a week to stay home and tend an egret with an injured wing."

Jessie didn't know what to say.

"A few years after that, you taught yourself to dance by watching old music videos from the eighties."

Jessie wasn't sure if she should laugh or blush.

"A person can learn a lot from Paula Abdul and Janet Jackson," he continued. "And your first cat was a bobtail named Mr. Babbington."

"Uh...did I drop my diary somewhere?"

He laughed, then struck a pose with his chin pinched between his fingers, as if trying to recall some elusive but significant fact. "And if I had to guess, I'd say that the best birthday present you ever received is after your father met a comic book artist vacationing in Belize. He drew you as the main character in your own super-hero story."

Jessie shook her head. "I think it's safe to say that you have me at a disadvantage."

His smile broadened, revealing his teeth. "My name's Rubio Mora. Your dad was my boss, among other things. I've seen a lot of pictures of you."

Jessie winced. "That's...probably not a good thing."

"You were your father's favorite subject, but I'm sure you knew that already. And this is Greta Steiner. She basically keeps the place from falling down around our heads. And thankfully her English is much better than her Spanish."

"Pleased to meet you," Jessie said.

Greta changed instantly, the centurion replaced by a mother hen. "Oh, you poor thing, you have come all of this way and not phoned ahead. We could have had a nice cottage ready for you. And I have American soap operas to thank for my English, by the way."

"A cottage isn't really necessary..."

"Necessary?" She shot a look at Rubio. "This is the one and only child of Dr. Archibald Alomar, and she says welcoming her isn't necessary?"

Rubio shrugged, still grinning.

"My dear"—she took the carry on from Jessie's shoulder—"after all your travels, you're deserving of a hot shower and a strong cup of coffee. And if there's one thing that Costa Rica does better than your Uncle Sam, it's grow fine coffee beans. Come along now, and don't bother protesting. Arguing with me isn't known to come to much good for anyone."

Before Jessie could mount a protest, she was taken by the elbow and led toward the door. She looked back at Rubio for assistance, but he clearly knew a lost cause when he saw one. He waved goodbye, and then Jessie was outside, her escort determined to force hospitality upon her.

Jessie didn't really mind. A shower sounded fantastic. Besides, she was distracted by something Rubio had said. *You were your father's favorite subject.*

It made her miss him all the more.

****

When Jessie stepped out of the bathroom thirty minutes later, her hair in a towel, a butterfly with lavender wings flew in from the open window.

The small room they'd given her was not even quite a bungalow. Other than the bathroom with its water that never quite seemed to get hot, there was only a single bedroom, the full-sized bed occupying most of the floor. The bed was draped with a canopy of white linen, though Jessie had cast the fabric aside in order to array the contents of her carry on across the comforter. The butterfly alighted on the pair of panties she intended to wear.

She sat on the edge of the bed, legs crossed. Greta had given her a bathrobe that was at least one size too big, which made it all the more comfortable. She watched the butterfly close its wings and open them again.

"So now what do I do?"

The butterfly made no reply. Or perhaps it did and she was simply unable to hear it.

Maybe over dinner tonight she'd explain to Rubio and Greta why she'd come. Was dinner the best time? Or should she wait until morning? They seemed like nice people, so surely they'd understand.

She thought of the things that Rubio had said. They were all true. She hadn't enjoyed a memory of Mr. Babington in years. If she'd known that her father was down here telling stories about her—

The butterfly took to the air and wove an uncertain pattern toward the open window. It rendered a figure eight and then disappeared from sight.

"Thanks for the visit."

As she dressed, Jessie turned on the little fan that stood where a nightstand otherwise would have been. The room had no air-conditioning. Though the temperature was probably in the upper eighties, the village was well shaded by trees that Jessie couldn't identify. Combined with the breeze that carried in from the ocean, it kept things rather comfortable and reminded her of her outrageous AC bill back home.

She put on pants with a drawstring waist, white sandals, and the least wrinkled top in her bag. She'd have to learn to live with clothes in need of pressing until she located an iron somewhere in Cerro Viejo and pleaded with the owner to let her borrow it. Then she located the room's single electrical outlet and spent twenty minutes with her hair-dryer and brush. She eyed herself in the mirror and decided she didn't look her best but not bad for a world traveler.

"Here we go, then," she said and stepped outside.

Nothing had changed here in generations. The village had that look about it. Oh, the brands of candy bars sold at the general store were new, as were the satellite dishes affixed to a few of the rooftops, but fathers still fished and ferried tourists for a living, and children still kicked soccer balls and interjected their speech with American slang.

They smiled at her as they passed. Her hair and skin were lighter than theirs, but otherwise she didn't seem any different, and she certainly didn't *feel* that way. She suspected that daughters here in Cerro Viejo tried to make their fathers proud and were forced to put up with girlfriends as high-maintenance as Li. In fact, the only difference between them was the one Jessie had faced her entire life. The villagers could hear the treetops tossing in the wind. They heard the soft sounds of their babies at night.

She checked her phone when she felt it shake.

Update?

She one-thumb typed as she walked toward the clinic. *Later.*

Weather?

Perfect.

Lucky U. Cloudy here. Evil frogs?

Jessie smiled faintly. Li had read about venomous frogs in Costa Rica. Now she was worried it was some kind of epidemic.

Been bitten four times already, Jessie told her.

Find hunk to suck out toxin.

I have to go. Duty calls.

Call me 2nite and spill.

A stoneware urn propped open the clinic door. Jessie removed her sunglasses as she stepped inside. Greta Steiner appeared to be singing while she dug through a filing cabinet. Rubio Mora, his back to the door, studied a clipboard and drummed his pen against counter.

"Hello again."

Greta looked up from her work. Rubio turned, saw her, and smiled. "I see you survived our guest room. Sorry it's a little on the cramped side."

"It's fine."

"We thought you might be hungry." He jogged around the counter, stooped down to a mini-fridge, and came up with a cellophane-wrapped tray of pineapple and banana. "If you're anything like your dad, you're a fiend for fresh fruit."

"It looks wonderful." And that was true; the sight of it reminded her that she hadn't eaten anything in the last several hours but a bag of airline peanuts.

Greta provided a plastic fork and bottle of water.

"Have a seat, dear, and get something in your mouth. You need to put some honest meat on your bones."

"I don't know about *that*, but thank you, anyway." She peeled the plastic wrap away and inhaled, savoring the scents. The banana had been cut into coin-sized slices, and the pineapple was divided into little triangles. "You grow this locally?"

"Sure," Greta replied. "You buy a fresh pineapple here for fifty American pennies. How much does it cost where you come from?"

"Oh, probably about five dollars."

Greta said something harsh in a different language, but Jessie interpreted it perfectly well.

"We didn't know you were coming," Rubio said. "I guess we might have cleaned the place up a little. But I'm glad you're here. I wasn't sure what to do with…with Archie's stuff." He looked away briefly, staring at the wall, then let out a sigh that Jessie imagined she could hear. "I'm so sorry this happened."

"Me, too."

"Archie was my friend."

"*Everybody's* friend," Greta added.

"Yeah." Jessie held the fork in front of her, a wedge of pineapple skewered on the end of it but no longer as inviting as it was moments before. "Dad had that effect on people."

"The kids called him *el ilusionista*," Rubio said.

"I don't know that word."

"It means *magician*."

"Ah. He showed them the old quarter-behind-the-ear trick, huh?"

"And the one where he pulled the big scarf out of thin air."

"Really? He practiced that one a lot. I'm glad he finally got it right."

The inevitable silence followed her words. Archie Alomar had come to life, and now that he was again among those who loved him, the room didn't seem big enough for anything as mundane as talking. Jessie concentrated on her fruit, enjoying the tang of the pineapple on her tongue.

"Anyway," Rubio said, trying to bounce back, "it's good to have you here."

"I'm sorry I didn't phone ahead. It ended up being sort of a last-minute trip. But someone had to take care of his personal effects, and by default, that someone ended up being me."

"Personal effects?" Rubio shook his head. "He left a lot more than that behind."

"What do you mean?"

Rubio pointed to a closed door in the corner, on which had been painted a line from the Grateful Dead: A BOX OF RAIN WILL EASE THE PAIN, AND LOVE WILL SEE YOU THROUGH.

"No one's been in there since he died," Rubio said. "I think you should be the first."

Chapter Ten

Jessie opened the door.

Her father was everywhere. The maps on the wall, the poems torn from their books, the figurine of Don Quixote charging a windmill—it forced her to momentarily shield her eyes. The smell of him lingered, and for a while she did nothing but let it fill her.

A hesitant touch on her elbow prompted her to face the bright world again. Rubio looked concerned. "Are you okay?"

"No."

"Can I get you anything?"

"A time machine."

He nodded as if understanding. "Yeah. I wish I could."

"Thanks. I'll be all right." She called herself a proper liar and went to her father's desk.

Pictures of her abounded. Her pigtail phase, her grunge phase, her I-am-teenager-hear-me-timidly-roar phase. One of the shots captured her signing the letter J; some kids flashed gang signs at the camera, while young Jessie Alomar had preferred American Sign Language. Her father had taught her that, too. The day after the doctors had confirmed she was deaf, Archie had committed himself to learning ASL, and they'd mastered it together.

Rubio crossed the room and pointed to what looked

like a finger-painting. "This was a gift to Archie from the children. If I'm not mistaken, that's the thumb print of every single kid in Cerro Viejo. They adored him. They really thought he was Santa Claus. Sometimes I wondered the same thing myself."

"How long have you worked here? You might have told me that already, but with everything going on—"

"Your dad hired me on his second day in the office. I was with some friends from the university's biology department. We came for the turtles. He was out for a morning walk on the beach when I was in the middle of stabilizing the sprained ankle of our team leader. We got to talking, and he told me I could have a job with him as soon as I finished my paramedic training. And ever since then, I've been getting my paycheck here. A *small* one, mind you, but a paycheck."

Jessie lingered at her father's chair. The memory of him returned to her with such ferocity that she had to grip the seat back to keep from sliding. How many times had she come upon her father like this in his study, with him bent over his desk and Jessie asking, "Whatcha doin'?" Without fail, her father would say, "Nothing important," even if it was, and minutes later the two of them would be doing something together.

Rubio moved his hand, trying to catch her eye. She looked at him. "I can't tell you how sorry I am. Do you want me to go?"

"It's hard, that's all."

"If it's any help, and I know it's not, my dad died when I was eight. I've been there."

"Did you have other family after he passed?"

"My mother and five brothers and sisters."

Jessie wanted to feel sorry for him, but that place

where sympathy normally lived in her was a desert, a dry Sahara waiting for a single cool breeze. She had no siblings with whom to share her pain. Her mother had passed away so long ago that Jessie couldn't even remember her, and ever since, she and Archie had been together with no one else in between. And now there was no *between*, because you had to have two to make that work.

"He taught me how to bake a pie," Rubio said.

Jessie thought she'd misread his lips. "He what?"

"Pie. Banana cream, actually. That man was a baking fool."

She smiled, feeling the mist of tears but holding them off. "He was, wasn't he?"

"And you?"

"Baking?" She shook her head emphatically. "Invite me into your kitchen only if you have the fire department on speed dial."

He laughed.

"You think I'm joking." She picked up a coffee mug, imagining she felt the impression of a certain hand. "There was a reason we kept two fire extinguishers in the house when I was growing up."

"Sounds like an interesting home."

"We also had the doorbell rigged so that it flashed the hallway lights when you rang it."

"Good idea."

"But when I was sixteen and dating Bobby Levingston, Dad threatened to disable the light so I wouldn't know when Bobby showed up to take me out."

"He didn't like Bobby?"

"I think he had a personal bias against black leather

jackets."

"Ah, Bobby was a bad boy."

"Wannabe bad boy. I think now he's a lawyer."

"So your dad was right about him all along." He grinned.

"What can I say? I rebelled against his wisdom but I never actually doubted it." She looked down at the desk, a simple affair made of particle board, with a single drawer. On the floor inside the kneehole rested a very familiar satchel. Archie had bought it in Calcutta during his tenure in the Peace Corps. Jessie had always seen it as a combination of a portable library and Aladdin's lamp. Genies lived in there.

Rubio tapped the desk to get her attention.

She saw the motion and looked up.

"You don't need to rush," he said, "but eventually we'll need to get it all out of here, the desk, the coat rack, the chair, everything."

"The desk? I'm sure the room's next occupant won't want to sit on the floor."

"Yes, well, I wish there was going to be a next occupant."

"What do you mean?"

"They're pulling the plug."

"The plug?"

Rubio ran a hand through his black hair, clearly frustrated by something beyond his control. "Your father funded half of this medical practice with grants, endowments, and his own bank account. The other half of our funding comes from a hospital in San Jose, and they tell me they no longer have the resources to maintain it. So the supplies we have on hand right now are the only ones we're going to see, and after the end of the month, Greta and I will no longer be on the payroll. Archie basically held the whole thing together with glue and good will."

Jessie absorbed this with an equanimity that surprised her. No event was so astonishing that it was going to move her from this support of her father's chair. She'd intended to come to Costa Rica and settle his affairs, and that meant selling his business interests, but apparently there were no buyers. As usual, Archie had strapped together a little house of heaven here, but with the passing of *el ilusionista*, the house was falling.

"I talked to a woman from the hospital," Rubio continued. "Her name is…Gavina Herrera. Gavina is…she's one who holds the purse strings. And she wasn't very interested in hearing my side of the story. She said she sympathized, but she didn't really sound like she meant it."

"What happens to the village?"

"It goes on, I guess. The people here are strong, inventive. They'll make do."

"And what if there's an emergency? What if someone needs help?"

He held up both hands and shook his head.

Jessie didn't want to think about it—at least not right now. She pulled the chair from under the desk and slid into it, putting her hands on the armrests and pretending she could feel him there. The drawer drew her eye, and below it, the satchel sat and waited.

"Do you want to be alone for a while?" Rubio asked. "I have plenty of stuff to do."

She cocked her head to the side. "Did my father ever take you fishing?"

Rubio narrowed his eyebrows. "Yes. Once. We

went out for sailfish but didn't catch anything. Why?"

She opened the drawer to see what her father had left behind. "Just curious."

****

On the top of a stack of books lay a grenade.

Jessie withdrew her hand as if she'd found a viper.

"What's wrong?" Rubio hurried around the desk and peered down. "Is that…live?"

"There's a note tied to it." She leaned closer, and if Rubio said anything else, it was lost to her as she gingerly reached down and lifted the paperboard note by the corner.

NEXT PATIENT, PLEASE TAKE A NUMBER

The note was marked with a number 13 and fastened to the grenade's activation pin.

"This must me a joke." She turned the note over.

GOOD LUCK FROM THE CREW, HAITI '94

She picked up the grenade, tossed it, and caught it. "Doctor humor."

"Now why didn't he ever tell me that he had that in there?"

Jessie placed it on the desk. Heavy and filled with what was likely sand, it was probably intended to serve as a paperweight. "Dad never liked to reveal all of his secrets at once. Did he tell you about the time he bought me a pony and managed to keep it for a week without me finding out?"

"Where does a person hide a pony for a whole week?"

"You'd be surprised."

The books turned out to be ledgers. Archie was fluent with email but resisted with medieval tenacity all suggestions to handle his finances electronically. This set of mostly matching account books dated back to when he was twenty-five, their columns filled with his exacting penmanship. Jessie turned the pages, hoping to see a bit of poetry or other interesting tidbit scrawled in a margin, but there were no hidden codes here.

Rubio said something.

"I'm sorry?"

"I asked if you found anything important."

"Just more things to box up and ship home."

"And where's home?"

"I thought you knew everything about me."

He smiled. "Only a few highlights. And…maybe a low light or two."

Jessie leaned back in her chair. "Such as?"

"We should probably keep working."

She crossed her arms and waited.

"Okay, fine. You asked. Let's see…Archie told me one time that when you were in elementary school, you cut your own hair, and it was so bad that the beautician had to nearly make you bald to straighten it out."

"That's it? That's not so bad. I went to a school for the deaf until I was in junior high, and we used to do weird things just on general principle. Cutting your own hair was rookie stuff."

"There was also the time your braces made a boy's lip bleed when he kissed you."

Jessie opened her mouth but said nothing. Had her father actually *told people* that story?

"I thought that one was pretty funny."

"He *said* that to you?"

"What, it's not true?"

"Yes, it's true, but…" She went back to the ledgers, stacking them neatly on the desk. She felt

Rubio's eyes on her. "By the way, I never let anyone tease me who hasn't known me for at least three hours. That's a firm rule."

He positioned himself in her line of sight. "I think it's sweet."

"A bloody lip is not sweet."

"And I'm not teasing you. I'm just...trying to get your mind off the fact that you're having to go through your father's belongings. Humor is the only thing I have."

"Thanks." She drummed her fingers on one of the books. "I can see why he liked you. He always surrounded himself with optimists."

"Like you?"

She shook her head. "There are certain mornings when my pessimism wins world championships. For the most part I do okay. But every now and then..." Pushing the ledgers to the edge of the desk, she lifted the satchel and unfastened the worn leather strap. "And honestly, this is one of those times."

The next item she extracted was his thermos. Jessie cradled it, one of the familiar artifacts of her youth. How many times had she seen him pour coffee from this dented metal cylinder? "It's not quite empty," she said, giving it a shake.

"That was always Greta's first job in the morning. Cranking up the coffee pot."

Jessie remembered the smell of their house in the morning as the machine brewed what her father called *my motor oil breakfast*. He'd gulp it down as he fixed her waffles and braided her hair with his nimble doctor's fingers.

She set the thermos aside and took out his first-aid

kit. Like a doctor of yore conducting house calls, he always traveled with the tools of his profession. He'd modified a roll-out canvas tool bag with slots for instruments, bandages for lacerations, and cherry suckers for the kids. Sand and salt lined the bag's deep wrinkles.

"…growing up with a doctor in the house," Rubio said.

Jessie had missed most of what he'd said. "Excuse me?"

"Having your dad be a doctor—it must have been hard to play hooky from school."

"I was never even foolish enough to try. If I wasn't puking, I was in class. Every summer he'd take me somewhere new. We'd spend two months in some faraway place, and he'd try to heal everybody in a hundred-mile radius before summer was over. I spent my fourteenth birthday in Vietnam."

"You had an interesting childhood."

"I have to admit that it was nice being the fair-haired foreign girl who got all the attention. But when they found out I was deaf, then they just thought I was odd."

Rubio picked up a framed portrait. Jessie knew that one well. She'd just received her master's degree and was smiling unreservedly at the camera. The photographer—her father—had captured her in a moment of reckless joy. "This was the first one he put on the desk the day he unpacked," Rubio said. "When he caught me staring at it, he told me who you were, but he never said anything about your being deaf. It was months later that it finally came up. I guess he didn't consider it a big deal."

"Most of the time it's not. But there are days…"
She glanced into the satchel again, but saw only one
thing remaining. It appeared to be a bundle of papers
secured with a black shoestring.

Placing it on the desk, she unlaced the string,
remembering the day she'd learned to tie her shoes on
her own. Silly, to be thinking of that now. But the
memories in this room were storm clouds, their
lightning striking from random directions. She needed
to finish this task and wait for the rest to pass.

The documents in the bundle turned out to consist
of one badly wrinkled map wrapped around a stack of
photographs. The pictures were scenes of Tortuguero
wildlife, portraits of smiling patients in front of Greta's
check-in counter, and the obligatory shot of the sun
setting over the ocean. The map turned out to be of the
topographical variety, revealing a highly detailed
representation of the region's forests, landmarks, and
elevations. It was folded too many times, as if it had
been riding in someone's hip pocket. Cerro Viejo was
underlined in red ink. The only other mark on the map
was a circled area about three inches from the village,
which translated to a little over a mile.

Jessie sat back in her chair and folded her hands in
her lap, realizing that they'd finally stopped shaking.
There, the first part was over. She'd delved into her
father's favorite possessions without being swallowed
up, and now her hands had settled…though her cuticles
weren't in terrific shape, now that she examined them.
She vowed to deal with them tonight in the comfort of
her borrowed bed.

She closed her eyes and breathed to make sure she
was actually okay—yep, all systems were go, which

was a mid-level miracle—and when she opened them again, Rubio was frowning and leaning over the map.

Even before she asked, Jessie suspected that something was wrong. Her instincts flared, but she was too exhausted by recent events to sit up straight and pretend to be enthused. "What's the matter?"

Rubio traced his finger around the circle that her father had drawn. "I know this place."

"Yeah? What is it?"

"It's where your father died."

Chapter Eleven

Jessie sought refuge in the clinic bathroom. She hadn't even bothered to follow her own travel guideline and wipe down this foreign toilet seat. Elbows on her knees, forehead in her hands, she tried to return to a land of stability because the planet's axis had tilted a few unexpected degrees.

Maybe she just needed sleep. Wasn't that the cure-all elixir? Just pound out a good ten hours in the sack and wake up a tougher woman. Go to bed as the orphan Jessie Alomar and wake up as a combination of Margaret Thatcher and Joan of Ark. And a little bit of Marilyn Monroe wouldn't hurt, either.

The implication of that circle on the map confused and worried her. All that she knew of her father's death was that he'd been hiking and had fallen down a hill. According to the official report, which she'd had translated at her attorney's office, the distance of the fall hadn't been extreme, but Archie had landed badly and…and broken the first and second vertebrae in his neck.

"Stop it," she whispered to herself.

But stopping wasn't so easy. The map remained, the map and its damn red-ink circle.

Why had he marked his hiking destination when no other location was noted on the map? According to Rubio, her father walked nearly every morning when it wasn't raining and had come to be very familiar with Tortuguero National Park in general and this area in particular. He wouldn't have needed a map, unless he wanted to make sure he remembered a specific location.

Jessie dug her phone from her pocket. She didn't have much signal, which wasn't a surprise because her body felt the same way—running on one bar.

She typed, *Are you there?*

She stared at the phone's screen, waiting. Before the advent of text messaging, she would have spent this moment alone, just a woman hiding in what the British called the loo and waiting for her heart to paste itself back together.

4 U? Always.

Those three words, though not expressed in the Queen's English, said as much about friendship as anything could.

You're not driving while you text, are you?

Promised U I wouldn't. Wassup?

Well, what *was* up? The authorities were going to shut down the clinic, and Jessie felt somehow responsible. At the same time, she was having to deal with her father's favorite possessions, each one heavy with his psychic imprint.

It's hard, that's all. I wanted to hear a familiar voice. The irony of that last bit wasn't lost on her. *Dad has some great employees. They might lose their jobs now.*

Sux. Thought he had biz partner.

His partner is a hospital and they're closing up shop. The village will have no meds, and Greta and Rubio will be unemployed.

Who & who?

Greta was Dad's office manager. When Archie's medical practice had been located in Flagstaff, Li's mother had filled that position, so Li understood the kind of person it took to compensate for Archie's laid-back and sometimes absent-minded demeanor. *Rubio was his right-hand man.*

Can't this Rubio guy take over 2 keep shop open?

He's not a doctor. Paramedic.

Oooh. They look hot in uniform.

Despite everything, Jessie smiled. *He's not bad.*

Describe not bad.

Jessie was ready to move on to other subjects—or to simply get out of this bathroom and face whatever came next—but now that she thought about it, Rubio was probably just the kind of man that would turn poor Li into one of those cartoon characters with stars in her eyes. *Truth? He's six feet tall, dark Latino hair, darker eyes, and I've already seen him with his shirt off.*

U lie.

Actually, it's true.

4 real? Married?

I don't know. It hasn't come up.

Details about shirt stuff!

Later, I promise. But I need to go. Lots to do.

U tease!

Jessie returned her phone to her pocket, and three minutes later she emerged from the bathroom with what she hoped was her second wind. She found Rubio and Greta standing in front of an open cabinet, taking inventory of their supplies. Jessie knew they were worried about running out. Apparently her father had brokered one of his famous alliances with the hospital's board of directors, but now that he was gone, they were pulling up stakes.

"How long will it last?" she asked.

Greta darkened at the question, but Rubio looked a bit more optimistic. "That depends on how lucky we get. We've got a decent stock of various antibiotics, but we're not so strong on other—"

"One week," Greta said. "That is my guess. Ten days at most."

Rubio shook his head. "Don't listen to her. She's gloomy, especially when she's speaking English."

"I am *not* gloomy." Muttering, she returned her attention to the cabinet.

"See," Rubio said, "gloomy." Jessie assumed he mouthed the words without making a sound, as Greta didn't react. "She gets mean when she's gloomy."

Jessie smiled but only when she was certain that she wasn't in Greta's periphery.

Evidently getting a kick out his newly discovered game of speaking silently, Rubio continued in that vein. "She has a soft heart but likes to pretend she's a Nazi. Archie was nuts about her."

Jessie lowered her head as if studying the clinic brochure in front of her, but she looked up through her lashes at Rubio.

"Last Thursday I put a frog in her filing cabinet. I don't know what she was yelling because it was all in German, but she definitely wasn't very—"

Greta spun around, shouting something that Jessie couldn't read but fully understood. Laughing, Rubio held up his hands in self-defense and retreated as she gestured and yelled. In seconds she'd backed him against the very filing cabinet where Jessie suspected he'd planted his saboteur frog. Rubio dashed to Jessie's side, took her by the elbow, and walked backward as he admonished Greta to calm down, grinning all the while.

"We're going now," he said to Greta, taking Jessie captive as he made for the door. "You need to take a nap and dream about being a nicer person."

Jessie looked back but had no hope of making sense of Greta's threats.

"Yes, yes," Rubio said, "I'm sure you're right about everything."

Greta threw a pencil at him.

Rubio dodged it. "I love you!" he shouted at her, then swept Jessie out the door and into the sanctuary of the late Costa Rican afternoon. They jogged a few steps, then Rubio turned to make sure they weren't being pursued. "Her aim is improving."

"Lucky you."

"Truly. What would that woman do without me pestering her all day?"

Jessie recognized the friendship the two of them shared, one that was close enough that flying pencils and practical jokes became part of the normal workday. And that was nice. Too often adults outgrew those things. But if the clinic closed, would Rubio and Greta ever see each other again?

Jessie couldn't answer that. Not now. Not when there was one piece of her journey remaining to be traveled. "Can I ask you a favor?"

"Of course. Anything." He put his hands on his hips and waited.

"Could you take me there?"

"Where, exactly?"

"To where my father had his accident."

Rubio sobered. The joviality of moments before

gave way to a still-fresh pain. "I'm not sure there's much to see."

Jessie stood there, looking up at him. She knew, better than most, that sometimes the spoken word wasn't necessary.

"You're serious about this?"

She said nothing, just kept on staring at him.

"You're just as stubborn as he said you were. All right. I'll grab a couple of bottles of water and some insect repellant. Go get anything you think you might need and meet me back here in fifteen minutes."

She watched him go.

After a moment of contemplation, she decided there was nothing she needed other than her imitation-designer mirror shades. They were the only armor available to her, so she pulled them on, took a breath, and waited.

Chapter Twelve

The setting sun worried her, just as it always did.

Her world shut down in the dark. She couldn't read lips. She couldn't pick up the numerous visual clues that helped her navigate the human race. Over the years, Jessie had come to rely so heavily on visual input that now her eyesight bordered on the supernatural; Sherlock Holmes had perceptive skills of the second tier in comparison.

She'd already used her phone to jump online and find the facts. The sun was scheduled to set this evening at 6:01. That gave her two hours. Of course, she could've simply put it off until the morning, but this pilgrimage wouldn't wait.

She and Rubio walked a narrow trail through the tropical forest north of Cerro Viejo. He kept his head turned toward her without being reminded, which was nice, except now he came close to running into low-hanging branches because he wasn't keeping his eyes on the path.

". . . and so I promised Archie I'd try and get into a medical program, though I'd probably make a lousy doctor."

"He made you promise?"

"He threatened to bring out a Bible so I could swear on it."

"I guess he saw something in you that made him

believe you'd be good at it."

"Do you know the kind of hours those guys have to work during their residency? They have to sleep in broom closets when they're on call."

"But the money…"

"Yeah, the money." He'd brought along a day pack to store their water, and now he shifted its weight on his shoulders. "My mother said the same thing."

"We're both wise women."

"Maybe so. But that's not why I love doing what I do. I know that having lots of money can be useful. I mean, your father was able to do a lot of wonderful things because of his savings and investments, and you don't get that kind of bank account by being a paramedic."

"Or a grant writer. That's the job I'm currently neglecting. But you probably already knew that."

"Archie mentioned it, yes. Sometimes he had a…what's the phrase? A one-track mind?"

"Sorry he put you through all of that. Hearing about my boring life all day can drive people to madness. There have been documented cases."

Rubio smiled. "It wasn't like that. All that information is coming in handy right now. And besides, I sort of didn't mind listening to him talk about you."

"We call that being a glutton for punishment."

"Perhaps."

Jessie studied him. "What is it that you're not telling me?"

"What are you talking about?"

"You have a look in your eye."

He laughed. "One thing he didn't tell me is that you're apparently telepathic."

"Comes with the territory."

He shook his head. "I'll tell you later."

"What's wrong with right now?"

"We're almost there. It's just another two hundred meters or so. But we'll have to leave the path, which means we'll need to be careful. Keep an eye on your feet."

"Why?"

"Anything. The ground can be uneven. And there could be snakes."

Jessie stopped. "I think this is where we turn around and go back."

"Snakes are not that big of a deal."

Jessie gave him her best you've-got-to-be-kidding-me look.

"Seriously," he said, not quite managing to hide a smile. "Besides, it's not the snakes you need to worry about, anyway. It's the frogs." He pointed to a small amphibian in the shady soil near the path. It was bright orange and no bigger than a thumbnail. "See that? It's a dart frog. It may not be very big, but in Colombia, the old Chocó Indians would touch their blowgun darts to the frog's back and scrape off just enough poison to make their darts toxic."

"And this is supposed to make me feel better about traipsing around out here? Sorry, but I didn't bring my steel-toed boots."

Rubio nodded as if he understood. "You're right. I apologize. Archie told me that he raised his daughter to be as brave as any man, but I guess he was exaggerating. That's a father's prerogative, so it's cool."

Jessie crossed her arms. "So that's all you've got,

huh? A dare."

"Maybe."

"I don't have a history of turning them down."

"So I've heard. If you want to see where he spent his last day, we may have to get a little dirty."

"Fine. We'll go. Heaven forbid I show my sissy side to someone I just met a few hours ago. But…did he really say that about me? That I was brave?"

"He called you Artemis, goddess of hunting and the moon."

She didn't know how to respond to that. It sounded just like something her father would have said, intermingling his love of mythology with his freestyle way of tossing out compliments to those he loved. It made her secretly proud to hear that he talked about her like that to strangers.

"So how about it?" Rubio asked.

Jessie knew she had to go, despite the waning daylight. "Just keep the dart frogs at bay, or I'll squish them with my overpriced American shoes."

"I can hear them hopping for cover right now."

****

Rubio asked himself just what the hell he was doing.

He'd intended to spend the evening job-hunting online, as the final word from the implacable Gavina Herrera was that the clinic was on its own, destined to shut its doors and leave the people of Cerro Viejo without local medical attention. Now they'd have to travel an hour by water taxi and then another hour overland to see a doctor, and sometimes two hours was too long to save a life.

But now, instead of finding a way to rescue the

village or searching the wilds of the Internet for fresh employment, he was journeying through the fading light with the woman from the picture on Archie's desk. Rubio remembered perfectly the first time he'd seen that photo. It had been sunset like it was now, the light slanting through the office window and falling across her face…

He scowled at himself and said, "Is this your first time in Central America?"

Jessie didn't reply.

Of course not. Rubio was walking in front of her, stepping over vines and weaving around moisture-dripping plants, so there was no way for Jessie to know he was speaking. For a moment he'd forgotten she was deaf.

He stopped and turned around. "Are you doing okay?"

She glanced down at herself, her shoes caked with mud, her fingers wrapped around a can of mosquito spray. "Is this how every tourist ends up on her first day?"

"No, that wouldn't look very good in our brochures."

She removed her sunglasses and slid them high on her head. "Are you sure this is the way?"

"I've only been out here one time, and that was the day your father…I mean, they called me out here when they found him. There's a ravine there. In the late seventies, archaeologists found some remnants of a conquistador expedition along the bottom, but otherwise it's just wilderness."

"That sounds like an odd place for my father to be hiking."

"Well, he was eccentric."

"The understatement of the year. One time he adopted a motherless hyena."

"A what?"

"A feral dog from Africa. It didn't go over so well with the neighbors."

Though Rubio enjoyed just standing here and getting to know her, darkness was not far away. If he were responsible for getting Archie's daughter lost in the woods, the doctor was likely to return in spiritual form and haunt him. And that was one gringo you didn't want to upset.

"We better keep moving," Rubio said. "The dart frogs only strike if you stand still."

"I think I'd prefer the hyenas."

Rubio took the lead again, reluctantly turning his back on her. He wondered what it was like, not being able to hear these endless insects or the water as it dripped from the leaves. Every time his foot touched the ground, he became more aware of the sound. Was it like floating in outer space?

"I used to go hiking on the weekends," she said from a few feet behind him. "I'd leave early on Saturday morning and drive to a ranch just outside the city. It belonged to my friend's parents. But a year ago they sold it and moved to Florida. Since then, I haven't been burning as many calories as the surgeon general probably recommends."

Rubio thought about looking back and responding, but the whole thing felt awkward. If she wanted his input, he supposed she'd ask for it.

"I bought one of those elliptical machine thingies," she continued. "Basically it became a grade-A way to collect dust. If exercise equipment was priced according to how often you'd actually use it, every treadmill would go for about eleven bucks and change."

Rubio smiled. He enjoyed the quality of her voice. It reminded him of when he was swimming underwater and conversations would reach him from the beach. How did a person learn to talk when they couldn't hear their own words?

They kept walking. Rubio pushed plant fronds out of the way, the western sun making a chessboard pattern on the ground.

"Eventually you just give up," Jessie said. "Working out is for sophomores in college and professional athletes and middle-aged guys who use the gym as a singles' bar. Maybe one day I'll hit the lotto and have enough time to work on my glutes. Thank God coffee doesn't have any calories. Hey, I think I may be babbling."

Finally he turned around. "I own a set of dumbbells, but they haven't come out of my closet in six months. And you're not babbling."

"Thanks. I guess you have the kind of job that helps keep you in shape."

"And I swim. Rich people pay to put pools in their yards. I have the best pool of all, and it's free. I'll show you if you want, but right now…"

"I know. Lead on."

Rubio looked up, reacquired his bearings, and half a minute later got them to the edge of a gulch. The foliage stopped here, giving way to a scar across the forest floor. The ravine ran several hundred meters in both directions, its sloping walls made of loose soil and the occasional protruding lip of stone. Vines crawled down the side and mingled like serpents at the bottom. Overhead, bright toucans winged across the sky.

Jessie stepped up beside him. "This is it? The mark on the map?"

"The general vicinity, yes."

"But there's nothing out here other than endless plants."

"Maybe that's what he was doing. Archie was an investigator. He liked to look at beetles and take pictures of flowers."

"Do you know the…the exact spot?"

Rubio knew what she was asking. Archie had slipped and fallen somewhere along the length of this ravine. One of the village boys had been sent to find him after he failed to return for several hours. But Rubio hadn't seen the precise location where the authorities had covered his body with a plastic tarp.

"Rubio?"

"I don't know. There might be trampled weeds and tracks of the ATV the police used when they…when they brought him back up."

"And we could find that place?"

"Are you sure you want to?"

"No. Not at all. But I'm not turning back now." She seemed to gather herself. "Show me where he died."

Chapter Thirteen

When Jessie was eight years old, her father had built a carnival in the backyard. The ring-toss had come first, constructed of plywood and dowel rods. Next was the duck pond, consisting of a wading pool half-set into a hole he'd dug by hand and populated with rubber bathtub ducks. He'd used a permanent marker to write a number on the underside of each one. Every afternoon for a week she got to pick one and claim its corresponding prize.

But what she remembered most about that crazy, wonderful private circus was not the live sheep named Chester nor the cotton candy machine, but rather the foundation he'd made for the dunk tank. The chair mechanism itself had never functioned properly; he'd designed it himself, and he wasn't able to get the lever to release the chair with any consistency. Still, her friends had loved the outrageous thing, even though it worked only half the time. But the morning he'd poured the concrete slab below the chair, the two of them had left their footprints in it before it fully dried. Years later the carnival gave way to a deck and koi pond, but the impressions in the hardened concrete remained, Jessie's smaller prints trailing behind her father's larger ones.

The same thing happened now as she walked the ledge. On her right was the tangle of the forest with its dark crabwood trees and dazzling patchwork of purple bell flowers. On her left, the ground fell away immediately, forming a twenty-foot slope that dropped at a steep angle to the gully floor. Behind her, the sun hung low in the sky, throwing her shadow in front of her, where she imagined her father's footprints to be. She perspired in the light humidity.

"Did he come out here often?" she asked.

Rubio walked several yards ahead of her. He turned around, the sunset clearly illuminating his face. "If he did, he didn't tell me about it. As far as I knew, he kept to the paths and trails. But he could also be unpredictable."

"Tell me about it."

"I guess that was part of his charm."

She indicated the ravine, the bottom of which was completely obscured by serpentine vines. "So…what is this? A dry river bed or something?"

"I don't think so. The entire national park used to be an archipelago. They say the region was a series of islands made from volcanic rock, but over time, sediment filled in most of the gaps, and we ended up with this sort of swampy paradise. The gorge here is just a natural feature of the land's formative years."

Jessie knelt at the edge and touched the soil. Damp from the constant moisture in the air, the clumpy dirt was easy to manipulate. Stuff like this would simply squish if a grown man put his foot down in the wrong place. He'd turn his ankle, lose his balance, and tumble down…

She stood up, brushed off her fingers. "Let's keep going."

Though Rubio clearly didn't want to oblige, he led her farther along the rim. She felt momentarily sorry for him. He'd met her only hours ago, and now she was asking him to confront the death of his mentor and friend. In her grief, Jessie had forgotten that she wasn't the only one who missed him.

She watched him as they walked. He moved confidently, not in the least intimidated by the proximity of the brittle cliff. Before leaving the clinic, he'd changed into a pair of hiking boots, and they looked as if they'd carried him many miles. Had they ever taken him to the States? She detected no hint of an accent when reading his lips.

She glanced down at her phone, thinking of sending Li a picture of Rubio from behind—just to get her mind off things—but she had no service this deep in the outback or the jungle or whatever you called this place.

Rubio stopped so suddenly that she almost ran into him. He turned and put his hand on a short tree with leaves as dark as jade. "This is a cocobolo tree, one of only three or four in the entire park. They used to be abundant throughout our country, but the wood is so beautiful that people go out of their way to harvest the trees. You don't find them in the wild very often these days."

"Do you think that's why my father came out here? To see the tree?"

"Do you?"

"How would I know that?"

Rubio cast his eyes into the ravine, the bottom of which was a nest of weeds. "This is where the police were working when I got here. Archie was...he was lying down there. I remember it because I sat right here with my back against this cocobolo and closed my eyes when they brought him up. I didn't want to see."

Jessie saw the casket rolling from the plane again. Standing there on the tarmac, she'd wanted to close her eyes, but unlike Rubio, she hadn't had the luxury.

She crouched at the edge. Even days after the event, considerable evidence remained of those who'd been involved in bringing her father's body up the slope. Having spent a lifetime depending on the accuracy of her eyesight, she noted even the smallest detail, the grooves where ropes had worn into the soil, the divots where tripods had stood as they supported cameras. But it wasn't enough.

She looked up at Rubio. "I need to get closer. I need to go down there."

"I knew you were going to say that."

"Am I that predictable?"

"No. But you're Archie Alomar's daughter. I wouldn't expect anything else."

****

Rubio sat down beside her, his legs over the edge. "Since we don't have a rope, I think it's best if we go down like this, using our hands behind us for support."

"You mean a crab-walk?"

"Is that what it's called?"

"We used to have crab-walk races in PE class in elementary school."

"What's PE?"

"Physical education."

"Ah. We played *fútbol*."

"We call it soccer."

He nodded. This morning when he'd taken his daybreak run, he hadn't imagined that twelve hours later he'd be sitting beside the woman from the picture on Archie's desk. Earlier during their walk he'd accused her of being telepathic but hadn't explained himself. She'd ask him what he was thinking, and he'd inexpertly changed the subject by mentioning snakes. But the secret he hadn't told her was that he'd sort of fallen for the face in that photograph. The more Archie talked about her, and the more often Rubio saw that framed portrait on the man's desk, the more he wanted to meet her. And now what was he doing?

Crab-walking her into a pit, he thought. *Terrific.*

"Are we going or not?" Jessie asked.

"Sorry. I just...wanted to make sure you were ready."

"I'm not ready at all. I don't think I could ever be ready for this. But still."

"Yeah. But still." He started down slowly.

The ravine wall angled in a way that Rubio could see would be dangerous if he wasn't careful. Had he stood up and tried to jog down, he would've quickly lost the fight to gravity and ended up tumbling to the bottom. He pictured Archie standing at the top, the soft ground folding unexpectedly beneath his foot. Though the thick vegetation normally might have cushioned him, anything could happen during a fall, even one from a short distance. The safest way to descend was working your way down feet-first in what Jessie called a crab-walk. Rubio stayed a few feet below her just in case she slipped and he needed to arrest her slide.

"I suppose we should have brought gloves," she said from behind him.

Rubio agreed, but turning around and saying so would be too inconvenient. He knew this had to be hard on her, visiting the site where her father lost his life.

Archie was right as hell when he said she was stronger than she realized.

"Notice I'm wearing my sensible shoes," she said. "If you were intending to make fun of the pampered American chick in the open-toe pumps, then I'm going to have crush your hopes."

Rubio flashed her a smile just to let her know that he wasn't ignoring her. But for the most part he concentrated on sliding down the wall of the shallow canyon.

"And this might surprise you," Jessie went on, "but I've been accused of being a tomboy."

Rubio reached the bottom, stood up, and turned to help her to her feet. "Actually that doesn't surprise me at all."

She accepted his offer and let him tug her up. She swatted the larger clumps from her pants. "And I talk too much when I'm worried."

"I'm sorry. I know this is hard."

"Don't sweat it. I'll do my best to wait and have my total girlie breakdown tonight in my room. Right now I'm the dragon lady."

Rubio wasn't sure what to say, so he took a few steps back and gave her space to look around. Many of the weeds and flowers here in the gulley's basin had been broken and stomped underfoot. You didn't have to be a professional tracker to see the signs of recent activity.

Jessie gave it all a lengthy inspection, arms crossed defensively over her chest. The setting sun left half of her face in shadow as she gazed up at the precipice from which her father had fallen.

Rubio cleared his throat to get her attention, then

realized she couldn't hear him. So he shifted his weight deliberately, catching her eye. "Can I ask you a horrible question that you shouldn't ever have to answer?"

She tipped her head a little to the side, as if trying to convince herself that she'd correctly read his lips. "If you phrase it like that, do you expect me to answer?"

"I don't expect anything. But I loved Archie—not like you do, but in my own way. And so I want to ask."

She never uncrossed her arms. "Ask already."

So Rubio did.

Chapter Fourteen

"What was the last thing you said to your father?"

She'd been expecting something heavy like this, a question about her dad, a question that no one ever expected to answer while standing in weedy ditch in a foreign land.

"You don't have to say anything," he told her. "But I had to ask."

"Why? What difference could it make?"

"None. But the day after he died, I sat there in the beach and tried to remember our last conversation before he'd gone out the door. I think we'd been talking about sports, but I'm not sure. And I really want to remember."

Jessie relaxed her arms, but now her hands sought refuge in her back packets, sliding her fingers into them like she used to do when she was fifteen and trying to get away with something. "I spoke to him on the phone the day before the accident. Before our call got cut off, I said that I loved him. That's what I always said, ever since I was little."

"And what did he say in return?"

"The call dropped before I heard his response. But I know he said what he *always* said. That no matter how much I loved him, he loved me more. It was kind of a ritual between us."

"That's good. That's very good. He deserved it. I

just wanted to make sure."

"Why?"

He shrugged. "I suppose I'm looking out for him."

"Since when did my father need looking after?"

Rubio held up a hand defensively. "I didn't mean anything by it. I know how much he cared about you, and I'm glad to know that you felt the same way about him. You hear stories all the time about ungrateful adult children going their own way. It's good to hear that sometimes it works out and nice guys don't always finish last."

Jessie inspected the ground at her feet; perhaps her father had been lying right here when they found him. "I'm not sure this is the way nice guys are supposed to finish."

She didn't bother looking at him for a possible response. Who was he to question her relationship with her own father? Sure, he was Archie's friend and protégé and all of that, and he knew her father as the patriarch of lost causes, but he didn't know Archie was also the man who'd baked cinnamon cookies for her and taught her about her period when the time came because she didn't have a mother to do it. And this place, this chasm, this goddamn dirty hole in the ground was where he'd died.

Jessie sent her eyes across the flowers and into the shadows painted by the setting sun, trying to give them something to do other than dropping tears down her cheeks. Those eyes had learned to become missiles, firing long and hard and rarely missing their target. A cigarette butt rested thirty feet away, probably cast off by a policeman. A bush with several broken branches might have gotten in the way of the gurney when it was being hoisted up the hill. The prints in the semi-hardened mud represented many different shoe sizes and tread types, and by following them, Jessie got a fair idea of the route the rescuers had used when they descended. With the sunset on her right, Jessie walked, picking out little places where evidence of human contact remained.

"There were more than half a dozen people down here at one point," she announced, "but no more than a dozen."

When she glanced at Rubio, she caught him in mid-reply. "…though by the time I got here, I'd say there were eight. So you're right."

She returned her eyes to the ground. Animals had also walked here, but not for at least a week. Jessie wasn't very savvy when it came to wildlife tracks, but she recognized dog prints. She doubted there were any wolves or foxes here, so these were likely made by standard canines, perhaps the dog she'd seen in the village.

She sank to her knees and plucked a weed topped with a purple flower. Turning it slowly through her fingers, she pulled the scents into her, inhaling what smelled somewhat like honeysuckle and damp wheat. What was she missing?

She felt Rubio's footsteps before he appeared in front of her. "It's getting dark," he said.

"Just a few minutes more."

"Is there…anything I can do?"

"How about some of that insect spray?"

"Sure." They'd put the can in his day pack before climbing down. He retrieved it and handed it to her, and she applied a thin film to each arm. The stuff smelled terrible. Maybe that's why the mosquitos stayed away.

"Did he tell you about our camping trip at the Grand Canyon?" she asked.

"That's one I haven't heard."

"We went there the week after school was out when I was sixteen. I was determined to hate the entire ordeal, because when you're sixteen, you either love something to the point of obsession or you despise it with every gram of your being. So boy bands were wonderful and trips with the old man were torture. There's no in between when you're that age. But of course I ended up loving it. We rode mules. Mine was named Confucius, and he had one white ear. Dad and I were hunting fossils at an empty spot along the canyon floor when he quoted the real Confucius. He said, 'Everything has its beauty, but not everyone sees it.'"

"That's hard to remember sometimes. There's no beauty in what happened here."

"Would my father agree with that?"

"You don't think so?"

"He wasn't afraid of dying, that much I know. He thought of it like some kind of last great hoorah, an adventure where the curious professor finally got to find out what waited on the other side. This is a peaceful place, with colors and plants and smells everywhere, and a big fat sky. So yeah, I think he would have found it beautiful."

A minute passed. The breeze completely faded, so that everything was still.

Rubio held out a hand. "It's time."

He was right. Jessie permitted herself one last sigh, then accepted his help in getting to her feet, even though she could've managed perfectly well on her own. Their contact, however brief, infused her with a surprising amount of strength.

He led her back to the slope and picked the least demanding route to the top. She followed him slowly, leaning forward and using her hands for support as she ascended. She focused on not slipping, but her eyes must have still been drawn to the canyon floor because she noticed something partially hidden in the grass.

"Wait a sec," she said.

"What is it?"

But Jessie didn't answer. She was already in motion, sliding back down the slope and running to what looked to be a pair of watching eyes.

****

The eyes were buttons, sewn into the face of a doll.

Jessie held it in both hands, almost cradling it. The head was made of dark green fabric, so it had been camouflaged within the foliage. No wonder the police hadn't seen it, as its arms and legs were also green, though they were constructed of some kind of fibrous material she couldn't immediately identify.

"Plantain peel," Rubio said.

"I'm sorry?"

"Plantains. Like bananas. The doll's limbs are dried plantain skins."

"Like a cornhusk doll."

"I guess so. I've never seen one of those."

Jessie turned the doll over, studying it from all angles. She passed it through her fingers, noting how it changed from rough to smooth as she moved from its limbs to its soft, batting-filled head.

"What's it doing out here?" Rubio wondered.

"I was about to ask you the same thing. Are there

children nearby?"

"There's *nothing* nearby. No one comes to this part of the park. The tourists are asked to keep to the trails and waterways. There's not much out here to see. But kids, you know, they go wherever they want. This could've been sitting out here for months."

"That's not true."

"How do you know?"

"This fabric is still clean. And the arms and legs would be in a lot worse shape if it had been lying out here in the elements for that long."

"Maybe."

"*Probably.*"

"Okay, so what if you're right? What difference does it make?"

Jessie moved a little to her right so that her shadow didn't obscure Rubio's face. "It doesn't make any difference at all. Unless it does."

"I don't even know that means."

"It could be important."

"Look, I understand that you want to find meaning here, some kind of closure, but this is only making it worse. There are no answers out here."

Was he right? Was she seeing revelations where there were only coincidences? This doll had nothing to do with her father. Right?

"Hey, I'm sorry," Rubio said, his eyes softening. "I can't imagine how hard this has been on you. If you want to search around some more, say the word. I'll help any way I can."

"That's sweet of you, but it's not necessary. What you said is true. But it just seems unfair that he should...he should be gone so quickly." The tears encroached, and she blinked to hold them back. "I feel like somebody owes me something, and maybe if I dig around out here until dark, I'll find whatever it is."

"And doing so will make everything better?"

"That was the plan, yeah." She wiped her eyes.

Rubio touched her lightly on the arm. "Nothing I can say will make this any better, but just so you know, I've had my moments, too. When I heard what happened, at first I didn't believe it. Then later that day, I waded into the ocean and started swimming without thinking about how far out I'd go. I ended up so exhausted that I almost didn't make it back to shore. I figured it would've pissed Archie off to no end if I died for no reason like that."

Jessie nodded. She realized how tightly she was clutching the doll, and she made a point of releasing some of the pressure in her fist.

"Tell you what," Rubio said. "Let's head back to Cerro Viejo, and we'll ask around about the doll. There's a chance it belongs to one of the kids there. Maybe they know what it was doing way out here. How does that sound?"

"It sounds like you're being chivalrous."

"I don't know about that. I just want help. This is the best I can do."

Jessie looked at the doll's eyes, but there were no answers there, either. "I suppose I should consider myself lucky."

"How's that?"

"I could've ended up with a far less understanding guide."

"Don't say that yet. You haven't seen the bill."

"This isn't a free tour?"

"Are you kidding? I'm charging you five U.S. dollars for that bottle of water. Haven't you heard that Costa Rica is one giant tourist trap?" He almost said it with a straight face.

At that moment, Jessie advanced him in her mind from stranger to friend. Just like that, he'd proven himself to be someone worth knowing. He could've reacted a hundred different ways to her tears. But he chose empathy, and that put her at peace.

"Okay," she said, holding the doll against her chest. "We'll go. But we'll ask around at the village when we get there."

"You bet."

"And we'll see if anyone knows anything."

"Definitely."

She motioned for him to lead, and he picked his way up the slope, choosing what looked to be the safest path.

Jessie bent herself to the task, literally, tucking one of the doll's arms into her pocket so she could lean down and use both hands to climb. Minutes later, she reached the top, her fingers dirty but the rest of her in fine shape, at least as fine as she could have been, considering the fragile state of her emotions. Rubio was already heading back the way they'd come, but Jessie wasn't so quick to leave. She stared down into the gulch, where the shadows of dusk had by now claimed nearly everything. She marked that place on the map of her heart.

Then she turned and left it alone, at least for now.

Chapter Fifteen

Rubio had bigger things to worry about than finding the owner of the doll.

In two days, he had to serve as Archie's proxy and travel to San Jose to sign whatever papers the hospital required to make the clinic's closing official. He dreaded that visit for two reasons. One, putting his signature down meant moving on, and he wasn't quite ready for that yet. And two, *Señorita* Gavina Herrera.

The day they'd met, she'd smiled at him often while she spoke with Archie about the clinic. By chance, he'd run into her again a few hours later. She was five years older than him but could've passed for twenty-five, with the sterile good looks of an urban professional and all the right hobbies—yoga, Pilates, and charity auctions. Their relationship lasted only a few months and had ended badly, but Rubio was the kind of man with rose-colored hindsight; the good memories always burned the brightest.

He glanced over his shoulder. Archie's daughter looked left and right, her keen eyes taking in every detail of the tropical forest. Did she realize how much she resembled *su padre*? But for all their similarities, the differences between them were as vivid as the stars now appearing against the dark eastern sky. Archie was jolly, all the way from his graying sideburns to his scarred right foot, where he claimed to have been bitten by a rattler in Colorado. Jessie, in contrast, was reserved. But Rubio ascribed that to her deafness.

She caught him staring. "Say it."

Rubio, a little embarrassed, slowed his steps. "Uh, say what, exactly?"

"You're thinking something but not saying it. What's wrong? I wore waterproof makeup, so I know it's not running even though I'm sweating—or *glistening*, as real ladies do."

"Glistening?"

"You're not familiar with the word? It's the socially acceptable form of perspiring. It makes sweating in strange countries sort of sexy. Or not."

"That's…not what I was thinking."

"I know. You had my father written all over your face."

Rubio stopped walking. "How do you know that?"

"Handicapped people develop a sixth sense."

"You don't seem very handicapped to me."

"I have a sticker on my license plate to prove it."

"That doesn't prove anything."

"It proves I can get the best parking places."

Rubio noticed that she'd moved very close to him. The daylight had all but vanished, and in a few minutes, she probably wouldn't be able to see what he was saying. He could have touched her by barely lifting his hand. "We should get going."

Jessie nodded.

Rubio got them moving again, wishing the night wasn't robbing him of his chance to talk to her. He sensed the tension in her and wanted to do what he could to alleviate it. He owed that much to Archie. She was courageous for coming out here and facing the site of his death, and Rubio felt helpless for not being able to do more than lead her back and forth like some kind of Hispanic sherpa.

That made him smile, and he felt a little better.

When they finally reached the village, night had settled over the world, and the colored lights strung from the eaves of the cantina looked like a constellation. On the weekends, when the honeymooners from the nearby lodges congregated here, the bartender hired musicians to perform a mixture of mariachi and American rock. But tonight the establishment was relatively quiet. Though the kitchen was enclosed, the taproom itself had only one wall, leaving the place open to the warm evening air. Rubio returned a few waves.

The clinic was one of the few buildings in Cerro Viejo that was locked at night. Rubio used his key and turned on the light, then fetched two bottles of water from the same refrigerator that held their medical supplies. "I have a few patients tomorrow," he said, "but we can make the rounds in between appointments and see about finding whoever lost that doll."

"Is eight o'clock too early?"

"I'm one of those annoying guys you hear about who gets up at dawn and goes swimming."

"Ah, I should've known. Well, at least you're not a jogger."

He made a face. "I may be guilty on that one, too."

"I see. And getting up early on Saturday mornings?"

"On occasion."

"This is getting serious. You don't drink protein shakes, do you?"

He laughed. "That's where I draw the line."

"Good. I was starting to think my father had worked with a crazy person." She smiled at him. "But anyway, I'll see you in the morning."

"Do you want me to walk yourto room?"

"I'll be all right. And thanks, by the way. For today."

"No problem."

She turned, stepped from the clinic, and closed the door gently behind her.

Rubio leaned on Greta's counter and sipped his water. Other than the faint buzzing of the overhead fluorescent, the room was perfectly quiet. The building's concrete walls cut off the noises of insects and amphibians from outside. Still, he was far away from understanding what it was like to live without sound. He heard his own respiratory process as his breath passed in and out. He heard the water moving in the bottle when he took a drink. And if he concentrated, he could even hear Archie's voice as the mischievous doctor said, "If only you could meet my daughter, Rubio my boy. Maybe once I'm back in the States, you can pay us a visit. That girl needs to get out of the house every now and then!" And then he added, "Of course, if you ever laid a finger on her, I'd have to murder you with tools from my garage and sink your body in the river."

"Here's to you, doc," he said, hoisting his bottle. "Here's to you."

He left the clinic, shutting off the memories as well as the lights.

****

So U went where he died?

I had to see.

&?

And nothing. That's just part of the process.

Sorry, grl. Wish I coulda been there.

Lying flat on her bed with her phone held in both hands above her face, Jessie wished the same thing. If she could have reached through the ether and pulled Li into the room, she wouldn't have hesitated. You had friends, and then you had people who seemed to be you with different names. *I found something out there*, she typed.

True luv and high adventure?

A toy. A kid was out there.

What R U talking about?

I don't know. But I think there was a reason Dad went there.

Huh?

Jessie wasn't sure how to explain herself. Was this a hunch or just a daughter not ready to let go? *There's an explanation for what he was doing out there, but I haven't found it yet.*

Sounds like BS.

You're probably right.

No gunman in the grassy knoll, babe.

I know. She supposed that Li was probably correct. They'd known each other since their junior year in high school, when Jessie had transferred from the deaf academy and entered a world where kids either stared at you or pretended you weren't there. Li had been her roommate in college, her ears, and her priest when Jessie confessed to sleeping with Jamal Walker from chemistry class. Li hadn't recommended any Hail Marys but she *had* demanded all the details.

So what's your plan, Stan?

Don't know, Joe.

Just don't push it too hard, k?

Jessie almost agreed, but her thumb poised over the keypad, unwilling to promise anything. *Goodnight, sister.*

Night.

Jessie let the phone fall to the bed. She stared at the lazy ceiling fan overhead. With the windows open, the room was balmy. It smelled of plants and sea salt—nothing at all like home. If she wanted, she could've walked a few hundred yards to the east and come upon the Caribbean at night. The very word conjured pirates in her mind and beautiful people in skimpy clothes and the possibility of finding treasure washed up on the shore. In that instant she wanted more than anything to be rich enough to buy a sailboat, one that required two to work the lines, and together she and her phantom companion would do nothing but roam from one coastal town to the next, drinking piña coladas and lying in each other's arms.

She turned her head and there on her pillow was the doll.

Damn thing. If she hadn't found it hidden in the weeds, Jessie's thoughts wouldn't have been so restless. Maybe she could've slept. But she'd mentioned it to Li, and then Li had said that thing about the grassy knoll, and one link in the chain invariably led to the next, so Jessie lay there and wondered when she'd become such a conspiracy theorist. She almost wished that someone really *was* responsible for what happened to her father, because then she'd have a target for the bullets of her sadness and rage.

Sensing the danger of such ideas, she got up and went to the tiny bathroom. She washed her face and spent some time examining the ever-aging condition of her pores. Had she spent more time with her skin as a teenager, maybe she'd be better off today. Archie had been pretty terrific at covering all the motherly duties as well as those of the macho dad, though he hadn't really been on the cutting edge of moisturizer use. But at seventeen, Jessie had been the only chick in school who could throw a tight spiral with a football, and you better believe the boys thought that was cool.

She made sure she deposited the moist towelette into the proper bin. Three cans stood near the sink, asking her to divide her recycling accordingly. That only served to remind her what a slacker she was when it came to being green back home.

She turned out the light and went to bed.

What if Li was wrong? What if an unknown person *was* responsible for what happened?

"Cut it out," she snarled at herself. Unless she wanted to be up all night, she needed to think about something else, such as sailing the Caribbean or the color of the Costa Rican sunset or how Rubio's ass looked in his khaki pants. But the darker thoughts were more insistent. Contemplating them, Jessie again remembered the words of Confucius her father had taught her. Not only did the old philosopher talk about beauty, but he also knew the perils of anger.

"'Before you embark on a journey of revenge,'" Jessie whispered, "'dig two graves.'"

That was no decent way to fall asleep.

Chapter Sixteen

She opened her eyes the next morning, and a hundred butterflies covered her bed. They rested in vibrant bands of color, preening themselves, slowly working their wings. At some point in the night they'd entered through the open window, and for whatever reason, they'd taken a liking to the white comforter with its islander pattern embroidered along the edge. The butterflies startled her, and she hung in a half-sitting position, weight on her elbows, hair in her face. Their wings blinked open and closed; it was like watching flower petals in time-lapse photography.

"Good morning," she said breathlessly.

Two of them took flight, weaving non-direct patterns to the window and the morning world beyond. The others—dozens of them—remained on her bed.

Jessie wanted to take a picture but couldn't reach her phone without disturbing them. If she'd dreamed last night, she couldn't remember the plot or who was involved, which was rare for her. Perhaps she was dreaming now, looking at a landscape of stained-glass wings.

She didn't move, not wanting to break the spell.

These were not the monarchs with which she was familiar. The lavenders and pale blues gave these specimens an ethereal quality, as if they'd originated in a fairy wood. In fact, now that she considered it—

They flew.

As if answering a call only they could hear, the butterflies erupted from the bed. Wings flickering, they poured through the funnel of the nearest window. A moment later they were gone.

Jessie held very still, hardly breathing. She stared at the window through which they'd departed, but she saw only treetops and the orange morning sky.

****

"One ticket for a birth at midnight in two days, what do you say?"

Rubio sighed and dug out his wallet. "Is this even legal?"

Finn Vargas chuckled. "Since when has that stopped me?"

Rubio couldn't help but grin; this man always had that effect on him. Vargas was fifty years old and baked hard by a lifetime of dancing and drinking under the sun. He lived in a little cabin on the shore and seemed to enjoy some kind of magical pact with the ocean. He and the Caribbean had long ago agreed that, instead of growing old and dying, Vargas would one day wander into the waves and be reborn as a sea turtle, to roam the coast until the time came to shed that skin for the next.

"Let's make it official, my friend." Vargas pulled a curled notebook from one of the many pockets of his guide shirt, licked the tip of his pencil, and scribbled Rubio's name in the slot he'd just purchased.

"What are my odds?" Rubio asked.

"I put them at three to one."

"That's not so bad."

"Three to one is what I tell everybody." He tore off a tiny slip of paper. "Here. Your receipt. May the luck of the pre-Columbian gods be with you."

"Since when were you religious?"

Vargas's smile returned. It came and went like a lantern in the fog. "Hey, man, I was baptized by the Catholics when I was a baby, by the Baptist missionaries who thought I was feral at the age of fifteen, and by a prostitute named Maria when I was twenty-one. You see these?" He shook his tangle of beads and seashell necklaces. "I got my rosary, my Egyptian ankh, and something the children made me at the craft show last spring."

"And a rabbit's foot in your pocket?"

"Better." He leaned close, as if imparting a great secret. "A condom." He stepped back and shrugged. "Like American Express, you don't leave home without it."

Rubio shook his head. "I'm sure Hanna appreciates being the centerpiece of your raffle."

"Capitalism, man. I didn't invent it. But I *did* read Donald Trump's autobiography."

Rubio glanced down at his receipt, but the handwriting was indecipherable. "I better be getting to work."

"You do that, Rubio Mora, you do that. And while you're staring into people's throats and checking old dudes for hernias, I'll be escorting three lusty American housewives on vacation from Nebraska, each one better looking than the last."

"Story of my life."

"Hey, if you want, maybe the five of us can go for drinks tonight at one of the resorts. Get a little liquor in them, you might end up as lucky as me. You know what a sucker they are for the noble savage." He struck a pose, chest out and head back, as he suspected the aboriginals might have looked before they were spoiled by the weaknesses of European settlers.

"I'm sure it'd be great, but I'm not Indian."

"Since when did that matter? Not everyone can be so fortunate as to be a Bribri. We're a small but heroic tribe. But you know what? For fifty U.S. dollars, I can probably get you on the roll as an official member."

Rubio laughed and headed for the clinic. "Take it easy, Finn."

"I'm serious!" Vargas called. "Everyone loves native people. A guy with your looks and tribal papers could be in Hollywood right now. Let's make it forty!"

Rubio left the man to his schemes. Finn Vargas led excursions to the turtle beaches by night, but during the daylight hours he could be found hustling, carving whistles out of wood, and telling stories that were so outlandish they had to be at least partially true.

I should be more like him, Rubio thought. Men like Vargas didn't worry about establishing a career and building a financial portfolio. Rubio had worked hard to get where he was, riding San Jose ambulances in twelve-hour shifts and putting away more money than he spent. He had saved lives, and what could be more fulfilling than that? But he still felt as if something were missing. Whatever it was, it eluded his grasp.

Vargas had gotten along very well with Archie Alomar. They traded tales and played cards and spoke to one another in Portuguese, though neither of them knew the language very well. Archie seemed to be the only one who could get an honest answer out of the grinning charlatan. When word of Archie's death reached the village, it was Vargas who tipped his head back in grief and shouted at God until he was hoarse, then fell to his knees and wept.

"Today no swimming?" Greta asked in broken Spanish as Rubio let himself into the clinic.

"Not in the mood."

"Meeting tomorrow, yes? Big rich hospital woman."

"Thanks for reminding me. You realize that when I come back, you and I will be down to our final pay period? I think you should use some time today to look online for a job."

Greta growled a reply, then switched to English to find more words to express her frustration. "…and the Wi-Fi is down, most likely because those damn monkeys have been playing with the dish on the roof again, so even if I wanted to search the classifieds, I couldn't. And it doesn't matter, anyway, because we have nine appointments today and that's a lot of paperwork that I have to complete whether we're closing up shop or not!"

"Why is everyone yelling this morning?"

"This is not yelling. This is the voice women use when explaining things to men."

"Ah, right. I knew I recognized it. Who's first this morning?"

Greta handed him the clipboard. "Possible flu at the Reyes house."

Rubio scanned the list, looking for anything that sounded like a priority. Since he'd been temporarily entrusted with the health of the people of Cerro Viejo, he was overly cautious when it came to what seemed to be everyday nicks and illnesses. Though he had medical training and had earned citations for his actions in emergencies, he was no doctor, and he had no intention of letting anyone get seriously sick while it was his hand on the tiller.

"You're very good at this, you know," Greta said in English.

He didn't look up from the clipboard. "Very good at what?"

"I see the look on your face when you think about the people here. But you don't need to worry. You're taking very good care of them. They trust you. They'd follow you anywhere. Mothers are wishing their daughters were either old enough to marry or not already wedded, because they adore you."

Rubio dismissed the notion with a shake of his head. "They say never to date your patients, your students, or your boss. Besides, when they look at me, they're probably just thinking of Archie, hoping that some of him rubbed off on me."

"Some of him has rubbed off on us all, but you're wrong about what they see. Men like Dr. Alomar...as good as they are, they're outsiders. Like I am. Our skin is too pale and our ideas too mixed up by commercialism. You, though, you're..."

"A foolish idealist?"

"That's not what I was going to say."

"Overworked and underpaid?"

"You're a *believer*, Rubio. You have a city education but a love of the country. You haven't been corrupted by life—at least not yet. Not to mention the fact that you're tall and handsome as the devil's doorman. But now you have to go to the exam room because I don't want to give you too many compliments so early in the morning. Go on, shoo!"

"Okay, I'm going. And thanks, by the way."

"Thank me by healing the sick."

"I'll do what I can." He headed for the examination room to prepare for his first appointment, but he stopped halfway there when Jessie stepped through the clinic door.

She wore jeans that fit her in the snug way the Americans preferred, with the cuffs rolled up an inch where they met her white athletic shoes. Her top was white linen, unbuttoned halfway, with a T-shirt beneath that matched the stripe on the side of her shoes.

Greta waved from behind her desk. "Hello, Miss Jessie."

"Good morning, Greta."

Rubio realized he was staring, and so he quickly smiled a neutral smile and said, "I hope you slept better than I did."

"It's already been a strange morning, but the bed was great."

"I'll take your word for it. I haven't slept in an actual bed since I took this job."

"So...what? You sleep on a straw mat like a monk?"

"That doesn't sound very comfortable," he admitted.

"You hang upside down like a bat?"

Rubio almost told her the truth, then decided that gentlemen probably didn't talk about their beds with women they'd met only yesterday. "Let's just say I have a somewhat unusual bachelor pad. Have you eaten yet?"

"I was about to ask if there was anywhere in the village where a woman could buy a plate of *gallo pinto.*"

"That can definitely be arranged. Let me see this first patient, then I'll walk you over to what passes for our local restaurant."

"I can manage. Just point the way. I'll take a raincheck on your guide service until after you're finished doing your rounds. But then I'm laying claim to you." She pulled the plantain doll from where it was hanging on her back pocket. "You can show me where to find the owner of this."

Rubio had forgotten about the toy. It was clear that Jessie had not. Was she taking this too far? Was she letting her sadness turn into obsession? Rubio was no psychologist, but he knew that humans could go to extremes when propelled by the need to lay their own sorrow to rest. "I'll do what I can, though I'm not promising we'll get anywhere with our search."

"I never ask for promises." She gestured quickly in sign language. "That means thank you."

"You're welcome. But I think I may need to ask a favor in return."

"Name it."

"I have to go to San Jose tomorrow and meet with the hospital administrators about shutting this place down. It might help if you're there. I'm not sure about the kind of paperwork involved. But since you're the executor of Archie's estate—"

"I understand. That's why I came. I'd be happy to go."

"Great. We'll need to leave fairly early. It's only a hundred kilometers as the crow flies, but the road is nowhere near a straight line, plus it's full of holes, so we won't make very good time." Rubio didn't mention

Gavina. The last time they'd spoken, she sounded as if she might be reconsidering their decision to split, and Rubio wasn't necessarily comfortable with the idea of being alone with her behind closed doors. There had been a time when he wondered if he were falling in love with her, but that day had passed. Having Jessie there would hopefully dissuade Gavina from being her usual forward self. "We can get something to eat along the way."

Jessie said that sounded fine, said goodbye to Greta, and took one step toward the door before stopping and saying, "I noticed there are a lot of butterflies here."

Rubio paused in the doorway of the exam room. "Butterflies?"

"Yes, this morning I..." She looked vexed but also enchanted, like a woman under the effects of a wizard's spell. "There were a few of them in my room."

"Sleep with the windows open?"

"Yes."

"It happens. If the night gets a little cool, one or two of them sometimes make their way inside."

"One or two. Right."

"I have a friend named Finn. He says butterflies are lucky. He'll go out of his way to avoid accidentally injuring them."

She nodded. "Okay, then. Thanks. I'll see you a little bit later." Smiling uncertainly, she left the clinic.

Rubio looked at Greta. "What was all that about butterflies?"

"What do you think? The young lady is her father's daughter. Dr. Alomar once put a chair on the roof so he could sketch pictures of the sunrise. His child is bound to be a little strange."

"I suppose so." But *strange* wasn't the first word that came to mind when he thought of her. He admitted to himself, if not to Greta, that he found her intriguing.

Then he recalled Archie's warning about his mangled body ending up in the river, and he smiled to himself and met his first patient of the day.

Chapter Seventeen

I have a friend named Finn. He says butterflies are lucky.

If that were true, then Jessie had luck enough to run through a few casinos and come out ahead. Enjoying her breakfast of rice and beans, she looked around as if trying to see Cerro Viejo for the first time again. This was not an impoverished *National Geographic* village with barefooted children. The families here worked at the resorts nestled along the banks of the causeways and seemed like the residents of any small town in America, with the exception of vehicles; because they lived in a national park comprised of just as much water as land, their use of motor vehicles was restricted. The air was clean, and the people smiled a lot.

Jessie saw why her father had loved it. The people benefited from free enterprise and democracy without being corrupted by them—at least not yet. She supposed even that would change, given time. But for now, it was still a land of butterflies and good fortune.

After paying for her meal, she strolled along the main road and eventually made her way to the clinic. Rubio met her at the door, wearing fresh scrubs and a bracelet of soapstone beads. The beads flashed as bright as polished ivory against the dark skin of his wrist.

"You'll have to teach me some of that," he said as she approached.

"Some of what?"

"Sign language. This is about all I know." He held up his hand in the Vulcan sign.

"Live long and prosper," Jessie said.

"Ah, so you know that show."

"Are you kidding? Dad was a science-fiction nerd. I grew up hearing him quote Yoda and Doctor Who. What he wanted more than anything was to be the first physician on Mars."

"Mars? He would've been perfect there. But I hear it's *really* cold, so I don't think I'd be joining him. So, uh, do you want to see what we can find out about the doll?"

"Of course. But are you serious about learning to sign?"

"One of the kids here, Madelina, she wears hearing aids in both ears. Something about an infection when she was an infant. But I thought if she and her family could learn a bit about how signing works…"

"It's not as difficult as it looks. But I only know American Sign, ASL."

"Shouldn't be a problem. Nearly everyone here speaks English."

"I've noticed that. I can't imagine the States being entirely bilingual, but here it's apparently the norm."

"Well, not every town is as closely associated with the tourism industry, but in certain parts of the country, like this one, you need English if you're going to get a job. We have tourists from all over the world— Germany, England, Israel—and so we need to have a default language. Someone told me once that I have a funny accent, and I explained that I learned to speak English by watching American police shows and

British comedies."

"I have trouble sometimes with British accents," Jessie admitted. "The words aren't always shaped the same. Of course, a similar thing happened when I visited Atlanta. I went for weeks without knowing what they were trying to say with the word *yawl* or *yall* or however on earth they pronounce *you all*."

Rubio laughed. "Come on. I think the best place to start is at Mama Tioni's house. She looks after about half a dozen kids in the morning while their parents are at work. She lives in that yellow house there behind the grocer's."

Jessie walked beside him. They kept their pace slow. The day was turning out to be just like yesterday—perfect. "Is the weather ever bad here?" she asked. "Or is it always like this?"

"Let's see…no snowstorms, no droughts, no hard freezes, no tornadoes, no smog. But we do get a lot of rain."

"Rain? That's it? Do you even own a heavy coat?"

"I have a windbreaker."

"Must be nice."

"It's all relative. Every once in a while I'd like to see it snow. In the movies, they catch the flakes on their tongues. Have you ever done that?"

"Sure. I've been to Denver in the winter, New York at Christmas…"

"What do they taste like?"

"Water. And they last only a second before they melt."

"I'll trade you a sloth for your snowflakes."

"A what?"

He stopped her by touching her arm, then pointed

to treetops. "See that white branch? Look about two meters to the right of it."

Jessie's well-trained eyes found it immediately. Clinging to a limb behind a partial covering of long green leaves was something that looked like a cross between a monkey and a koala bear. It didn't move, clasping the tree as if carved there.

"That's a sloth? I've never seen one in real life. Outside the zoo, anyway."

She didn't catch Rubio's response until she looked away from the creature. "...but they're usually around if you're patient and know where to search."

"Is it...sleeping?"

"Just wait."

Jessie stared at it, letting her senses take over. A vagrant breeze wandered through the village as if lost, touching her neck as it went on its way. Beside her, Rubio smelled of shampoo and just a touch of cologne.

The sloth lifted an arm and ponderously scratched itself.

"Hey, he's awake!"

"Yep, just barely."

After the sloth, things got only more amazing. Rubio showed her a massive ground mosaic made of glass and the painted lids of tin cans. He pointed out a lizard he claimed could walk on water.

"I get it now," she said. "Water-walking lizards? This is the part where you play around with the outsider and see how gullible she is."

"You think I'd do that to you?"

"You were a friend of my father. You're a rascal by association."

"Point taken. But actually, it's true. It really walks

on water. Flaps of skin on its feet create air pockets when it runs. As long it moves fast, it doesn't sink. It's officially a striped basilisk, but we call it a Jesus lizard."

"Nice."

"Four percent of the entire world's wildlife is found in our little country. It's more ecologically diverse than anywhere else on earth. If only our baseball team could manage to beat the Nicaraguans, we'd be on top of the world."

"Being on top isn't all it's cracked up to be."

"Perhaps. We Ticos aren't necessarily the most ambitious people."

"Ticos?"

"That's what we call ourselves. Ticos. What do you call yourself? An Arizonan?"

"Not on a daily basis. Mostly I'm just a woman in need of a personal stylist to do my hair every morning. After that maybe I could get around to labeling myself."

"You're not like him in every way, are you?"

"Dad labeled himself all the time, if that's what you mean. He was an activist, a liberal, a scholar, a ham-radio operator, and a member of Doctors Without Borders, not to mention a daydreamer and an unpublished poet."

"And his daughter isn't any of those things?"

"I'm some of those things some of the time, but I'm not all of them all of the time, if that makes any sense. Every day is a little different, depending."

"Depending on what?"

"On whether or not I wake up and find that I'm out of coffee." She realized she was talking about herself far more than usual, but she blamed it on the lizard; in a land where reptiles walked on water, you weren't expected to be your normal self. "Fortunately, they tell me that Costa Rica makes some of the best coffee in the world, and from what I've sampled so far, I'm not going to disagree. Not to mention it's a lot cheaper than the four dollars I pay for a cup back home."

"A cup of coffee costs *four dollars*?"

"Well, at the diner down the street it's only fifty cents, or a quarter if you catch Beatrice in a good mood when she's pouring the pot. But when I'm feeling wasteful, yeah, I've spent four dollars on one. Silly, isn't it?"

"Damn."

They reached the brightest house in Cerro Viejo, yellow with freshly painted white trim. From the overhang of the flat roof dangled a line of mobiles that looked as if they'd been made by children, their trinkets turning slowly in the intermittent breeze.

Rubio touched her arm. "Mama Tioni doesn't speak much English, so I may have to translate for you. Actually she *knows how* to speak it, but she chooses not to. Long story—something about her ex-husband, who was a Brit. Anyway, just so you know."

"I understand. I think."

Rubio pulled a shoestring attached to a brass bell near the door. Jessie knew what the bell supposedly sounded like, a sharp but not unpleasing noise that she imagined to be like the sudden appearance of the color orange. The wind, on the other hand, probably sounded much like long ribbons of pale blue.

The door opened, revealing the female version of Abraham Lincoln.

That was Jessie's initial impression of Mama

Tioni, who stood at least five-ten, with a lean and solemn face. She was not comely by any estimation, but there was a gravity to her that inspired obedience, even in those first few seconds.

As Rubio spoke to her in Spanish, Tioni's colorless eyes went to Jessie. After a few moments, she signaled them to come inside.

Rubio gestured for Jessie to go first, and a few steps later, she found herself in a remarkably ordered room full of undersized desks and finger-painted art. A young woman sat on a stool in the middle of the circled desks, making alphabet letters out of clay. Seven children around the age of five did their best to copy her example.

Jessie followed Tioni around the back wall, stopping at a whiteboard mounted on a wheeled frame. Tioni spoke as she turned, looking at Jessie for an expected response.

Rubio intervened. Jessie imagined his explanation. Please excuse my friend. She can't hear what you're saying. She's from the planet Neptune, where everyone is born deaf, but they sure can cook a mean fettuccine alfredo.

She extended her hand. "I'm Jessie."

Mama Tioni didn't like what she saw. That much was clear. Her cheeks were pitted like flaking paint, the echoes of untreated teenage acne, giving her the look of someone who didn't have time for pampered *Americanos* with frivolous agendas. She shook Jessie's hand, then picked up a dry-erase marker and wrote on the whiteboard in a surprisingly feminine hand: *I promise me not ever speak English. Okay this?*

"Yes, of course."

Ex-husband asshole from Liverpool.

"I've never been to Liverpool, but I know what you mean."

Said no Spanish in his house. He gone now. So screw him, no English now.

Jessie was liking this woman more by the second. "Gotcha."

Tioni said something to Rubio, who translated. "She says that she needs to take the kids outside for recess in a few minutes, but she has a little time until then."

Jessie nodded and addressed Tioni directly. "My father was Dr. Alomar."

Mama Tioni's somber face brightened, making her look years younger in an instant. She wrote, *He bake pineapple cake for me!*

"I know the one," Jessie replied. "I have his recipe in a box at home."

He not like others. Only two good man left. And now only one. She pointed her marker at Rubio, who shook his head in denial. *My heart hurt with you. Wish he here today.*

"Me, too. Thank you. But I was hoping you could help me with something."

Rubio conveyed Tioni's response. "She says she'll do everything she can, but she isn't sure she'll be of much help. She doesn't get out much. Babysitting the children while their parents are at work takes most of her time."

Jessie showed her the doll, with its round fabric head, cheery facial features, and limbs made of lacquered plantain peels. "I was wondering if you've ever seen this before?"

Tioni took the doll in her long, inelegant hands, turning it over twice before replying to Rubio and pointing vaguely westward.

"She says that she's never seen any of the children carrying it around, but she knows that Ina's father sells a lot of arts and crafts like this to tourists at the resorts across the water. Ina is the little girl there in the red."

Ina's fingers attempted to wring a recognizable shape from her clay. She and several of the other children were talking simultaneously, so that the room was probably filled with little voices—the constant chatter that so often tested the perseverance of adults; what was that like? "Would it be okay if we talked with her?" Jessie asked.

Tioni took to the doll to the girl's desk and knelt beside it. Jessie watched as Tioni displayed the doll and spoke with the animated face and patient pronunciation that all the good teachers mastered. She nodded her head several times, then smiled and touched the child on the arm in thanks. When she returned, she relayed her findings to Rubio.

"The doll isn't Ina's," he explained, "but she says her daddy makes them to sell to the rich white people in the fancy hotels."

"Rich white people?"

"Her words, not mine. She's referring to the resorts on the banks across the water. Her father is head of maintenance at a place called the—" His last word appeared as a jumble that Jessie couldn't interpret. Usually she was good at guessing and filling in the blanks when she missed someone's spoken word, but this time, the ability failed her.

"Where is he at?" she asked.

Rubio repeated himself. "Man-uh-toos." Then he took Tioni's marker and spelled it on the board: *Manatus*. "It's named for a big statue of a manatee out front."

"A manatee? Like a whale?"

"Something like that."

"You have whales here?"

"Other than the statue, no."

"Can we go there?"

"Can you wait till after my next appointment?"

"Of course." She didn't feel like waiting. She felt like swimming across the water and continuing her investigation. "I'll just…hang out in my room and catch up on some reading."

"We have Internet access at the clinic, assuming the satellite receiver is functioning properly again. Sometimes the spider monkeys get a little too curious. But you're welcome to use it if you want."

"That would be great, thanks."

They said goodbye to Mama Tioni, who offered to help again if they needed it, which Jessie wasn't ruling out. What had started as a trip to conclude her father's finances had already transformed into a kind of personal vision quest, so anything was possible. Maybe all of this was silly and pointless and wouldn't bring him back. Or maybe it was just an elaborate way of letting him go. Whatever. Jessie just wanted to know why he'd been out at that ravine.

They returned to the clinic, with Rubio pointing out flower specimens and explaining how the matrix of waterways affected Tortuguero's growing season and supported over fifty types of freshwater fish. He spoke of the industrious leaf-cutter ants and the way seed fibers of the ceiba tree were used to make cushions for furniture.

Jessie listened to him with her eyes.

Chapter Eighteen

"Keep the brace on for another two days, and don't forget your exercises."

"Thanks, doc," Esteban said.

"I'm not a doc," Rubio said, "but you're welcome. Just remember not to lift anything heavier than your coffee cup."

"Oh, I got something heavier, all right, but I'll let my girlfriend do the lifting there."

Rubio shook his head as Esteban laughed at his own joke. "I'm serious about this. That's the only way it's going to heal."

"Yeah, I'm too crude for my own good sometimes. See you around, doc. You know, you've got to admit that was funny." Chuckling to himself, Esteban left the clinic.

Rubio wondered if he should have joined the man in his laughter. Archie had possessed the kind of bedside manner that enabled him to be comfortable with any type of patient, from conservative Catholic grandmother to blue-tongued merchant marine. It was the kind of thing they couldn't really teach you in medical school.

Rubio stepped into the adjacent restroom and changed out of his scrub top, donning a white linen shirt with buttons of stained gallinzo wood. He leaned toward the mirror, bracing himself on the sink with one hand and inspecting his cheeks with the other. He'd shaved this morning as he did nearly every day, but by the afternoon the relentless genes he'd inherited from his grandfather were again asserting themselves. The old man's nickname had been Blackbeard, after the infamous pirate; they said he'd grown a mustache as early as thirteen, the envy of every boy in school. Rubio preferred the opposite extreme. But he didn't want to spend any time plowing a razor across his face when he could be hanging out with Jessie Alomar.

"Guilty as charged," he told his reflection.

She fascinated him. Rubio had come from a poor family and was the first to graduate from college. He'd traveled up and down the Central American coast—mainly on the Atlantic side—and had met people from every layer of the social strata. He'd danced in the *discotheques* of Mexico City and studied airborne pathogens near the Mayan ruins of Belize. He'd experienced more than one meaningful relationship along the way. But standing there in front of the mirror, with no one to impress but himself, he couldn't remember ever thinking about a woman so often after having met her so recently.

He washed his face and spent a few minutes tidying up the exam room. Maybe he was simply attaching Jessie to her father, for whom he was still grieving. He'd taken enough psychology courses to know the power of emotional transference. Was he reassigning his affection where it didn't necessarily belong?

He thought of how she'd fretted over *yall* and *yawl*, and he smiled. He'd first heard the phrase when he visited San Antonio with his college *fútbol* squad. A grinning Texan named Tom Pickering had asked them, "Hey, boys, you know what the plural form of *yall* is?"

They'd shaken their heads, having little idea what he was talking about.

"*All yall!*"

Pickering had chortled and slapped Rubio's bewildered friend Sergio on the shoulder.

Amused by this random memory, Rubio walked into the lobby to find Greta with a magazine on her lap.

"How y'all doing?" he asked in English.

She looked at him as if he were an alien descended from the mother ship. "Sometimes I don't understand a single word you're saying. The same thing was true with Dr. Alomar. Are all doctors secretly insane?"

"Why does everyone keep calling me a doctor?"

"You save lives, don't you?"

"I worked in an ambulance. That's not the same as stitching people up in the emergency room."

"You ever give someone CPR, make them breathe again?"

"Twice, yeah."

"See there? You're a doctor *and* a hero. The Chinese say that once you save someone's life, you're responsible for it."

"Sometimes I'm barely responsible for myself."

Greta turned the page and kept her attention on her magazine article. "You're lucky I'm not twenty years younger. I'd force you to marry me so I could beat some sense into you like only a wife can do."

Laughing, Rubio headed for the door. "I'll see you tomorrow, Greta."

"You have San Jose tomorrow."

"Right. I suppose that means I'll need to wear a

tie."

"If that Herrera woman tells you that we're shutting down, you have my permission to strangle her with that tie. Call me and I'll help you get rid of the body."

Rubio didn't reply, just let himself outside and squinted against the sun. What Greta didn't know was that the *Herrera woman* was more than just the chief financial officer at the hospital. Things would have been easier if that were the case. But there were pages written between them, a story with one of those endings that left its characters wondering what had gone wrong.

****

The water taxi pulled away from the jetty on the edge of the village. The little outboard motor looked like it hadn't been cleaned since the nineties, but it chugged along gamely, pushing the small craft across the water.

Wearing her silvered sunglasses, Jessie sat just forward of the driver in the center of the boat, her seat a wooden plank topped with the kind of cushion you took to pad the bleachers at high school football games. She wore a light jacket to deflect the random droplets that occasionally leapt the side of the boat.

What do you call the side of a boat? she wondered. Certainly it had an official name, such as prow or stern or some such term.

"Doing okay?" Rubio asked. He sat at the front of the boat, but faced her, so that his back was toward their destination on the opposite shore about two hundred yards away. "You're not prone to seasickness, are you?"

"Not sure. I live in a desert."

By the slight strain in his neck muscles and the way his mouth changed slightly when he spoke, she could tell he was raising his voice to be heard over the motor; silly man. "I've seen the deserts of Mexico. Beautiful place."

"Hey, aren't we supposed to be wearing life jackets?" She didn't ask because she felt as if she needed one, but simply to kid him a bit. "Isn't that standard procedure when shuttling clueless tourists around the canals at a national park?"

"I couldn't find one that matched your outfit. I didn't want you to be out of style."

"Very thoughtful of you."

"If we capsize, the rule is to stay with the boat."

"If we capsize, I'm screaming my head off, thank you very much." Taking her cue from him, she intentionally spoke a little louder. She'd been told more than once that she was sometimes difficult to understand, even on a normal day, much less when she was skimming across the current on a noisy bass boat. "So this hotel we're going to…"

"The Manatus."

"Right. Any chance they serve lunch there?"

"Have you not eaten yet? I thought that while I was seeing the last of the patients—"

"I didn't think about it. Stupid, I know. But I walked around the village and met a lot of people, and I texted a friend back home, and before I knew it, I was in a boat without a lifejacket and hanging on for dear life."

"For a woman about to drown for lack of a life jacket, you don't look very frightened."

"Nerves of steel."

"Is that right?"

"I taught myself to swim in the neighbor's pool. I went to a special school, and I got home about half an hour before the public-school kids. It was in September, still hot. I didn't tell my dad about it until after I could already swim from one side to the other."

"Brave girl. But how's that going to help against the hungry caimans?"

"I already have that one figured out."

"Yes?"

"I don't have to out-swim them," she said. "I only have to out-swim *you*."

He smiled. "Oh, is that how it's going to be?"

"You bet it." She pointed behind him. "Looks like we made it."

He turned around just as the driver slowed the motor, guiding the boat toward a wide, well-made pier. The hull nudged a bumper made from old tires, and a dock boy in white shorts and a matching polo shirt quickly lashed the boat in place. He reached down to offer Rubio a hand, and they clasped like men do, their thumbs hooked together and their hands forming one large fist between them. Jessie had seen it countless times, in gladiator movies and ball games, and she wondered why women never did that. Maybe she could start a new trend.

But, no. When the young man in white leaned down to help her from the boat, he held his hand differently, palm up, like a chauffeur waiting for the delicate fingers of the queen. Jessie accepted automatically, managing to say thank you even while she was thinking about one day surprising the hell out of some random fellow by grabbing his hand like a man.

Rubio spoke with the boat operator, giving Jessie a few moments to take in her new surroundings. Unlike the village grass on the other side of the causeway, the lawn here was tended by professionals, trimmed around a clearing to where the treeline began. Immediately in front of her, near the end of the pier, was an elaborate, two-level deck overlooking the water. Several round tables, just big enough for two, sported unlit candles and fresh bouquets, inviting couples to stop by at any time throughout the day and relax with an uninterrupted view of the sky. From here, Jessie couldn't quite see the ocean, as it was blocked from view by the village's strip of land to the east, but she could smell it, even if no one else could.

The dock attendant said something she didn't catch. She assumed it was *Right this way* or *Follow me*. She and Rubio trailed him along the pier, turned left at the deck, and jogged up a few stone steps to a path leading to paradise.

To the left, bungalows nestled in the trees, serene and without any of the commercial fanfare Jessie had expected. On the right, a bar and dining area—roofed but without walls—waited to serve mid-afternoon refreshments. There were a dozen tables, but only one was occupied; two newlyweds held hands while a waiter holding a carafe told them how his daughter kept asking for a puppy every morning before he came to work. Jessie read his lips from fifty feet away and was impressed by his honest smile when the coupled laughed. He seem interested in more than just reciting the wine list.

The attendant led them to the end of the path and

the resort's surprisingly small main building. It had a tropical look to it, more comfortable than luxuriant, which suited Jessie's mood. It was the kind of place Jimmy Buffett would have chosen if given the choice between it and the Hilton. Beside the door was a wicker basket holding several styles of umbrellas and marked with a hand-written note: FOR YOUR CONVENIENCE. Sudden showers were supposedly common in the park, though Jessie had yet to be caught in one.

"Cozy little place, huh?" Rubio said as he held open the door for her.

"I was expecting something more…I'm not sure…"

"American?"

"Not necessarily," she said, stepping into a lobby with polished hardwood floors. "I thought it would be bigger, for one thing."

"It probably doesn't serve more than a dozen guests at once. More exclusive that way. Not to mention a lot quieter."

"I'll take your word for it."

He didn't seem to know what to say to that. Though he appeared completely comfortable with her disability, even the most empathic people never really knew what it was like. But the reverse was also true. As imaginative as she was, Jessie couldn't envision the sound of a giggling toddler or the sexy swing of a jazz trombone.

Rubio spoke with the gentleman behind the counter. Jessie left them to it, roaming the lobby and gathering up the data of this new place and new experience. The walls and furniture were natural rather than elegant. The windows were immense, permitting the outside world as much access as possible. Just off the lobby was a room sporting two public computer terminals, neither of which was currently in use. The screen-savers showed images of cartoon toucans wearing aviator goggles.

Jessie resisted the urge to plop down at the keyboard and read the news. Without a doubt, the Internet was her favorite invention of all time, beating out even her ceramic hair straightener, because it allowed her to connect with humanity in a way that seldom required the power of hearing. In the forums and chat rooms, everybody typed and nobody spoke, and there was nothing more wonderful than being on even ground with the rest of the world. Your battles were much easier to fight.

She saw a shadow on the wall in front of her and turned as Rubio approached.

"We may have a lead on the doll," he said.

"What did he say?"

"The little girl, Ina, her father works here. His name is Arturo. He's in charge of general upkeep, but right now he's a few kilometers down the bank, helping the park wardens set up a wildlife camera. He should be back in an hour or so. But Lucas at the desk says he's seen Arturo working on dolls exactly like that during his lunch break."

"Any reason he'd be out at that ravine with my father?"

"I can't answer that."

"Did my father ever come here to the Manatus?"

"Probably. There's a billiards table near the bar. He was something of a hustler."

"Yes, he certainly was. That's one sport he never

taught me. I guess he wanted to keep me out of the pool halls." She looked around, too anxious to stand and wait for Arturo's return. "So what do we do in the meantime? Tromp around in the jungle and hunt venomous dart frogs?"

"We could get something to eat, if you'd like. They have a fish soup here that will make you never want to go home again."

Jessie didn't realize how hungry she was until he mentioned food. She wasn't normally a big eater, but like any woman with occasional issues, she had her moments that could be resolved only with ice cream or a bag of chips. "You talked me into it. Maybe I'll even accept when they offer to bring out some dessert."

"I'm sure dessert can be arranged, but don't expect your grandmother's pecan pie."

"What? How do you know anything about...oh. Right. My dear old pa sure was talkative, wasn't he?"

"He said he used his mother's recipe, and it was your favorite." He shrugged with both shoulders. "I didn't ask about any of this stuff. I wasn't being nosy. He just...liked to tell me about you. You were his number-one topic of conversation. I just happened to be in the room."

"You should've told him to button his mouth. God knows what kinds of embarrassing things he said to you."

"It wasn't like that. You just seemed to be on his mind a lot. Now let's go get that soup. I'll try to even things out by telling you plenty of embarrassing stories about *me*."

"And then we'll find Arturo?"

Rubio put a hand over his heart. "Promise."

She pointed at him in warning. "I never let anyone break a promise to me."

"And I've never broken one."

She thought about that, liking the sound of it. "Fair enough. Let's eat."

Chapter Nineteen

Sometimes when you're eating, you think about dining at the place where the food originated. Jessie did it all the time with spaghetti. Of all the far-flung countries her father had dragged her when she was young, Italy was not among them, and more's the pity. Rome reportedly contained a variety of things that appealed to the romantic in her, as well as to the closet history nerd and amateur art critic. As she sat across from Rubio sending her tastebuds into happy hysterics, she tried to imagine where she'd be if she found the home of this lobster and shrimp in its luscious coconut sauce, but she couldn't place it.

"Our chef specializes in Afro-Carib recipes," the waiter explained when she asked him. "He attempts to combine the best flavors from the two cultures."

"He succeeded," she said.

The waiter gave a half bow. "I will be sure to inform him."

After the waiter departed, Rubio said, "You know, I thought I remembered hearing something about you being a budding vegetarian."

"It was a phase. Just like leg-warmers."

"Leg what?"

"Let me ask *you* something for a change."

"Please, go ahead."

"What do Ticos think of Americans?"

"In general, or what do we think of you personally?"

"I mean just taking us on average."

Rubio dabbed his lips with a napkin that matched the wooden shades that had been partially lowered to intercept the afternoon sun. The dining area boasted only a single wall, on the other side of which was the kitchen. Pillars of polished wood trimmed in brass supported a rooftop that made the restaurant look like an elegant pavilion. The open-air effect was liberating. Jessie enjoyed an uninterrupted view of the water.

"It's like this," Rubio said. "People in my country see people in your country as having it really easy."

"Having *what* really easy?"

"Life."

"Example?"

"Well, do you have a garage?"

"Sure."

"There are many people in Central America who don't even have houses. You have a house for your car."

"Does it make any difference that half the time my garage-door opener doesn't work?"

He smiled, but only faintly. "There's a certain amount of envy, and maybe even a little frustration at how it seems that so much gets wasted in the States. But at the same time, we're in love with all of you. Nearly every Tico under the age of twenty-five wants to be a hip-hop star in California."

"Every *American* under the age of twenty-five wants to be a hip-hop star in California."

"See there? We're all just the same. Everybody in the world watches the same sitcoms and reads the same cheap thrillers, though most of us have to wait a little bit for the translated version. Well, not *everybody*, I suppose. But a lot."

"I'm sorry for having a garage, but I'm *not* sorry to be sitting here eating this shrimp." She swallowed her last bite, relished it, and washed it down with sparkling water. She was about to change the subject to something less political when she realized she was doing it—having lunch with an actual member of the male gender. Omigod.

"What is it?" Rubio asked. "That look on your face…"

"Nothing. Just…wait a minute. That meeting tomorrow, with the hospital officials—"

"It's going to be bad news."

"How bad?"

"There's nothing we can do about it. Money for lost causes is tight these days, whether you live in the San Jose of Costa Rica or the San Jose of California. Archie worked for no salary *and* he acquired funding from the States for half of the start-up costs."

"And the people of Cerro Viejo?"

"We've talked about this. They'll be fine. They've survived for a long time. It's only a couple of hours to medical care."

"You know as well as I do that two hours might as well be two hundred. If someone gets an infection, they currently need to walk about fifty yard to the clinic for help. Getting out of the park requires riding in a damn boat at a turtle's pace and then hoping to get a lift when you reach dry land. No one is going to bother. They'll just choose to be sick."

"I've said all those same things already."

"And what did the hospital say?"

"They said to find them a free doctor."

"That's possible, right? There are volunteer organizations. What about the Peace Corps?"

"Greta looked into it. The Peace Corps prizes its licensed physicians very dearly, and they send them only to the most sensitive locations. We're not one of those. Most of the families in the village are poor by city standards, but the weather is perfect and there's an adequate amount of food, so no one has us at the top of their list of desperate cases. Look around. Some might just think this is paradise. And the Peace Corps doesn't work in paradise."

"So you're just shutting down."

"This isn't my fault. I don't have any control over what stays and what goes."

"I know. I'm sorry. I mean *they're* shutting you down."

"Well, *she* is, specifically."

"What's that mean?"

"*She* is Gavina Herrera. She and I have…worked together before. We met because of your dad. I really don't see her being flexible on this."

"Sometimes people surprise you."

"Not this people."

"We'll see."

The waiter returned just in time, no doubt prompted by the telepathy mastered by all expert wait staff. As he gathered their empty plates, he asked about dessert.

"I was planning on it," Jessie said, "but honestly I think I'm too stuffed. But tell me what you have just so I know what I'm missing."

"From the Caribbean side," the waiter replied, "we have key lime tart with an orange mango sauce."

"I shouldn't have asked. My willpower seldom lasts beyond the words 'key lime.'"

"And from our African heritage, we have baked bananas as they make them in—"

Jessie didn't catch the last word, as its shape on the waiter's lips wasn't one with which she was familiar. But she was curious to know. She looked at Rubio. "Where did he say?"

Rubio repeated the word, but it didn't help, so he spoke each letter individually: "G-A-B-O-N."

"Gabon?"

"I've never heard of it, either."

The waiter intervened. "Gabon is a country in western Africa. It is a tropical land, like ours, and one that I am told is very beautiful. The chef has family there."

"Okay, you sold me. Baked bananas from Gabon, please."

"Very good. And for you, *señor*?"

"Make it two." As the waiter hurried away, Rubio said, "I have a confession to make."

Jessie tried to guess what was coming next. In the second of silence that followed his words, she thought half a dozen things, none of them very likely. When someone told you they were about to confess something, making wild assumptions was part of the game.

Rubio leaned forward, elbows on the table. "There are nuts falling on the roof."

Jessie had read him wrong. She shook her head. "I'm sorry. They tell me I'm one of the best lip-readers around, but I don't always catch everything. Could you repeat that?"

"Nuts. They're hitting the roof every few moments."

Jessie made a face as she tried to comprehend this enigmatic statement. "Nuts."

"Yes."

"What kind of nuts?"

It was obvious that Rubio was enjoying this. "Almonds."

"I see. And these almonds…they're landing on the roof as we speak?"

"Every couple of minutes, yeah."

"Uh huh. And they're…falling from the sky?"

Rubio pointed over Jessie's shoulder.

She turned around. From here, she had a full view of the bar, its pristine glasses held upside-down from a rack on the ceiling, its bottles gleaming in the reflected light. There was no wall beyond the bar, which opened onto the resort's lawn and eventually led to a pool where an elderly couple sat with their feet in the water.

Jessie looked back. "I don't see anything."

"Nuts fall for those who wait."

Puzzled, Jessie returned her attention to the bar and the grounds beyond. What was she doing? Sitting here over two thousand miles from home with a handsome paramedic and waiting for almonds to drop from the clouds…and two days ago she'd been cloistered at home with the curtains drawn and only her sadness for company. In other words, she was *potentially* having a good time, though she wouldn't make a formal declaration of such until she texted Li tonight—

Something rolled off the roof, fell, and disappeared

in the grass.

"Well, what do you know?" The object had been brown and smaller than a golf ball. She turned to Rubio. "That was an almond?"

"Those trees you see there are wild almond trees. This time of year, the nuts occasionally fall from the branches. They make a bit of a noise when they strike the roof. I've been watching them fall behind you for the last twenty minutes now."

"And here I thought I commanded your full attention."

He grinned. "They're kind of hard to ignore."

She looked again, waited, and sure enough, a minute later, another specimen tumbled overboard and bounced once when it met the ground. Turned around in her seat as she was, she had a clear view of the main office, where the man from behind the desk was standing outside near the umbrella bucket, talking to a man in a red beret.

The innkeeper pointed at her, and the man in the hat followed his finger. For a moment, his eyes met Jessie's. He was small—barely over five feet—his cheeks punctuated by deep grooves, like a series of parentheses on either side of his face. Looking at him was like locking gazes with an animal.

"Rubio?" she said. She didn't know if he responded or not. "Is that Arturo, the guy we're searching for?"

The words had no sooner left her mouth than Arturo spun around and ran away.

Chapter Twenty

"Where's he going?" She shot up from her chair, almost knocking it over. Rubio said something as he got quickly to his feet, but her peripheral lip reading rarely worked.

Not waiting to see if he would follow, she took off after the man.

What was happening? She instantly felt absurd, a grown woman of average cardio health giving chase across the yard of a peaceful, upscale resort. When was the last time she actually ran? Not jogged. Not plodded along on a treadmill. But honestly bared down and put her ass in serious motion?

Rubio was probably shouting something behind her. But she didn't take her eyes from the fleeing figure. Arturo darted down a shaded path between two of the bungalows. The trees were so thick that it seemed as if he'd raced into the mouth of a cave. If Jessie ran in there without caution, would she be attacked? The thought of being ambushed was even more ridiculous than the idea of running, but that was what her life had suddenly become—surreal.

"Thanks, Dad," she muttered between breaths.

Rubio passed her.

Evidently he'd decided the same thing about the ambush, and he didn't want her running into the unknown. He moved by her effortlessly, like something carried along by the wind. The grace of his form captivated her, a perfect human body in flight. He might have been a Mayan hunter of old, bounding through the jungle in pursuit of a jaguar, his rhythm carrying him swiftly onto the path and the darkness beyond.

Jessie increased her speed and tried to catch up.

Would she have run like this had it not been Archie's ghost she was trying to catch? As she reached the path and pointed herself through the trees, she discarded the question. There was no time for self-psychology when you were trying to run a man down.

Fifty feet away, Rubio stood in the middle of the path, blocking Arturo's escape. He'd caught up with the man and corralled him, and now the two of them yelled back and forth, both of them breathing hard.

Jessie slowed. Her throat boiled. She stopped and bent over, letting her lungs remember the old days before she turned them into rocket engines.

When she stood up, hands braced on her hips, Rubio said, "He recognized you."

"What?" Her chest rising and falling, she approached them, letting her eyes adjust to the gloom. The branches were so thick overhead that only swatches of sunlight made it through.

"Arturo here," Rubio said, not looking winded at all. "He knows who you are."

"Why on earth would"—she took several long breaths—"the sight of me make anybody run away?" She realized what she'd said. "Wait. Don't answer that. I'm sure my friends could give you plenty of reasons."

Rubio motion for Arturo to say something. The little man, clearly uneasy, shifted his weight back and forth, his beret now clutched in one hand. He wore heavy work boots and a military-style belt.

"Well?" Rubio prompted.

Arturo looked at Jessie and said, "Your father, *señorita*, he, uh…he leave chest at my house. I believe you came to take it."

"Chest? Sir, I didn't come here to take anything."

"No?"

"I don't know anything…about any chest. Rubio and I just wanted to ask you a question."

Arturo seemed to think it was some sort of ruse. "You…you no take it back?"

Jessie wiped a line of moisture from her forehead. Great. Now she was sweating. "Look, it's like this. The three of us can walk like normal people back to the restaurant. For one thing, we need to pay for our food so the waiter doesn't send the Costa Rican national police after us. Second, I left something there I want to show you. I think it might be one of the dolls you make."

"Doles?" His accent made him hard to read.

"May we just have a minute of your time? Please?"

Eventually he nodded.

Jessie made an about-face and headed back up the path. Rubio fell into step beside her, but Arturo maintained a careful distance behind them, as if expecting an attack.

"By the way," Rubio said as they walked, "he didn't say 'chest.'"

"Looked that way to me, but heaven knows I've been wrong before. What did he say?"

"Chess."

"Chess, as in the game?"

"I suppose so."

"My father left a chess set at Arturo's house?"

"I'm not sure. Maybe we should ask. Sounds strange."

"Strange? You know, the longer I'm here, the stranger this place gets."

"True. And you haven't even seen the giant albino scorpions yet."

"Just how giant are we talking about? And are they anywhere in our general vicinity?"

"Just kidding."

"Brat." She slugged him on the arm, careful to conceal her smile.

****

Now remember, pumpkin, the knight moves two squares this way and one square here.

Staring down at Arturo's chess board, Jessie heard her father's lesson as perfectly as if he'd been pushing the pieces across the board.

The knight is funny that way, isn't it? Nobody else can move like that.

"Nobody else," she whispered.

Arturo had brought them to his home, one mile from Cerro Viejo. They'd ridden in his army jeep, something that looked straight from the set of an old *M*A*S*H* episode. In halting English, he'd explained that Archie had bought the chess board from an artisan in San Jose. It was made of alternating squares of red and white marble. The pieces were carved by hand from mahogany and birch, each one unique. The bishops were old Indian rain gods. The queens were pregnant, symbolizing rebirth. It was an expensive set, and Arturo had made it the centerpiece of his house.

"When doctor die, I think everyone say I stole it," Arturo said, kneading his beret in his hands. "I think you come to get it."

Rubio gave him a reassuring squeeze on the shoulder. "We're not here to take anything. You can keep it. I'm sure he would want you to have it. Jessie and I just want to talk."

Keep your knight off the edge of the board, pumpkin. It's more dangerous near the heart.

Rubio gave a little wave of his hand, getting her attention. "Are you okay?"

"I was never any good at chess."

"That makes two of us. Maybe Arturo here could give us some lessons."

"I wanted a pony when I was nine. Dad bought me a chess set instead." She looked at Arturo, then nodded to a shelf in his tiny kitchenette. "Those dolls there. You made them?"

"*Sí.*"

"They look just like one I found at the place where..." She took a breath, then let it slowly out. "Where my father died."

"I no give him one."

"You didn't?"

He shook his head briskly. "Not make in many months, very long time. Too busy."

"Do you sell them to tourists?"

"No. No one buys. Too plain. Make for—"

Jessie failed to catch the rest of it. She asked Rubio for help.

"He said he makes them for the children. Specifically for his sister's kids."

"But he hasn't made any of them recently?"

Rubio and Arturo spoke for a few moments, and Jessie intentionally kept her eyes from straying back to the chess board. She hadn't played since she was a child and only vaguely remembered the rules. But she recalled the lesson well enough. Things were more dangerous near the heart.

"He says the last time he recalls giving one as a gift, it was to his niece, Britney."

" Britney? That's not a very Spanish-sounding name."

"Arturo's sister is married to one of the park biologists, who's an American."

"So…maybe the doll belongs to her?"

"Hard to say."

"Any reason that Britney would be at the ravine?"

"Maybe she was out with her father. He travels all over the park as part of his job. If he had Britney with him…anything's possible."

Jessie tried to put the pieces together in her mind, but for some reason, her thoughts strayed to Rubio. Why was he doing any of this? And how had she gotten so lucky as to find a guide who was so…intriguing? What had Tioni said? *Only two good man left.*

And now, with her father gone, there was only one.

"Could we visit with Britney and her father?" she asked.

"How did I know you were going to say that?"

"Rumor has it that I'm stubborn."

Rubio consulted Arturo, who was looking more comfortable by the moment. Now that he was convinced they weren't going to repossess his chess board, he visibly relaxed and seemed willing to help.

"He says his brother-in-law, David, lives near the

park entrance, not far from where you boarded the water taxi. You know it might not be her doll, right?"

"Arturo made it, didn't he?"

"Looks that way."

"And he doesn't sell them. He gives them to family members. That means one of those doll recipients was out there at some point fairly recently. Remember, the doll didn't look like it had been lying around out there for very long. This David guy, the biologist, he may have the answer."

"And if there is no answer?"

"Why are you suddenly playing devil's advocate?"

"Maybe I just don't want to get my hopes up."

"Sorry. You're hanging out with the queen of high hopes. If you're looking for a realist, you'll have to wait for the next deaf woman from Arizona to show up on your doorstep. As for me, I'm hailing that taxi." She held out a hand to Arturo. "*Gracias.*"

"*De nada.*"

Before she left, she reached down and picked up the knight from the white side of the board. She moved it two places forward of its position, then one space to the right. Then she turned and made for the door.

Chapter Twenty-One

Someone once told Rubio that all American women were insane.

Not just flighty. Not simply unpredictable. But downright random. They got mad at you for inexplicable reasons and then got all lovey over the most insignificant thing. They could be as practical as nuns on Tuesday and buy three pairs of shoes on Wednesday, just because of the sale sign hanging in the window.

"They say it's supposed to rain tomorrow," he told her.

Jessie sat across from him in the boat as it skimmed the water, her hair tossing about in the wind. "What did you say?"

Rubio replied by mouthing the words but not making any sound. "Rain. Tomorrow." It was fascinating to communicate in silence. "What's the sign for rain?"

Jessie put her hands in front of her, palms down, and lowered them in a series of short pulses.

"I get it," Rubio said silently. "That looks like rain. Show me another one."

She put one fist on top of the other, then raised and lowered it.

Rubio tried to guess. "Looks like…"

She signed rain again, then followed it with the

second symbol.

"An umbrella!"

She smiled.

"Another." Rubio felt like a boy requesting magic tricks from a traveling magician.

This time she bent the fingers on both hands and opened and closed them like jaws.

"That has *got* to be a crocodile."

She gave him a thumbs up.

"Another!"

She put an L-shape in front of her mouth and clipped her thumb and index fingers together. It looked like a little beak.

"A bird?"

She nodded.

"I was never very good at playing charades," Rubio admitted. "I must be getting lucky. Or you're taking it easy on me. Give me something harder."

She bit her bottom lip as she pondered it for a moment. Then she adjusted herself on the wooden seat, straightened her back, and made a series of three distinct motions. The first was two curved index fingers, followed by the pulling of her palm away from her chest, and finally a pair of peace signs that sort of snapped up and down.

Rubio shook his head. "I take it back. I don't want anything harder."

"It means 'giant albino scorpion.'"

Laughing, he shook his head. "No way!"

"Actually it means 'big white scorpion,' but that's close enough."

"How many words do you know in sign language?"

"As many as it takes."

"That must be thousands of things to have to memorize."

"You're bilingual. It's no different than that. Well, it's a *little* different than that, but it still just comes down to memory. But the signs themselves don't have as much meaning without facial movement and other signals. You have to find a way to convey tone of voice without using your voice."

Rubio's fascination only grew as she explained the nuances of being hearing impaired. She seemed so complete, as if she weren't missing anything at all. Suddenly he wanted to know the sign for a dozen different words that came to him all at once—ocean, paramedic, monkey, father—but he didn't want to come across as being uncool. Regardless of his nationality, the one thing a guy wanted to be when sitting across from a girl in a boat was cool.

Jessie pointed at him, then spread her fingers across her face two times.

"What does that mean?" Rubio asked.

"Just making an observation."

"An observation about what? Me?"

"Never mind."

"Hey, that's no fair."

She turned her head as if suddenly intent on a red-feathered bird circling the water.

"You can't even hear me now," Rubio said to her profile.

She didn't look at him or respond.

"You're doing that on purpose."

When she still didn't reply, he sighed, smiling to himself as he touched her leg.

She turned her head.

"Okay, you win," he said. "Maybe you can tell me later."

"We'll see."

Yes, it was true: American women were insane.

****

When the water taxi brushed the pier, Jessie stood up too quickly and almost lost her balance. She righted herself by spreading her arms, deploying them like counterweights until she regained her balance. During these brief moments, she suspected that both Rubio and the boat driver shouted various helpful phrases such as *Are you okay?* and *Easy does it now!* But she kept her feet and clambered onto dry land.

The sun hung low in the west. Jessie slid her sunglasses to the top of her head.

Rubio appeared in front of her. "It's a bit of a walk. Arturo's sister lives about half a kilometer along that road right there."

"I was raised on yards and miles. I don't know kilometers."

"Um…it's five hundred meters, which is…maybe six hundred yards or so? I'm not sure of the conversion. Why is that, by the way? The yards and miles thing, I mean. That system doesn't seem very logical."

"It's not. But it probably comes down to money. It would cost billions for the U.S. to make the switch to metric. We have an awful lot of road signs."

"We have a road that runs south to Chile and north all the way to Alaska."

"Okay…"

"That's not very impressive as far as national highlights, is it?"

"Well, in Kansas there's the world's largest ball of twine."

"Now *that's* something to talk about."

They started their trek along the gravel-topped road that led away from the busy docks, where several different tourism outfits shuttled their patrons from bus to boat and back again. Jessie's eyes settled on a tree carving depicting a woodland nymph reaching for what appeared to be hummingbirds. In her research, she'd read that Costa Rica featured a hummingbird preserve or nesting ground or some kind of thing, but she doubted she'd have time to visit it. Everything seemed so rushed now, as if her father's trail might fade if she didn't hurry. In her haste, she'd almost toppled out of the boat, and where would that have ranked on the embarrassment scale?

Rubio turned and walked backward so she could see his face. "Want to know something else interesting about this country?"

"Certainly."

"Our president lives in his own house."

"What do you mean? Our president has his own house, too."

"Yes, he has the White House, right? But when our president is elected, he doesn't move anywhere special. He gets to live at home, in his own neighborhood, on his own street."

"That doesn't sound very safe."

"Oh, they definitely increase security. There are men in Italian suits hanging around on his front lawn with guns under the coats. But it's not like in the States. We're a bit more…"

"Laid back?"

"It keeps us grounded."

Jessie imagined the political landscape if the president's home shifted the center of government around the country every term. "I don't think Americans like being grounded. It doesn't make for very exciting TV."

"Archie once told me that he hadn't watched television since Walter Cronkite died. I didn't know who that was, so he made me look him up online."

"That was Dad for you. If I asked him a question, he'd usually refuse to answer until I'd tried to find it myself. When I was growing up, that didn't always go over so well with me. And then he'd always say that thing about the fish."

"The what?"

"He said that instead of giving me fish to eat, he wanted to teach me how to fish. That really annoyed the shit out of me when I was twelve."

"And now?"

"Oh, I don't know. I suppose that if I ever have kids, I'll expect them to fish for their lives, the poor things."

They continued to talk all the way to their destination, which Jessie found at least a little bit exhilarating. Walking beside a man and having a carefree conversation wasn't something she'd done in a while. Maybe her location was intoxicating her. The late-afternoon sun warmed her face, the tropical wetlands lurked mysteriously around her, and birds she didn't recognize turned circles overhead. Could she be blamed if she was at least a little bit tickled by the idea?

The house belonging to David and Verónica Zimmer stood on four thick wooden columns, like the pilings beneath a seaside wharf. It overlooked a bend in one of the canals, the water pushing lazily in the direction of the ocean, the sight of which remained cut off by the wall of jungle on the east. Broad flagstones led to a front door flank by a pair of soiled wading boots and a red tricycle with its tires caked in mud.

The door opened as they neared, revealing a man with pale blond hair and a gun.

Jessie stopped immediately, grabbing Rubio's arm. This must have been David, as he was Caucasian and wore a Detroit Red Wings T-shirt, but what was he doing with that pistol? She thought about running, but where would she go? Dive into the water? Head for the trees?

"Hey, folks," David Zimmer said, looking surprised to find them on his front step. "Can I help you?"

Jessie flicked her eyes to the gun and back to his face. "I...suppose that depends."

"What? Oh, sorry. It's not what you think." He quickly shoved it into a black nylon holster. "It's not that kind of gun. It fires tranquilizers. For the animals."

Jessie's body relaxed. She felt Rubio do the same.

"Didn't mean to scare ya," Zimmer said. "You have my apologies."

"That's all right," she assured him, releasing a nervous sigh. "We're just a little jumpy." She stepped forward and introduced herself, shaking the man's hand and noting the callouses on his skin. "My friend Rubio and I were hoping to speak with you for a few minutes."

"About the snakes?" He over-shaped the words to make them bigger—the typical response when someone realized by Jessie's voice that she was deaf .

"Snakes?"

"You're from the university, right? Here about the vine snake eggs?"

"No. We're actually wondering if you know anything about this." She showed him the doll. "I believe it was made by your brother-in-law."

"Arturo? Sure, he made it. All of my daughters have one." He darkened. "Why, is something wrong? Is Arturo in some kind of—"

"He's fine. We found the doll. We're hoping to return it."

"Return it, huh?" Zimmer studied her face, then Rubio's. "You two came from where, exactly?"

"Cerro Viejo."

"That's at least an hour from here, more if you're on one of the slower rigs. You traveled that far just to give back a lost toy?" He didn't seem to believe it.

"For starters, yes. We also wanted to ask you a question about where it was found."

Zimmer slid his hands into the pockets of his cargo pants. "Just what line of work are ya in, ma'am, if you don't mind my asking?"

Did Zimmer think she was a cop? Or maybe a criminal? "I'm a grant writer."

"Pardon?"

"I'm not here in any official capacity. My father…my father was Archie Alomar."

Zimmer's face went through a subtle transition. Confusion turned to recognition which in turn became sympathy. "You have my condolences. And I'm completely serious about that. Alomar was one hell of a good man."

Only two good man left, Jessie heard in her mind. "Thank you."

"He helped us out on more than one occasion," Zimmer continued. "My team does a lot of habitat work, and we've been known to get scratched up in the line of duty. Alomar always stitched us up and never charged us a single *colón*."

"Yeah, that sounds like Dad."

"We paid him back in beer. He seemed to like that just fine."

"And that *also* sounds like Dad."

Zimmer fell silent for a moment before saying, "I appreciate your bringing my daughter's doll back, but since I've got you here, I should go ahead and tell you."

"Go ahead and tell me what?"

"You better come inside," Zimmer said. "There's something you need to see."

Chapter Twenty-Two

Jessie stood in a living room that combined the best and worst of two countries. From the U.S., David Zimmer had imported a John Wayne lithograph, coasters from Graceland, and a stuffed catfish he said he caught in the Colorado River. These items somehow cohabitated with a hand-woven Costa Rican rug, watercolors depicting the Monteverde cloud forest, and a sea turtle sculpture made of recycled plastic bottles. Jessie couldn't remember seeing such an eclectic collection, at least not all crammed into a single room.

"Wife's at the market," Zimmer said, "so our hospitality is at half speed. I don't do a lot of entertaining, but I know where we keep the beer, if you'd like one."

"I think I'm fine," Jessie told him.

"Me, too," Rubio said.

"All right, then. Just hang tight for a sec. I'll be right back."

As soon as he was gone, Jessie tried to guess what this was about. What did he want to show them? In what way had her father touched this man's life?

Jessie assumed Rubio was speaking so that their host couldn't hear him when he said, "Interesting place."

"And then some." Even from here, her eyes picked out the tiny lettering on a magnet clinging to the fridge in the adjacent kitchen: GET YOUR KICKS ON ROUTE 66!

"Cute kids." Rubio nodded toward a shelf near the TV. Three girls grinned at the camera with all the merriment of elves. One of them, the youngest, had her father's pale yellow hair.

Jessie sometimes wondered how she'd fare as a mother. On certain days she wanted a child more than she wanted sunlight, but give her forty-eight hours and she'd realize what a drag it would be to wake up early on Saturdays because someone had turned the cartoons on too loudly, or to have to stop the car because they were pinching their sister, or to have to endure one of those infamous fits in the cereal aisle.

But looking at this photo, she felt the life bursting from it, and—oddly—she craved to know that feeling with a daughter of her own, someone to snuggle up in the nook of her body and make finger-paintings not for the sake of art but simply to get her hands messy.

She looked at Rubio. "Think you'll ever have kids?"

"My mother says that if I don't, she'll write me out of the will."

"That's a strong incentive."

"She says I'd be good at it, but sometimes I worry that I'd spend too much time being their buddy and not enough being their dad."

"Dads *are* your buddy."

"You're right. I guess it's the discipline thing that scares me. I'd love to play soccer or build a tree house with my son from dawn till dusk, but I'd probably be a big sissy when it came to punishing him when he did something wrong."

"There are worse things to be."

Zimmer returned, holding what looked to be an oversized sketchbook. The pad was hinged at the top, and as Zimmer lifted the cover, he said, "This belonged to your father. He did a lot of drawings, mostly of animals and insects. But he made the mistake of letting my kids draw on some of his blank pages, and they had such a good time that he let them keep the whole thing, including his illustrations."

Jessie accepted the pad, and Rubio moved closer to get a look.

The first picture depicted a shoreline scene. Archie had a fine hand for drawing. Though he lacked the formal training found in commercial artists, he possessed a layman's talent for transferring to the page what his eye saw in the world around him. This simple rendering wasn't going to win any ribbons at the county fair, but it was an adequate representation of a beach meeting the ocean waves.

She turned the page.

Three hummingbirds vied for airspace near a flower with fairly impressive graphite shading on its petals. Proportionately the birds were slightly irregular, but Archie had captured the flower with near perfection. His careful doctor's hands were clearly at their best.

After glancing up to see if Zimmer was providing any commentary—he wasn't—Jessie moved to the next drawing.

A lizard advanced along the sand, leaving a trail that looked vaguely like runes or ancient writing. The sun must have been positioned behind the reptile, as it followed its shadow toward wherever it led.

These drawings, though precious because her

father had made them, were not unlike the hundreds of others she already owned. Archie's sketches filled two boxes in her hall closet. If Zimmer had wanted her to see these, she appreciated the sentiment but found nothing here to bring back any part of him that she'd lost. She used her thumb to fan through the pages. The bottom half of the pad consisted of the drawings made by Zimmer's daughters, with their imprecise lines and seemingly random design elements—standard kid art. The best thing Jessie could say about them was—

A drawing flashed by, catching her eye.

Jessie went back to it, picking through the pages individually until she relocated what she'd seen, and she knew instantly that this was why David Zimmer had brought her here to his living room.

A woman sat on the shore, feet in the water. Archie Alomar was a casual artist who drew only images of wildlife…except for this. Her face was placid though lined from half a lifetime of experience, her eyes slightly downcast as if searching for her reflection in the water. Her hair curled far past her shoulders, simple but elegant, with a flower tucked into the strands above her left ear. She wore a peasant's dress with a scooped neckline. Her breasts were full, her waist a little too big to be called petite.

"Who is she?" Jessie whispered.

If either of the two men responded, she didn't know, for she was captivated by the woman's necklace. Lying on the hollow of her throat was a pendant, a tiny caduceus rod that Jessie had seen many times before…

"That's his lapel pin." She looked up at Rubio. "She's wearing my father's pin."

"Do you know her?"

"No." She turned to Zimmer. "Tell me about this picture. Who is this woman? Why did my father draw her?"

Zimmer's face betrayed his thoughts. He was stuck in the middle of something he didn't quite understand, and he wasn't sure how to extricate himself. "I think I better get those beers."

"Yeah," Jessie said. "I get the feeling I might need one."

Zimmer went to the kitchen, and Jessie returned her attention to the nameless woman on the riverbank, trying to guess where it all was going to lead.

****

Minutes later, they'd taken seats in the living room, Jessie choosing a vantage point that enabled her to see both men's faces without having to turn her head. She didn't want to miss anything. She held the open art pad on her lap. Her beer was as cold as it could be without icing up, and after a semi-long swallow, she put the bottle on a coaster bearing an image of the home of the king of rock-n'-roll.

"You know how the kids were with Alomar," Zimmer said. "They followed him around like he was Saint Nick." He tipped the neck of his bottle toward Rubio. "They do the same with you, I noticed."

"I try to have fun with them," Rubio said. "It won't be long before they're old and boring adults like the rest of us, so I try to encourage them to be silly while they can."

"Spoken like a wise man. Heaven knows I make every effort with my own girls, at least when I'm not out in the field. Anyway, he used to let the kids sit on the porch behind the clinic. He had a card table set up back there, and they used it for craft projects. Alomar had one of those hot-glue guns. My daughters liked to make birdhouses out of twigs, and they'd use that glue to hold 'em together."

Jessie smiled to herself. Her father had done the same thing with her when she was little.

"That doll you mentioned," Zimmer said. "My youngest, Sophie, she lost hers about a week and a half ago. Cried all night when she couldn't find it. I asked her sisters if they'd mind sharing, because their Uncle Arturo had made one for each of them, but that wasn't good enough for Sophie. She wanted her own. She had a name for it, but I forget it what it was. I know that sounds bad, forgetting the name of your daughter's favorite toy, but do you know how many dolls, action figures, and stuffed animals those three have between them? And they've named every one of the damn things. I may hold a graduate degree in biology, but that doesn't help me one lick when it comes to remembering the individual names of sixteen-dozen Barbies."

As he paused for a pull from his bottle, Jessie thought of Noxy. That was her prized plush elephant, purchased at a market stall in Calcutta. These days sweet Noxy occupied a cardboard box in the attic. Maybe it was time to dig her out again, just because.

"She'll be thrilled to hear that you two found it and brought it back," Zimmer said. "Where was it at, anyway? And if you say it was down at the dock, then I don't know what I'm going to do, because I've told 'em a thousand times to stay away from the water."

"Actually," Jessie said, "that's why we came. We found it in a…a strange place."

"Strange how?"

"How often do your daughters visit Cerro Viejo?"

"I take 'em with me almost every weekend. They stay at the babysitter's place while I do the rounds. We have nine watch stations set up the area. Those are places we're paying particular attention to, whether something's hatching eggs or making a nest or any number of things. I spend the better part of Saturday logging notes from the station and uploading them to our database. You'd be surprised how much of wildlife management has nothing to do with wildlife and everything to do with computers."

"We found the doll in the woods near the village."

"About a kilometer or so," Rubio added. "At a ravine well off the trail."

Zimmer looked unconvinced. "That doesn't make sense. My daughters swear that all of their toys can get up and move around when no one's watching, just like in the movies, but I'd still be skeptical about a doll walking that far on its own. Maybe one of those stray dogs carried it out there."

"Maybe," Jessie admitted.

"By the sound of your 'maybe,' I assume you don't believe that at all."

"It doesn't feel right."

"I won't be one to argue with a woman's instincts, that's for damn sure, but I still don't know what else could explain that thing getting so far from the village."

"When you're checking those stations on Saturdays, your daughters are at the sitter's?"

"They call her Granny. My folks passed away years ago, and so did my wife's. The girls have a tendency to adopt random senior citizens as grandparents." He smiled, and his love for his daughters was evident there. "Her real name is Beatriz. She's great with the kids and has raised God knows how many of her own. I pay her to look after them when I'm working out of the village, because my wife is usually at her own job on Saturdays. She's an assistant manager at the information center at the northeast corner of the pier, down where all the tourist buses park."

"So…maybe Beatriz would know something?"

"Your guess is as good as mine, ma'am."

"And this woman?" She held up the sketchpad. "Know anything about her?"

"Wish I did. Like I said, Alomar gave that book to my kids and they filled up nearly every page like a pack of wild Picassos. My wife noticed the drawing there and showed it to me. I knew as soon as I saw it that it wasn't like the other ones. This one was…different. You can tell he thought that woman was special. I was planning on returning that one to him, but then he…you know." He looked down at his bottle.

"Yeah."

"I'm sorry as hell for your loss, ma'am. I buried my dad ten years ago, so I've walked that path, and nothing that anyone's going to say can make the trip any easier. But you've got to keep on walking it and come out on the other side, just like he'd want."

Jessie's throat tightened, and the tears threatened to spring their trap again. Moments ago she'd been fine, but hearing Zimmer's words beckoned the sadness again; it was never far away.

"Here, let me see that." Zimmer got up and reached for the pad.

Jessie handed it over.

"I'll tear out my daughters' stuff so you can have

this back."

"No, please. That isn't necessary. He'd like them to have it, I'm sure. I'll just take the one."

Zimmer held her gaze for a long time, then nodded. "Fair enough." He opened the book to the unexplained illustration of the woman, then carefully pulled the page until it tore away from its ring binding along the top. "If you ever find out who she was, I'd really like to know."

Jessie stood up, leaving a half-full bottle of beer. "I will."

"I don't suppose you two would care to stay for dinner. My wife and the girls will be back in a few minutes, and we could have a regular sit-down meal, if you want."

"Thanks, but…I really need to—"

"Enough said. I can tell you have a lot on your mind. *Via con Dios*, ma'am." He extended his hand.

Jessie shook with a solid grip—one more thing her father had taught her.

Chapter Twenty-Three

"It will be dark soon," Rubio said, just for something to say. He enjoyed talking to her and was afraid of letting her slip away into her silent world. "We should grab a boat and head back."

Jessie didn't reply, just kept walking along the canal that led north into the park.

Rubio hadn't know her long, but he understood the look in her eyes. It reminded him of the photograph on Archie's desk, the one that had captivated him long before he'd met the woman herself. Though she smiled in the picture, there was something about her that hinted at layers underneath.

He touched her elbow. "We're still on for San Jose in the morning?"

"I don't think there's any way I can avoid it. As executor of Dad's estate, such as it is, I'll have to jump through whatever paperwork hoops they might have."

"We'll leave at eight, if that's okay."

She nodded and went back to her closed-off self.

Rubio thought of cavemen.

His thoughts traveled there instantly, all the way back to the time when humans first slogged out of the prehistoric mud and took up residence in the side of mountains. At some point in the incomprehensible past, a brute with a sloping forehead and rudimentary language skills had stood utterly perplexed when a female of his species ignored his advances in favor of her own thoughts. Man's confusion had been going on for that long.

Rubio chuckled.

Jessie must have noticed, because she turned to him. "What did you say?"

"I didn't say anything." He bit down on his smile.

"What's so funny?"

"Men."

"Men?"

"We haven't really evolved very much."

"You expect me to disagree with you?"

His chuckle became a laugh. "Looks like there's a boat available. Let's see about getting back before nightfall. The water taxis don't run the route after dark."

After a quick barter with the boat's operator, Rubio climbed aboard, but when he turned to offer his hand to help Jessie, she's already gotten herself over the side and seated. In the orange light of sunset, her hair look dusted in gold.

What had Archie told him?

If you ever laid a finger on her, I'd have to murder you and sink your body in the river.

"You're doing it again," Jessie said.

"Doing what?"

"Smiling. What's so interesting?"

"Just happy to be alive."

"Liar."

The boat's engine rumbled to life, scattering the birds.

****

Jessie ate dinner alone. Rubio had wished her

goodnight, and though Jessie had sensed his reluctance to leave, she was too exhausted to be flattered by it. The day had sapped her strength, not because its events were particularly rigorous, but because they were so freighted with emotion.

She sat cross-legged on her bed, its sheer curtains hanging down on three sides of her and making her feel like a Persian princess in a tent. Her meal consisted of fresh fruit, nuts, and a bottle of semi-cold mango-flavored soda. Beyond the open window, the night cries of insects and amphibians reminded her that she had left her former life behind.

But for how long?

Her father had fallen in love with this place for reasons that were quite clear, now that Jessie had wended her way through its trees and skimmed the crests of its waterways. Perhaps in San Jose there was bustle, but out here she'd found a native simplicity without having to give up most of the comforts of the industrialized world. As long as she could plug in her hair dryer and fall asleep on a memory-foam mattress, she considered it civilization.

Her pillow jiggled slightly.

She reached over it and found her phone, its vibration level set to its usual jackhammer intensity.

Knock knock.

With her banana in one hand, she typed with the other. *Who's there?*

Emerson.

Jessie tried to guess where Li was going with this one, but when nothing came to her, she had no choice but to step into it. *Emerson who?*

Emerson nice boobs, babe!

Jessie groaned. *I don't even want to know where you got that one.*

Heard nephew say to friend. Make U miss jr. high?

Nothing makes me miss junior high, thanks.

U OK?

Things got interesting today.

?

Not sure yet, Jessie replied. *Dad had a lot of friends. Talking to all of them and getting this sorted out might take some time.*

ISWYM.

By now Jessie was familiar enough with Li's shorthand that she didn't have to ponder that one: *I see what you mean.*

U have hospital 2morrow? Li asked.

Yes. Not looking forward to it.

Be brave. U will K some A.

We'll see.

Shirtless guy?

It took Jessie a moment to realize what her friend was talking about. Then she remembered telling her that she'd seen Rubio running around without his shirt. A lot had happened since then. Rubio had turned out to be more than just a running paramedic with the body of a Greek javelin-thrower. *He's not bad*, she typed, amazed at her own power of understatement.

Best thing you said about a man in 4ever.

I have discriminating tastes.

Lower your standards. Works 4 me.

No matter what else happened in this world, Jessie would never get tired of Li's slightly off-center perspective on love. *I'll let you know how it goes. I'm going to finish dinner and drag my bod into the shower.*

Wait!

Yes?

Wouldn't kill U 2 have a good time.

Jessie sighed the sigh of someone who had no decent rebuttal. *Talk to you tomorrow.*

Deal. XXXOOOXXX.

Jessie put the phone down, pushed her plate to the side, and sank back on the pillow.

Sometimes there was wisdom that could be found only in staring at the ceiling. Of course, this time her ceiling was the white fabric that was draped between the four posts of her bed, so the effect wasn't quite the same. She'd come here simply to sign on the necessary dotted lines, close her father's accounts, and collect anything personal he'd left behind. But it seemed as if he'd made the entire place personal; he was slopped all over it, recklessly, like someone flinging paint. And it was *good* paint. The people here truly cared for him, and now that he was gone, his clinic would close, and he'd dwell only in their memories.

The life he'd left here was apparently too nuanced to be so neatly tied up and put away. Maybe the doll she'd found meant nothing, or maybe someone had been out there the day he'd slipped and fell. What would David Zimmer's daughter be doing at the ravine? And if she *hadn't* been out there, then how had her doll found its way there?

And who was the woman in the drawing?

Without looking, Jessie reached through the gauzy drape and found the illustration on the nightstand. She held it in both hands above her face. The finer details left a bit to be desired, but clearly this represented her father's best work. Jessie tried to envision the circumstances that resulted in this drawing being created, but the woman with her bare feet in the water gave no secrets away.

She lowered the thick paper and let it fall to the bed. Someone had once wondered that if a tree fell in the woods when no one was around to hear, would it make a sound? The question had fascinated Jessie when she was in school. It came across like a paradox or a Buddhist koan or some other philosophical mumbo-jumbo that wasn't ever supposed to be answered. She'd finally come upon a suitable answer, which she turned into a paper in sophomore English.

If a tree falls in the woods and only Jessie Alomar is there, does it make a sound?

The answer was no.

"The impact of the tree against the ground makes waves in the air," she said to herself, just as she'd written all those years ago. "But those waves can become sound only when interacting with a working receiver. Without that receiver, those waves just roll out in all directions and fade away."

And there was her problem: she'd never been able to keep things from fading.

Sensing a sleepless night, she banished her sullen thoughts and got out of bed in search of her toothbrush. This wasn't anything that a little bit of minty freshness couldn't cure.

That done, she returned to her bed, brought out her tablet, and lay down on her stomach, as she used to do with books when she was a girl.

After a few minutes, her mind drifted from the story. What would Rubio do if their trip tomorrow resulted in the end of the clinic? He came across as a man capable of anything, so she wouldn't be surprised if he opened a nonprofit to save the world or took up male modeling. If she had his cell number, she might do something rash and send him a text message. That's the kind of mood she was in, compelled to send partially coherent texts to men she barely knew.

Li would have approved.

She tapped the screen to turn the page, tried to pay attention to the words, failed.

There was always tomorrow. The two of them were going to spend at least part of the day in San Jose, and maybe they could stop and eat at a place normally too trendy for her. She wanted to know more about him. She wanted to look at him and realize that—amazingly enough—he was actually interested in whatever she happened to be saying.

Then something horrible occurred to her. She closed her eyes, groaned, and dropped her forehead to the bed.

What the hell was she going to wear?

Chapter Twenty-Four

When Jessie emerged from her room the next morning, Rubio was leaning against a palm tree about twenty feet away, sleeves rolled halfway up his arms, hands in the pockets of his loose-fitting slacks. His shirt was tucked neatly into his waistband, his slender belt clasped with a buckle that might have been real silver. His glossy black shoes completed his transformation from yesterday's liberal islander to trendy urbanite.

"I didn't know you were already here," she said. "How long have you been waiting?"

"I knocked. Twice. Then I realized that…well…"

"That I was ignoring you?"

"No."

"That I'd changed my mind and wasn't coming?"

"That's not what I mean. And you know that."

"You're right, I do. You mean that you knocked and then remembered that knocking on my door is about as useful as showing slides of your family vacation to Stevie Wonder."

"Something like that."

"Don't sweat it. Stevie doesn't get easily offended, and neither do I. Besides, I need to apologize to you."

"What on earth for?"

"For not having the foresight to bring an outfit suitable for business. I didn't anticipate sitting in an office full of people with ties while I signed away my father's life down here."

"Do you see me wearing a tie? It won't be that formal."

True, Rubio wasn't wearing a tie, but he still looked perfect for the occasion, a combination of professionalism and cool. The way the dark skin of his neck and chest contrasted with the white of his shirt…Jessie reminded herself not to stare like a teeny bopper with nothing better to do than flip through the pages of *Teen Weekly* all day.

"You look fine," Rubio said. "Or at least good enough that no one in the hospital will say anything about it until after we're gone."

She crossed her arms. "Isn't it too early in the day to tease wayward foreigners?"

"Seriously. You're great. You want me to sing your praises in poetry or something?"

"Well, it wouldn't be the worst thing that could happen to a girl."

"Maybe later. Let's just get a boat and try not to get our sort-of fancy clothes all wet."

"Agreed."

In reality, Jessie was pleased by the ensemble she'd assembled. Though unprepared, she was a natural improviser, and she mixed and matched tops until she found a combination that didn't break every law of fashion when paired with a teal blue skirt. White sandals were perfectly acceptable summer attire, and by the grace of God she had a pair of white earrings to match. Her hair, which never behaved without a fight, ended up fairly obedient—another sign that the universe was rooting for her. In addition to her purse, she carried a crinkled envelope containing various documents relating to her father, his death, and her subsequent power of attorney. She was sick of looking at it.

From Cerro Viejo, they rode a water taxi along the same route they'd taken for their visit with the biologist, David Zimmer. Jessie donned her shades as the sun ascended, pushing another immaculate morning in front of it. She'd heard rain was expected, but she saw no sign of it.

When the boat finally docked at the entrance to the national park, the first thing Jessie did was head to the information center in search of Beatriz, otherwise known as Granny. Hopefully Beatriz could tell her about the woman in the drawing. But according to the staff members on duty, Beatriz was currently leading a tour of the inner channels, and no, ma'am, she doesn't get cell reception out there, thanks and have a nice day.

Resisting the urge to grind her teeth in frustration, Jessie bought two bottles of water and waited with Rubio for the car he'd arranged. They spent the next hour in the backseat while their driver told them about his wife and kids and how his arthritis always warned him when the weather was about to change. Because she was sitting directly behind him, Jessie received none of his commentary, so Rubio repeated everything, silently inserting his own observations about talkative cabbies. Jessie got the impression that Rubio liked the idea of being able to talk to her without making any noise, as if they were sharing a secret. And in a way, she supposed they were.

But she was also perceptive enough to notice the lag time in his smile and the way his eyes occasionally darted to the window. Was she making him nervous?

She signed the question as she spoke it: "Are you worried about something?"

"Damn, and I thought I wasn't being obvious."

"You're not. At least not to most people."

"That's what I get for riding in the back of a taxi with a psychic."

"I could break out my Tarot cards if that would make it easier."

"Nah, I'd be afraid of what I might find out." He sat back in his seat. "But you're right. This whole meeting has...it's just...complicated."

"Whenever someone says 'it's complicated,' they usually mean they don't really have a good explanation."

"You're not going to let me off the hook, are you?"

"You don't have to tell me. I'm just asking as a friend." This was no sooner out of her mouth than she questioned her own choice of words. But it was true. They *had* become friends, even though they'd known each other for only a matter of days. And that was some kind of record for her. "It's not really my business at all."

"No, it's fine. I don't mind. The situation is...not something that I've discussed with a lot of people. Or *any* people for that matter. It just sort of ...came and went."

"*What* came and went?"

He paused for another moment, then said, "The woman we're going to meet today, from the hospital financial department, her name is Gavina Herrera."

"Okay."

"Gavina...she and I..." He seemed unable to find the words.

"You've met before?"

"To say the least."

Jessie was no dummy. She knew what he was trying to say. He'd shared something with this woman, a fling or full-blown affair. No big deal. Happened all the time.

"We…dated," Rubio said.

Jessie was surprised, but not by the fact that Rubio had once had a romantic relationship. To the contrary, a man like this probably couldn't walk down the street without women turning to watch him go. What surprised her was her own emotional response. She felt a little defensive and didn't know why. "So you two were an item." She shrugged with one shoulder. "Nothing unusual in that."

"You're right. I shouldn't let it get to me. The whole thing didn't last very long, and I haven't seen her in nearly a year. I'm just hoping the weirdness level in the room doesn't get too high today. I guess I've never really been very good at forgetting old flames."

"The optimist in you wants to remember only the good times. I know how it is." She couldn't help but wonder what Herrera looked like.

"The two of us…what we had, it couldn't get us over the bad spots. When you're with someone, you want to feel like they're your bodyguard, and vice versa, and that one of you would jump in front of a bullet for the other. But more often than not, it felt like it was every man for himself, if that makes any sense."

Jessie hadn't intended the conversation to take such a serious turn. But now that she was here, curiosity compelled her to press on. "The two of you never took a second shot at making it work?"

"What's the sign for 'disaster'?"

She smiled and showed him. "That means 'wreck.'"

"Close enough. It comes down to her being this arrow fired straight into the sky at her career, and me willing to take a few left turns and sometimes stop along the way."

"To smell the roses?"

"Exactly. Life's too short to live entirely by your appointment book." He smirked at himself. "And that's the extent of my personal philosophy. I'm full of clichés. I'm afraid I don't get any more complicated than that."

Jessie sensed his desire to change the subject, and so she did, asking about the trees beyond the window and the weather and the type of music on the radio. He replied with his usual enthusiasm, and she wondered if he was actually enjoying her company or if he was just really good at faking it. She didn't try to figure it out, because right now it didn't matter. The only things she knew for certain in this world were that Costa Rican roads were bumpy as hell, that chocolate could cure everything but heartache, and that Gavina Herrera was a fool.

****

San Jose dazzled her. With its winding, switchback streets and busy markets, it reminded her of old European cities, but its digital billboards and determined pedestrians made it seem very American. She said as much to Rubio.

"That's probably close to the truth," he said. "There's still a lot of old-world attitudes here, but with every new generation, we get more...California. The kids don't want to shop for lunch at the corner fishmonger, and they don't shop for music in a record store. Lunch is whatever they can get at the drive-through, and they stream their music online. See those skateboarders there? Can you tell their nationality by looking at them?"

Jessie turned to see half a dozen teenage boys with wild hair and knee-length shorts. They wore their Yankees caps sideways, their skin tones dark and light.

She turned back. "I see what you mean."

"I love them all," Rubio said. "They have an energy that could really be put to use if they manage not to get burned out by the time they're twenty-one. I'm tired of seeing the young people of my country—or of *any* country—just turn into old people without doing anything productive in between."

"Where I come from, we'd call you an idealist."

"And your father wasn't?"

"Oh, he was the high royal majesty of idealists. That's why I can recognize one from a mile away." She saw what she assumed was the hospital through the window over Rubio's shoulder. "I think we're almost there."

Rubio glanced that way. "I'm really not looking forward to this. Shutting the clinic down means Greta will have to find work somewhere else, and I hate the fact that I can't do anything about it."

Jessie knitted her fingers in her lap. She'd tried to think of some way to save the clinic, but without an unexpected financial windfall—did they have a lottery in Costa Rica?—she saw no opportunity to make things right. "I wish Dad had left me a fortune," she said softly.

"Don't worry about it. None of this is your fault. We'll all be fine. In fact, this is probably the incentive I need to take everyone's advice and enter medical school."

"The look in your eyes says you're not so enthused about that advice."

"I really need to start working on my poker face."

"It wouldn't help. I have X-ray vision."

"Well, you're right. Med school is something you're supposed to do in your early twenties, when you're too young to know any better. But I'm thirty years old, and I'm too much in love with my life to be willing to spend most of it as a sleepless intern."

"You'd rather spend it as a sleepless paramedic?"

"It's not the same. The shifts are long, but I still have enough time to go out and...and *breathe*. Last summer I went horseback riding in El Salvador and took ballroom dancing lessons in Cancún. You can't do that if you're working eighty hours a week in a hospital."

"So how are your dancing skills?"

"I'm not going to win any prizes, but I promise not to step on your toes in a fox trot."

"I'm afraid it would be *me* doing the toe-stepping."

"If you tell me that deaf people can't dance, I'm not going to believe you."

"No, deaf people can do anything they put their minds to. The problem happens to be my total lack of grace."

He laughed. "Maybe we'll stick with the horseback riding, then. Any experience with that?"

"Does riding an elephant count?"

"A what?"

"An elephant." She signed it, moving her right hand down from her nose, pantomiming a trunk. "My father took me to India when I was thirteen."

The taxi pulled into the hospital's U-shaped drive, parking under a porte cochere that matched the color of the San Jose sky.

Rubio said, "Wish we had that elephant right now. I'd rather be riding away from this place as fast as it could carry us. Guess I just have to man up and get it over with."

Before Jessie could respond, Rubio swung open his door and got out.

She met him on his side of the car just as he was pulling back from the passenger's window, having paid the cabbie for the ride. As the taxi drove away, Rubio slipped his wallet into his back pocket, turned toward the hospital's glass doors, and visibly steeled himself for battle.

"Contrary to popular belief," Jessie said, "I can't read minds. I'm not sure what you're thinking right now, but it doesn't look good."

"Trying to decide which part of this I'm dreading more, closing down the clinic or seeing Gavina again."

What Jessie did next was something she hadn't planned; it just happened, and she surprised herself by doing it. She was a person who lived by gestures, by motions, by meaningful body language that often said more than words could convey. So it felt only natural when she offered her hand, palm up, fingers slightly spread.

Rubio looked from her waiting hand to her face, then back again. Smiling softly, he took her hand in his and—bolstered by their shared warmth—headed inside.

Chapter Twenty-Five

Rubio enjoyed elevators the way other men liked cars.

Put a guy behind the wheel of a '69 Camaro, regardless of what country he was from, and he instantly traveled through time to when he was a boy, shifting gears in imaginary races. Men fantasized in cars. For Rubio, who marched to the beat of a dyslexic drummer, those boyhood dreams were scrambled. He'd been raised by a single mother who instilled in him not a love of hot rods and sports stars, but instead an appreciation for old movies and a love of the ocean on a summer evening. So whenever he rode in elevators, his mind wandered, and he imagined himself to be someone else, perhaps a secret agent about to meet his Russian lover in the top-floor penthouse or Steve McQueen on his way to save the day in *The Towering Inferno*.

"You're smiling," Jessie observed.

"Long story."

"Maybe later?"

"We'll see." The door gave a *bing!* he knew Jessie couldn't hear, and when the doors parted he reluctantly released her hand. For the last three minutes, he'd been hyperaware of the shape of her fingers and the heat that formed where their palms met. What business did he have holding the hand of a woman he'd known for only a handful of days?

It's been much longer than that.

True. He couldn't deny the voice in his head that argued he'd been at least slightly infatuated by her since the moment he saw her photo on Archie's desk. The more he heard about her, the deeper his intrigue. When she'd shown up without warning at the clinic, Rubio wondered if Archie had pulled some strings from heaven.

"These places all smell the same," Jessie said as they moved along the hall.

"Do they? You'd think there would be some variation by nationality."

"Nope. Same scent, some shine on the floor, same lame-ass art on the walls."

"Now *there's* a term I never heard Archie use."

"What, you don't agree? Look at it. Meaningless floral patterns and landscapes of places so generic they could represent almost any place on earth. And that ocean scene there? I think there must be a really bland art studio somewhere that produces the most boring pictures possible and sells them to hospitals, banks, and dentist offices all over the world."

"All right, you made your point. Lame-ass is official."

"Thank you. And by the way, in case you weren't paying attention, the fact that I can say 'ass' in front of you is a sign that I'm comfortable with you. Sometimes men need things spelled out for them."

"More often than not."

"Which is my way of saying that I'm glad I'm not going through this alone. My dad invested a lot of himself in this project. It hurts to be putting it away."

"Agreed."

Having gotten their bearings by way of the staff directory downstairs, they closed in on the island desk of an administrative assistant who guarded a pair of heavy oak doors. She looked up as they approached.

Rubio introduced himself in Spanish, explaining that he had an appointment, and she told him that *Señorita* Herrera would be with him shortly. Then she indicated the modern steel-and-leather chairs in the waiting area. They looked uncomfortable, favoring form over function.

He and Jessie sat down beneath a particularly lame-ass picture of a waterfall.

Jessie crossed one leg over the other and plucked up the nearest magazine, a celebrity-gossip rag. "You know, it doesn't even matter that this is written in Spanish, because all anyone ever does with these things is look at the pictures of how the other half lives."

Rubio didn't reply because he was sitting beside her and his lips were not directly visible. Instead, he surreptitiously observed her, the way she bobbed her foot, the thickness of her hair.

He looked away, knowing a danger zone when he saw one.

Their lives may have temporarily intersected, but he couldn't see them running parallel, at least not for long. She was an American, more like the people in that magazine than she would ever believe. Rubio's greatest shortcoming—at least in his own estimation—was the desire to live for the day at the expense of tomorrow. Americans, Europeans, and an increasing number of Ticos bought houses larger than they needed, lived on credit cards, and waited for easy retirement days. Rubio had never been like that. He made his money to spend it, not on material goods but on experiences. He'd bought his own plane ticket when he volunteered with earthquake relief in Haiti. He'd stood five meters from the cryptic faces on Easter Island. He'd attended music festivals, bullfights, and ballets. Could such a life be reconciled with hers?

"I can almost hear you thinking," she said without looking up from the page.

He waited, but she didn't take her eyes from the magazine, so he couldn't provide a response—not that he had anything sensible to say. She'd caught him thinking about her. If he opened his mouth now, he'd only further incriminate himself.

He glanced at the clock above the secretary's desk. Three minutes remained until their meeting. He pictured Gavina in her office, poring over financial statements or perhaps staring out over the city skyline.

Finally he could stand it no more. He tapped Jessie on the knee and shaped the words without making a sound. "Is it too late to turn around and run?"

"Where would you go?"

"I hear Nova Scotia is nice this time of year."

She closed her magazine. "If it helps, I'd rather not be here, either."

"A part of me wants to blame Archie. I can't help but feel like…like he…"

"Abandoned you?"

He nodded. "Yeah. I know that's not fair of me to think that way."

"This microwave is shot."

Rubio had no idea what she just said or how it applied. "Excuse me?"

"That's why I called him that night, the last time I ever talked to him. I called to vent about having to buy a new microwave. That was the substance of our last conversation. I never heard his voice again."

Rubio opened his mouth but had no more words.

"It's okay to feel like the universe or God or somebody screwed you over," she said. "That's part of the package, and it sucks. I get up every morning and it's still there, pissing me off."

Rubio, humbled, leaned forward, elbows on his knees. If only he could tell her—

"Miss Herrera will see you now," the secretary said.

Rubio stood. "Here we go."

Jessie joined him, returning the magazine to the table. "There's strength in numbers, right?"

"So they say."

Together they walked through the office door.

****

Gavina Herrera stood at the window, arms crossed, talking into her Bluetooth earpiece. She wore a dark three-button jacket over a white shirt, with a matching pencil skirt that stopped strategically at her knees and revealed a pair of legs that reminded Jessie of those showoffs from her college days. Gavina's two-inch heels probably went for a hundred and fifty dollars, which was enough *colones* that Jessie didn't even try to do the math.

Preferring not to take in any further details, she inspected the room.

According to corporate lore, a corner office represented a career milestone, giving its occupants a certain amount of self-governance, despite the proximity of their superiors. Gavina had maximized her independence, decorating her surroundings with pieces of formless modern sculpture, diplomas in wrought-iron frames, and—somewhat incongruously—a foosball table. This unexpected game table was set into a sandalwood cabinet, each of its hard resin soccer players painted so as to be individually distinct. This was not the battered foosball unit of the co-ed lounges in dorm buildings, but the expensive showpiece of a woman who wasn't afraid to roll up her sleeves and challenge the men who visited her office. Jessie had no doubt that guys thought it was extremely cool.

Gavina ended her phone call, smiled almost subliminally, and addressed Rubio in Spanish. Jessie had seen the woman's eyes roll over her, but otherwise she might have been invisible as Gavina circled her desk and welcomed Rubio with one of those platonic kiss-greetings made famous by Russian gymnasts and jet setters who imitated the French.

In English, Rubio said, "This is Dr. Alomar's daughter, Jessie."

Jessie had spent the last several minutes prepping herself for this moment, and her diplomacy didn't fail her. She stood tall, shook firmly but politely, and fixed a political smile to her face.

"So very pleased to meet you," Gavina said. She wore her hair gathered behind her head, with a few strands hanging artfully loose on one side of her face. Jessie guessed she was a woman who could have afforded contact lenses but opted for these Armani glasses because they gave her the look of a boardroom veteran.

Or a substitute teacher about to strip at a bachelor

party, she thought.

Squashing this renegade thought, she managed to say, "Thank you for taking the time to see us."

Gavina hesitated.

Jessie had seen it before, this uncertainty on a stranger's face, this pause before they connected the dots and realized that, yeah, you were deaf, and no, you didn't need any special treatment. There was a word Jessie had always liked: *hangfire*. She'd once read a murder mystery in which the narrator had described the tiny amount of time between the drop of a gun's hammer and the discharge of the bullet as hangfire.

As soon as Gavina's hangfire passed, she motioned toward the chairs in front of her desk. "Please, make yourselves comfortable, and I'll see about locating some spring water. I don't know about you, but I'm an absolute *fiend* for hydration."

At least, that's what Jessie *assumed* she said. Gavina spoke so quickly that Jessie missed every third or fourth word, but she'd become remarkably adept at patching the holes in people's sentences. The word 'fiend' actually came across as 'fee,' but Jessie guessed that the former was a more appropriate match, all things considered.

She sat beside Rubio, whose eyes swept the room like radars, picking up Gavina's blip and tracking her from the mini-fridge and back to her chair.

Gavina gave them both a bottle and spun the top on her own as she settled into her seat, which was probably so finely crafted that it didn't creak when she moved. Back home, Jessie's office chair made noises every time she shifted in front of the computer. She knew this to be true because not only had Li informed her of the racket on more than one occasion, but the problem was so severe that she felt the vibration of metal against metal whenever she spun too quickly to the left.

Gavina folded her hands on her desk blotter. "I want to start by saying I'm very sorry. Dr. Alomar seemed like quite a gentleman, and the work he was doing up at Cerro Viejo was commendable. You have my condolences."

"Thank you," Jessie said, far beyond the point of wanting any more condolences.

"I wish that we'd had the pleasure of working with him for many years to come. He really did a lot to improve what we call the region's quality of place."

Jessie considered the phrase and wrote it off as meaningless marketing lingo. *Quality of place* was right up there with *repatriation of the remains*. But according to the diploma on the wall, Gavina had studied at Georgetown, and ambiguous language was just the kind of thing you learned in Washington D.C.

"It's unfortunate," Gavina said, "that we had to meet under such circumstances."

"Thank you," Jessie said, realizing belatedly that she'd repeated herself.

Gavina turned to Rubio. "It's good to see you."

Jessie didn't catch Rubio's response, because it would have put her in what she called tennis-match mode, swiveling her head from one side to the other in hopes of not missing anything. Instead, she kept her eyes on Gavina and her apparently poreless face.

"Has it been that long?" Gavina asked him, not quite smiling. "From the looks of things, you've been taking care of yourself. Still getting up at sunrise to go running?"

Nope, Jessie mentally replied, *I sleep till noon, then spend the day hungover.*

"And the knee? It's not bothering you anymore?"

Knee? Jessie thought. *Nothing that a little duct tape won't fix, thanks for asking.*

"Too bad," Gavina said, unaware that her conversation was being edited. "I guess that means I'd no longer be able to keep up with you on that hill by the park."

Yeah, I'd pretty much leave you in the dust, lady, now can we cut the frilly shit and get this over with?

"No, sadly these days all of my running happens on the treadmill, but I still manage to hit it three times a week."

And I manage not to groan when people lay it on so thick. Suddenly she didn't want to be in here, at ground zero of SFZ, the Subtle Flirtation Zone. "Excuse me, do you have a restroom I can use?"

Gavina touched the side of her glasses, adjusting them slightly with a gesture that was as feminine as it was subconscious. "Yes, of course. Just step back out into the reception area. The women's room is just to the right."

"Great, thanks." Jessie felt better even as she stood up, because evidently Gavina wasn't *that* important, otherwise she would've had her own private bathroom.

She left them alone, to say whatever it was they needed to say.

Chapter Twenty-Six

As soon as the door closed, Gavina said, "She seems nice."

Rubio chose his response with tact. He knew a little about the way women communicated. He'd been raised by a single mother and her girlfriends. He paid attention when they revealed the secrets of their gender. And so by now he was quite certain than when one girl said another was nice, it was just a euphemism for *dull, quaint, harmless, plain*, and *generally underwhelming*.

In Spanish he asked, "Aren't there some papers you wanted me to sign?"

"Interesting." She leaned back in her chair. "Since when is any subject off limits between us?"

"Things change."

"True enough. I know *I* have. What about you? Still the same white knight out to save what's left of the world?"

"Someone has to."

"But at what expense? I started out as an accountant, remember? I can do the math. And I understand that if you keep giving more than you get back, you don't last for long. The numbers just don't balance out."

"It's never been about the money."

"Sure it has. You're just too stubborn to realize it." Then she showed him her smile. Not the workday variety. This was the full-on masterpiece, the one that bent hearts. "Damn, it's great to see you again, Rubio."

Even though they'd broken up a year ago, it still made him feel good to hear that. Maybe she was just playing to his ego, but Rubio figured any heterosexual man would have felt just a little macho upon hearing such a thing from a woman as cool as Gavina. Her power suit curved her body like the sea drawing slender shapes in the sand.

"You've gotten a new office since then," he said.

"Promoted twice in eleven months. But who's counting, right?"

"And from here?"

"Oh, I don't know. Perhaps I'll see about getting a work visa and moving to New York. What do you think? Too cold for me up there? You know how I love the sun. What was it you told me once? That I'm a—"

"Daughter of the sun god. Yeah, I remember." In fact, the memory returned so swiftly that it startled him with its clarity: he lay on the beach beside her, mesmerized by a few grains of sand that rested on her brown, naked back as she sunbathed. He blinked a few times, trying to force the image to dissolve. "Look, I'm trying to be a nice guy here, but what's about to happen is that you're going to tell me I'm losing my job and Cerro Viejo is losing its medical practice."

"I already told you as much on the phone. It's out of my hands. I don't make all the decisions around here. Without Dr. Alomar's support—"

"There's no other way? There's not a government subsidy out there or a partner willing to put up the money?"

"Do you think I *want* to do this to you? Believe

me, the last thing I desire right now is for you to sit there and glare at me like that. Honestly…you've been on my mind lately. The men around here have no idea who I really am. Without you to talk to, sometimes I feel like there's no one who truly…*gets me.* So please don't say I'm the villain here."

Rubio was impressed. Gavina had never been one to open up, even when they were lying in each other's arms. So this slight admission of loneliness, fabricated or not, was something of headline news. "I'm not blaming you. I'm blaming the accident."

"Accident?"

"Archie's death."

"Ah, of course. Sorry. And I really am. He was what the Americans call a character."

"I won't argue with that. And he was brilliant. And generous. And joyful. And so…so goddamn thankful just to be given the chance to be alive and take pictures of the flowers." A new fire rose in him, and he slid to the edge of his chair. "Do you hear what I'm saying? Dr. Alomar was the kind of man I hope to be one of these days. He went where he was needed, and he gobbled life down in huge bites. And he knew magic tricks that made kids laugh. So forgive me if I don't come crawling across this desk and ask to get back together with you, because the best man I know is dead."

Gavina took off her glasses and lowered her eyes. "I'm sorry. For everything."

Rubio surprised himself by believing her.

****

Jessie stood in the bathroom, leaning against the sink, facing a blank wall. She'd come to this hospital for business purposes, but now her only thoughts were of the personal nature. Personal as in wondering what Gavina was saying. Personal as in hoping that Rubio was immune. And what did these thoughts mean about Jessie's feelings for him?

"Thanks, Dad," she whispered. "Next time hire a right-hand man who's old and fat and doesn't look like I could eat him with a spoon."

Needing a lifeline, she took out her phone and sent Li a simple two-word text:

Save me.

****

Standing at the office window, Gavina pointed across the city. "See that star?"

Beside her, Rubio searched the skyline until he saw the sign affixed to the building a few blocks away. In the daylight, the neon was a pale pink without any flash.

"That's where we met for the second time," Gavina said. "Dr. Alomar introduced us, but a few hours on that very same day—"

"It rained."

"And neither of us had been smart enough to bring an umbrella. I was walking along in my usual caffeinated state, chugging about with my briefcase, and then the lightning flashed and the whole sky seemed to open up at once."

Rubio didn't necessarily want to travel back through time, but standing here next to her, it was impossible not to accompany her on the journey. "I ducked under the hotel awning. I was on my way to the gym. But I never made it."

"How long did we stand there before saying

something? God, it must have been three or four minutes. It was starting to feel a little awkward, standing around watching the pouring rain with someone I'd just met, and *then* you said—"

"'Come here often?'"

Gavina nodded. Her reflection in the window smiled.

"It was the best I could come up with," Rubio said.

"It made me laugh."

"Sometimes I get lucky."

"Sometimes we *all* get lucky. And sometimes we don't."

There wasn't much deep philosophy in that statement, but Rubio felt the truth of it just the same. Sometimes things didn't fall his way. But other times Jessie Alomar showed up on the clinic step.

Gavina never looked directly at him, but she met his eyes in the glass. "How do you feel about second chances?"

Rubio didn't immediately answer. It was a question worth considering. He sensed that he'd reached an important place in his life and that possibilities—both good and bad—abounded in every direction. "I'd like to think that I'm open to all options. But that doesn't mean that I would consider—"

"Wait. I know you have every right to turn around and walk out right now. In the time we were together, you never once heard me say I'm sorry. That's my fault. I tend to get caught up in myself, and heaven help anyone who gets in the way."

"What exactly are you asking me?"

"I wouldn't mind trying again. Not immediately. But with the operation closing in Cerro Viejo and you moving back to the city…I just thought that if we happened to shelter from the rain again together, we might consider…" She shook her head. "Sometimes I don't know when to shut up. Let's just start with my apology and go from there. How's that sound?"

"No strings attached?"

"You know me. I can't swear off the strings."

"At least you're honest about it."

"Have I ever lied to you?"

"You've got me on that one."

"So…a peace treaty then?"

Rubio considered turning away from her, but what would that accomplish? He prided himself on keeping a youthful heart but making grown-up decisions. And this was one of them. He believed in mending fences when you had the chance. Their affair might have been over, but holding onto resentment would only make him old before his time, as it did with so many others.

"Is it that hard of a decision?" she asked.

"Just weighing my options."

"And?" She gave him the slightest raise of an eyebrow, an unspoken challenge.

He finally nodded. "Apology accepted."

"Clean slate?"

"As clean as can be expected."

"I'll settle for that." She smiled, and then the door opened, and for a moment Rubio found himself at a strange intersection of desire, with his past on one side and a potential future on the other. Jessie entered the room with her face perfectly placid and betraying nothing, and Rubio wanted to explain himself and tell her about the agreement he'd just made, assuring her that it was simply to make amends and not to rewrite history. But then again, why did he feel like he owned her any explanation at all?

"So," Gavina said a little too loudly, "let's get down to all the paperwork. Then maybe we can move on to more pleasant matters." Instantly she was the professional again, a bombardier pilot in a dark blue skirt, moving to her desk and soldiering through the formalities as if the last five minutes had transpired only in Rubio's mind.

Jessie took a seat across from her, not meeting Rubio's eyes, apparently interested only in concluding her business here. She and Gavina became quickly absorbed in their business, handing documents back and forth and working through them as if Rubio were no longer in the room.

He wanted to laugh. This was but one more example of how men had never been able to understand women. Not even the brightest minds in history, the Shakespeares and the Einsteins, could have stood in this room and felt even a little bit in control.

It was turning out to be an interesting day, and it was far from over.

Chapter Twenty-Seven

"I think that may be everything," Gavina said, leaning back in her chair.

Jessie waited to feel something dramatic. She'd just finalized the dissolution of her father's partnership with the hospital, his last legal connection with Costa Rica. She wondered when she'd experience relief or a sense that everything was finally complete.

"Now, before we part ways," Gavina said to her, "I have a thought that I'd like to share with you."

"Of course." Jessie didn't hate this woman. True, at first she'd considered Gavina the enemy on the grounds that the clinic was being forced to shut down, and it hadn't made things any better to see her give so much attention to Rubio. But ever since she'd settled down to business, the woman had been nothing but polite. Could they have ever been friends under different circumstances? Probably not. But at least Jessie was no longer wincing inside every time Gavina fluttered her professionally curated eyelashes. "Please, go ahead."

"This may sound rash, but…" She tapped her fountain pen on her hand. "Would the two of you consider going out tonight?"

Jessie leaned a little forward in her seat. "Out?"

"I know it's silly, but I truly feel bad about what's happening here, and I want to leave you with a better impression, if at all possible. In other words, Ms.

Alomar, I want us to go out and have a good time so you don't fly back to the States thinking I'm a total bitch."

"I don't think that about you."

"No, but you're close. I can tell. I'd feel the same way if our positions were reversed. So I was just thinking that…maybe I could invite a friend along, and the four of us could see the city this evening and talk about other things. We might even surprise ourselves and have a bearable time."

Jessie expected a trap. Normally she gave everyone the benefit of the doubt, but considering her recent tendency toward conspiracy theories, she was now a woman of high suspicions. "That sounds…fun. But we should probably get back to the village."

"The village will still be there tomorrow. Stay here. At least for this evening. Stay and enjoy the nightlife courtesy of a woman who's desperately trying not to come across as totally without a heart." Before Jessie could reply, Gavina looked at Rubio. "What about it? And don't tell me that you don't know how to dance, because I know better." She gave him one of the most tempting smiles Jessie had seen in real life, the kind she suspected would turn most men to wax caricatures of their former selves. "How about a double date?"

But Rubio was not wax. In fact, the look on his face surprised Jessie with its earnestness, and she delighted in the fact that he didn't respond predictably. Damn, maybe Tioni had been precisely right when she said there were only two good men left in the world.

"Jessie and I should return to the clinic."

"Come on, I'm not going to kidnap the two of you and cook you in a witch's kettle. We're adults, Rubio

Mora, and like adults, we can enjoy ourselves without letting other emotions get in the way. This has been a difficult meeting for more than one reason, and I think we deserve to be human for a while. And you're never more human than when you're dancing."

It sounded reasonable enough. Though Jessie's initial response was to decline the offer, now that she considered it, spending a night on the town with Rubio might be just what she needed. She wasn't much of a dancer, as she depended on the heavy bass to provide stepstones across the music, but there was a recklessness in her that encouraged her to try.

"You're bringing someone?" Rubio asked her.

Gavina gave him a little roll of her eyes. "Yes, unless you're thinking that a threesome is more to your liking."

By the sudden color in Rubio's cheeks, it was clear that he'd been considering no such thing. He looked at Jessie for help. "What do you think?"

What *did* she think? For starters, she thought that Gavina Herrera in her high-dollar shoes was probably still sweet on Rubio. Second, she thought that the evening had a high probability of being awkward for everyone. Finally, she thought that the idea of a double date, as Gavina had said, sounded nice, all other things aside. "Sounds fun," she said again, knowing that it was all far more complicated than those two simple words implied.

Gavina beamed. "Excellent! I'm not free until after five, but what do you say to an early dinner after that, and then a bit of innocent club-hopping?"

Jessie missed the details that followed. As Rubio and Gavina settled on times and places, Jessie glanced down at her vibrating phone.

Save U from what?

Jessie wasn't sure how to answer that. Maybe it was time to lace up some steel-toed boots and do the saving herself.

****

They spent the afternoon at the downtown market. Jessie pretended to be carefree as Rubio guided her through the merchant stalls, and for the most part she succeeded. She enjoyed walking with him through this new place, this labyrinth of artists and fishmongers and perfume salesmen calling out to her without knowing their raised voices were for naught. She resisted the temptation to spend money on handcrafted trinkets she didn't need. Her father had collected so much bric-a-brac from foreign bazaars that Jessie wouldn't have been able to find room in the house for any more.

When she returned from using the public restroom, she found Rubio standing in the center of the brick-lined street, holding a purple flower. He offered it to her as she approached.

Something came over her at this simple gesture, and she stopped a few feet away, lips slightly parted in wonder. She hadn't been given a flower in years. She was a foreigner in a beautiful country. She'd seen lizards that walked on water and butterflies without number alighting on her morning sheets. She divided her thoughts between her dead hero and a man with midnight eyes. All of this added up to pure distraction, but when Rubio held out that solitary orchid, everything focused, as if Jessie had spent all this time staring at the world's muddied reflection in the water only to finally look up and see it all become clear.

"It's called a *Guaria Morada*," Rubio said. "It's our national flower. They say that it brings people together and fosters understanding between strangers. It's a symbol of hope. If you smell it, you'll find that it doesn't have any special scent. That's because it was never filled with fragrance, but rather with the dreams all Ticos hope to achieve."

Jessie accepted it, knowing that her thoughts were perfectly visible in her eyes. "I don't know what to say."

"Say that you'll wear it in your hair."

"Like the woman in my father's drawing?"

"Precisely like her."

Jessie did just that, tucking the short stem above her left ear. "The last time I wore flowers in my hair, it was six years ago and I was the maid of honor at my friend Li's wedding."

"The *Guaria Morada* is good luck at weddings."

"Li ended up divorcing him after only seven months."

Rubio shook his head, laughing.

Jessie couldn't stop smiling. Her stomach felt that special lightness she hadn't experienced in...in longer than she cared to recall. "Thank you."

"My pleasure. Come on. Maybe we can find a candy store that won't try to take advantage of my weakness for coconut covered in dark chocolate."

"Hmm, that might be a weakness that we have in common."

"You like chocolate-covered coconut?"

"Never had it. But I am more than willing to sample some and find out."

Rubio seemed to appreciate that, and he led her

down the street. When Jessie caught their images in a mirror outside a clothing shop, she almost confessed to him what she'd been signing that day in the boat. She had pointed at him, then fanned her fingers twice in front of her face. Rubio had asked what it meant, but she'd said nothing, not quite willing to admit that she'd just told him that he was beautiful.

Flower in her hair, she accompanied him to wherever he wanted to take her.

Chapter Twenty-Eight

They met Gavina and her date that night under a half-hidden moon. When Jessie stepped out of the back of the cab, that was the first thing she saw, the bright lunar lantern partially concealed by a curtain of clouds. The sight of it further entranced her, as she was already at least a little bit spellbound by the day's events; touring the city with Rubio had been more pleasurable even than she'd anticipated. She'd relaxed a little more with every passing hour, and for the first time since her father had died, she called herself lucky. But where would it all lead when it came time to fly away home?

"There they are," Rubio said, pointing to a table at an outdoor bistro. "Looks like they saw us. I guess that means it's too late to turn around and run."

"We don't have to do this if it makes you uncomfortable." Jessie stood close to him so as to read his lips by the light of the curbside lamps. "Hanging out with her tonight isn't going to help the clinic stay open any longer."

"You might have noticed that I'm an optimist."

"Yes, and God knows that we could use a bit more of that in the world. But I can't help but think that maybe she's…I don't know, that she's using this to her advantage somehow. And that's totally unfair of me because I don't even know the woman."

"Maybe if we stand here long enough they'll get

bored and forget about us."

"Uh, she's waving us over."

"So much for forgetting us," Rubio said.

"Can you blame her? We're not very forgettable people."

"That explains it. We're rock stars, right?"

"Yes, and we're also stalling. Let's go. If it becomes unbearable, you have my permission to whisk me away without warning."

"You got it," he said, and they went to face whatever the night presented to them.

****

As he took his second sip of wine, Rubio remembered the witches.

If you don't eat all of your vegetables, his mother once said, *the Witches of Clean Plates will visit your room and pester you all night with their obnoxious laughter.*

Unlike his boyhood self, Rubio planned to clean his plate, including the broccoli, even though he'd never counted it among his favorites. The restaurant specialized in Italian cuisine, and the pasta primavera almost warranted its price on the menu. Half an hour into dinner, he'd permitted himself to meet Gavina's gaze only twice, and that was enough. She'd unpinned her hair, and it hung over her shoulders with the perfection of a shampoo commercial. She wore a cocktail dress that he'd never seen before and had intentionally left her glasses elsewhere. Her sex appeal was as evident as she intended it to be, so when she caught Rubio's eye the second time, he didn't give her the satisfaction of holding her stare.

And if you're up all night because of the witches,

his mother had warned, *then you'll miss the bus tomorrow and have to walk all the way to school.*

Gavina had introduced them to Trevor, a pharmaceuticals rep from Miami. Though he wore a tailored blazer and was equipped with the kind of handshake you expected from a salesman, Trevor had a habit of laughing a little too loudly whenever Gavina made a joke. Rubio knew that the man was underestimating her. Flattering her had never been easy.

So unless you want to walk to school tomorrow, you'll clean your plate and keep the witches away!

Those damn witches. Rubio tried to pay attention to the conversation—Trevor was giving his opinion on alternative energy sources—but he kept thinking about his mother's attempt to convince him to be a healthy eater. She would have appreciated this. Here he was, forcing down his broccoli not for its nutritional value but simply because it kept his mouth busy. If he said too much, he feared he'd give away his newly discovered secret.

He had a crush on the boss' daughter.

From the moment he'd seen that photo on Archie's desk, Rubio had been at least a little bit enthralled. He'd wondered what she was thinking when the snapshot was taken, and where she liked to go on Saturday night, and what silly movies she watched when no one else was around. The more Archie had spoken of her, the more real she'd become, and through nothing more than secondhand knowledge, Rubio had fallen for her.

But this—this was a different kind of falling.

This was the kind of falling you could do only when a woman at the seat beside yours gave you a glance that no one else saw, the kind of falling that happened over a few afternoons in the summer sun, the kind of falling you did when you felt that someone was falling for you in return.

But was she? This was the question that kept distracting him. More than once he'd had to ask Gavina or Trevor to repeat themselves when they'd addressed him. By now they probably thought he was intentionally ignoring them.

There was only one problem. Gavina would not relent. She was flirting with him on a level no one else detected. Like the sea that moved against the rocks until even stone gave way, Gavina knew how to move her hand, how to say things with a laugh, and how to convey with her eyes what she'd never say aloud. Her subtlety staggered him. Usually when she wanted something, she was as delicate as a surface-to-air missile, but now, for some reason, she'd dialed down her flirtations so they barely registered. She never brushed his foot with hers or accidently touched his fingers when they both reached for the wine. But there was an easy attractiveness to her tonight, a suggestion that she was open to compromise and that she just might be a changed woman.

Was it true? The last time around, had she met Rubio in the middle instead of refusing to budge on numerous topics, they'd still be together. If she were truly different now, could they have a second chance?

"….but I'm sure things are a little different than that in Arizona," Trevor was saying.

"For the most part," Jessie said, her legs crossed, her wine glass held near her lap. "We're close enough to California that sometimes we can't help but be a little bit strange."

"I was stationed in San Diego when I was in the Marines, so I totally understand the whole California thing. Hey, anyone need some more wine? I feel like I'm taking more than my fair share."

Rubio wondered where Gavina had met this guy. Trevor seemed almost like a stereotype, as if Gavina had rented him from a shop called Typical American Men in Nice Suits. He went to the gym. He played golf. He wore boxer-briefs. Somehow all of these topics had managed to come up in the night's conversation.

"What about you, Rubio?" Trevor said to him. "Gavi tells me that Costa Rica is one of the world leaders in recycling."

Gavi? That was a new one. Rubio waved a hand noncommittally and said, "I'd like to think I'm environmentally conscious, but I have my moments when I'm just as wasteful as anyone else." He said it without much thought, delivering an automatic response but revealing nothing of his thoughts. He looked at Jessie, but her gaze continued to leap from one face to the next, keeping up with the conversation using only her eyes.

Look at me, he thought.

But Jessie kept her attention on Gavina, who was saying something about leading the hospital volunteer efforts to reduce paperwork in favor of digital patient records.

Rubio shifted in his chair, intentionally moving the legs harshly against the concrete that comprised the restaurant's verandah.

It worked. Feeling the vibration, Jessie glanced at him.

He mouthed a single word: *Run.*

Though he was certain she'd understood, she looked back at Gavina as if no message had passed between them. Rubio wanted to run away from this round table with its salt shakers in the form of toucans, away from this neighborhood where students pretended to be poets, away from the strings of lights and pulsing beat of nearby clubs that promised anonymity on dark dance floors. He wanted just to walk with her and tell her of his dreams and maybe throw down his cloak if they encountered any puddles in need of chivalrous crossing.

But they didn't run. Trevor ordered more drinks and bread sticks, Gavina told them of a new unisex boutique she'd recently discovered and how they absolutely *had* to give it a try, and Jessie joined them with a kind of courteous grace that Rubio admired and decided at that moment to imitate. The evening could be an enjoyable one if he allowed it to be, and talking sports or cars with Trevor from Miami wasn't going to kill him.

And then Gavina reached across the table and took his hand.

****

Jessie drew back a little, not knowing how to react. Gavina had leaned forward and clasped Rubio's hand, and the angle was such that Jessie couldn't quite see what she said.

Her eyes went to Rubio's mouth just in time to get his response, "Yes, I remember. How could I forget?"

Gavina withdrew her hand, caught up in whatever memory she was reliving. Jessie watched her as she told the story of how she'd once been invited to a wedding and had dragged Rubio along so she wouldn't have to go alone. "...and during the reception," she explained, "Rubio here got to play the total stud hero when the bride broke a heel and almost fell down the church stairs. Luckily Rubio swooped in and caught her. The poor girl might have ended up in the emergency room at my own hospital, for God's sake."

Trevor gave another of his pre-packaged laughs. "Talk about being in the right place at the right time. My luck, I would've tripped on my way to catch her, and we *both* would've ended up on the ground."

"Don't believe a word of it," Gavina said, looking straight at Jessie. "Trevor spends the weekends playing basketball with teenage boys at a youth shelter. He's not about to let a falling damsel slip through his grasp."

"I'm sure he wouldn't," Jessie replied. At some point the entire evening had become someone else's; Jessie observed it from a safe mental distance, trying to decide whether or not this man-eater with the two-inch eyelashes was trying to seduce both of these men or only one of them. And if that one was Rubio, did Jessie have the right to intervene?

There went Gavina with the hand again, only this time she placed it on Jessie's. "Can I ask you something personal? And feel free to tell me to go to hell."

Go to hell, Jessie thought, then banished this renegade notion before it slipped out. "I'm not promising an enlightening response."

"Do men find it intimidating to ask you out?"

Jessie's first reaction was, *They're not exactly standing in line to get my digits*, but actually Gavina was right. "It's not just men," she said. "A lot of people would rather just smile politely and avoid conversation with me altogether."

"They're embarrassed?"

"They're out of their element. Unless they were raised in a household with a handicapped person, I make them feel...weird. Have you ever converged on a door with a person in a wheelchair? You're not sure whether to open it for them or let them get it themselves. Most of the hearing world is afraid of doing something politically incorrect."

"And your advice to the hearing world?"

"I don't know. Usually I don't even have good advice for myself. But I guess I'd tell them that we hear a lot more than they realize, even if we can't technically hear a thing."

"I'll remember that."

Jessie was glad when Gavina turned the spotlight of her attention elsewhere, even though that meant she went back to more *remember whens* with Rubio. Jessie had never been comfortable being the topic of discussion...and maybe that was an indication that she needed to expand her comfort zone to include herself. She loved people-watching and observing the world around her, so she shouldn't be afraid of letting that world look at her in return.

Whatever. There was no time for self-analysis when the man you were attracted to was being stalked by another woman.

But in the last thirty seconds, she'd lost the thread of the conversation because Gavina's perfectly lustrous hair hung in such a way that her mouth was mostly concealed. Making matters worse was the onset of twilight and the relatively weak lighting on the restaurant verandah. Jessie quickly fell through the cracks of whatever they were talking about around her.

She picked up things where she could. She jumped from face to face, snagging bits and trying to put them together in case someone turned to her and asked for her opinion. But this was one of those time when bits weren't enough. And instead of speaking up and letting them know they were leaving her behind, she concealed her weakness and committed the one sin that her father had always warned her about: letting the silence drag her down...

Chapter Twenty-Nine

Once upon a time there was a little girl named Jessie. She lived in a faraway kingdom where no one, from peasant to His Royal Majesty, possessed a sense of smell.

Sitting on the edge of his daughter's bed, Archie Alomar tells his story as he tells all of his best ones, with his green eyes animated under his bushy brows and his hands gesturing wildly.

The little girl grew up in a land where nobody could smell anything. Nobody! They went through their days unaware that roses were more than beautifully red and that horse droppings on the cobblestones were more than simply messy. It had always been this way, and the people of the kingdom went about their lives unaware of the good and bad odors happening all around them.

Archie perches on the foot of the bed, and he takes hold of one of his daughter's feet, little more than a protruding shape beneath the covers. He gives it a gentle shake. *Imagine how horrible that would be if you couldn't smell my cookies baking!*

His daughter—seven-year-old Jessie, the anchor of his life's ship as well as its sail—giggles at the thought.

But one fine autumn afternoon, young Jessie came upon an old wooden box, half-buried in the moist earth at the foot of a tree. She opened the box's lid, and

216

behold! Within the box were dozens and dozens of tiny little jars, and when she spun the top off of one—bam! The scent of a wet dog hit her right in the face!

Jessie, who has smelled wet dogs on more than one occasion, nods her head in understanding.

The next jar contained...springtime rain, the smell of it washing all the worries from the little girl's body. She tried a third one, the rich scent of a hayloft in a warm barn. The next one was even better...freshly baked bread.

By Archie's face, it is clear to that he is reliving each of these aromas as he describes them. He is a man who has known the extremes of loss and love, and they have shaped him like the wind slowly sculpting stone.

And so Jessie set about the kingdom to bring these smells, good and bad, to all the people. She stopped first at her own village, taking out a single jar of honeysuckle and holding it up to the nose of the town elder. But the elder glared down at her as if she were crazy and asked why she was thrusting this jar at his face. She asked him what he smelled. He told her that he could smell nothing, of course. No one, he said, could smell anything. Smelling was just a myth from the old days.

Archie lets his face grow serious. His daughter's powers of perception are acute, even at her age, and she will glean many things from even the simplest expression. Archie wants her to know that even though his story is make-believe, something that lives within it is very much the truth.

No matter how many jars she tried, and no matter how many people she tested, Jessie could find no one in her village that experienced the scents. When she put them to her own nose, she knew the wonderful smell of cut grass and the strangely pleasing odor of those little black snakes you burn on the Fourth of July. But no one else could. And so they said she was different, and the nice ones ignored her and the mean ones called her names like freak.

Archie takes care to shape this last word—*freak*—with special emphasis. His daughter has been called far worse in her young life, and she will certainly face crueler treatment in the years to come. People fear those things that are alien to them. And so Archie wants to armor her against these slings and arrows, to instill in her such self confidence that no amount of name-calling will ever assail her.

And so the little girl felt alone, different from everyone else around her. But she also felt delightfully blessed, because she now experienced the world in a way unlike anyone else in the kingdom. She knew the secret of breathing deeply. And in her many days to come, she would always remember.

The story concluded, Archie isn't sure whether to explain himself or not. Sometimes his daughter senses instantly the moral of his tales, and other times she's like any other girl her age, in need of an epilogue so the lesson sinks in. But tonight is not one of those nights. She lies on her pillow, hair spilling around her like an aurora, and in her eyes is a wisdom that shakes Archie with its depth. In her silent world, she's already learned a kind of extra-sensory perception, and she understands. Archie, not wanting to dishonor the moment by saying anything else, opts for sign language, moving his hands to say, *Do not forget this story.*

"I'll remember, Daddy," his daughter replies. "I

won't ever forget."

****

Walking those last few feet to the dance club, Jessie recalled it perfectly. There was once a little girl whose father told her incredible tales, each one wrapped around a piece of advice that he hoped would serve her on nights like this. She was nobody's dancer. Without being able to hear the music—or even to understand, fundamentally, what music *was*—she had to rely on the beat...or she had to be drunk enough that it didn't matter.

That second option had its appeal.

Gavina led them, of course. Here was a woman who knew the nightlife of San Jose well, who lived in a trendy loft apartment and drove a convertible. But if the heroine of her father's story had offered Gavina a jar of lilac scent, would she have been able to smell it?

Jessie had stopped trying to read their lips. Night had settled over the city, and though the streets were alive with neon signs and the headlights of passing cars and the glow of corner lamps, it wasn't enough to provide consistency. She knew that Trevor was speaking even though she walked behind him, and every now and then Gavina turned around so Jessie could see her face, but in return she offered only a polite smile.

Rubio touched her hand.

He walked beside her, and the slight brush of his fingers was all it took. She looked at him closely and made out the movements of his mouth. "I'm sorry."

She shook her head to let him know it wasn't his fault.

"We can go somewhere else."

Though Rubio was probably making sure he didn't let the others hear him when he shaped the words, Jessie had no way of sharing this silent communication. Had he known any signs beyond those for rain and crocodile, she could've spoken to him on the sly, but as it was, she could only shake her head again and give him a conspirator's smile. Dancing would be okay. The thought of being next to him among all those writhing bodies was inviting. Besides, she'd been bequeathed an adventurer's spirit, so even if the evening turned out to be a disaster, she would come out in one piece on the other side.

Or so she hoped.

****

Rubio walked into the pulsing chaos of the club and decided he had to stop the clinic from being closed.

The conviction came on him like that—suddenly— a defiance of the fate that had been presented to him. As he followed the others through the pools of darkness and colored light, he had no plan but he *did* have, at least, a promise. He would not let the people of Cerro Viejo be without what Dr. Alomar had taken such care to bring them.

Just how he was going to do this, however, remained unknown.

Gavina led them toward the bar with its curving, elegant counter top that resembled the wing of a plane. Its surface glowed faintly blue from lights embedded along its length, softly illuminating the faces of the twentysomethings gathered here. Rubio stayed close to Jessie and briefly wondered what she was thinking. The club was mostly dark. Reading lips would be difficult, and he didn't want her to feel as if she were alone—

especially now, when alone-ness was something both of them were finally trying to end.

Gavina leaned in closely so as to be heard above the beat. "First round is on me. It's the least I can do." She smiled at Rubio in a way that asked for a peace accord. She didn't want to be the villain in the saga of the clinic's closure. And more than that, she didn't want Rubio to forget what they'd had.

If Rubio were reading her right, she seemed as if she wanted them to start over at the midpoint of their relationship, when enough newness remained to make it exciting and enough confidence was shared between them that their intimacy wasn't slowed by self-consciousness.

An image of her returned to him unbidden, the night they'd had sex on the floor in her apartment, her oversized movie poster of *Gone With the Wind* hanging above them. By then she was brazen enough to get undressed while he watched, and in his memory he saw her standing naked in front of Clark Gable, one hand on her hip. Somehow Clark had maintained his cool perspective, though Rubio's had rapidly eroded.

But now?

He turned to Jessie as she took a spot next to him at the bar and asked, "Is this okay?"

She stood on her toes to put her mouth near his ear. "Sure is loud in here!"

Perplexed, he gave her an uncertain grin. "Uh…I agree."

"Can hardly hear myself think!"

"Um…yeah."

"Almost enough to make a person go deaf!"

He shook his head at her, finally letting himself

join her in the joke. "You're awful, you know that?"

"Just having fun at my own expense. Did you ever hear the one about the musician and the leopard?"

"Can't say that I have."

"Well, this really talented musician is walking through the wilderness, and when he sits down on a rock to play, his music is so beautiful that all the animals come to listen. Even the meanest predators lie down to hear his song. Then, suddenly, a leopard leaps out of the bushes, lands on the musician, and rips him to pieces. A lion asks the leopard, 'Why did you do that?' The leopard replies, 'Huh?'"

Rubio's own laughter surprised him, welling up from a place inside where Archie had apparently constructed a special house where now his daughter lived. "So a deaf leopard is hearing-impaired humor?"

"I have a thousand more just like it."

"I have no doubt."

"You learn to make fun of it," she told him, "or you let it get the best of you."

Gavina tugged his sleeve. "What are you having, hero?"

Rubio realized the bartender was waiting for his order. He glanced at Jessie and made a drinking motion, his crude version of sign language.

In response, she made a kind of knocking gesture with her right hand.

"Does that mean 'margarita'?" he asked.

She laughed in her near-soundless way. "It means yes, a drink sounds fine, and yes, a margarita is perfectly acceptable."

Rubio relayed the order. Beside him, Trevor regaled Gavina with a story about his recent afternoon of playing golf at a pro-am tournament. His partner had been an American golfer who was apparently famous, though Rubio didn't recognize the name.

On the dance floor, one song relented only to be replaced by another, the DJ's volume cranked so high it nearly burned the song's lyrics into the walls.

Jessie brought her hand to her chin and bounced it twice, her index and little fingers extended. "What's wrong?"

"Who said anything's wrong?"

"Your face, that's who. And your body."

"Did you ever consider reading people's fortunes for a living? You'd be good at it."

She made the sign again. "So I've been told."

He shrugged. "Nothing worth talking about here."

"It's about the clinic, isn't it?"

"Maybe we should just enjoy our drinks and not worry about it." He'd no sooner said it than the bartender presented their order, and though Rubio hoped for a distraction, Jessie just kept staring at him over the salty rim of her glass.

"I just want to do the right thing," he said. Everyone else had to raise their voice to be heard in these raucous surroundings. But because of the magical ability of his audience, Rubio needed to do no more than shape the words—which was good, as he didn't want Gavina overhearing him. "I don't want it to end like this. I don't want everything your father worked for to stop just because he's gone."

Jessie leaned toward his ear again. "Don't do it for him. If you're going to do it, do it for *you*."

"Sounds just like something he would have said." He took a sip of a his drink, looking for the solution that continued to elude him. "But I don't know how to make it happen. We just don't have the money."

"Have you considered robbing banks?"

"Let's hope it doesn't come to that."

"And the hospital won't budge?" By *hospital* she meant *Gavina*, as indicated by a quick flash of her eyes.

"I suppose the hospital could make it happen if they wanted to, but it's not a priority."

"Well, then it's simple. We make it their priority."

"How do you propose we do that?"

Gavina appeared between them. "Why don't you two knock down that alcohol, and the four of us can go make fools of ourselves on the floor."

Rubio could tell that Jessie hadn't caught a word of that. What did she think about dancing? *Could* she dance? It sounded like a silly question, but the way she perceived the world was so different from his own experience that he had no idea if dancing was something that was even feasible. But the thought of being out there with her, her body moving next to his...

He mouthed the word: "Dance?"

Her only response was to return her glass to the bar and extend her hand.

Rubio found it all so hard to believe. This was the woman from the photograph. The woman he'd wanted to meet. The woman who was unintentionally making him think about things he hadn't considered before.

He wondered, briefly, what would happen to them when her business here in Costa Rica was finished. Then he pushed it aside, put his glass next to hers, and took her hand.

Chapter Thirty

Jessie had always thought of dancing like walking on the moon. Like everyone else, she'd seen a thousand video clips of Armstrong and others gallivanting on the lunar expanse, but the idea of it remained an alien activity. It was simply too strange. No earthbound person really understood how the body reacted in so little gravity. You could watch the images of astronauts all day and still be no closer to actually knowing how it felt to move like that.

Without being able to hear the music, Jessie had never understood the inherent human desire to move along to the tune. To really know the moon, you had to be there, and to really know the impulse of dancing, you had to hear the song. But all Jessie had was the beat. Fortunately the beat was, by itself, a powerful thing. She counted on the big subwoofers in the corners to keep her from looking like a totally graceless freak.

Rubio led her to the center of the mass. Bodies jerked and twisted around her, and she became wonderfully anonymous. No one would notice if she tripped over her own feet. This gave her the chance to stop fretting about it and focus on the truth: she was in a foreign city, in the middle of a club full of sexy socialites, on a wild dance floor, inches away from dark-eyed Galahad who apparently couldn't stop looking at her. She'd notice that he'd rarely turned away from her all evening. And *that*, ladies and gentlemen, was maybe the most amazing thing that had ever happened to this particular grant writer from Arizona—and she had no intention of letting it stop.

If only she could dance and text at the same time. Li would never believe it.

****

Three songs later, the beat slowed down. Each time a new one began, Jessie felt the change in the heavy stroke of bass. This time that stroke was languid, and she knew by the way the dancers melted into one another that this was not a rapid hip-hop number, but a ballad.

Rubio stopped moving. Only a foot away from her, he stood there, a thin crease of sweat along his hairline. He looked uncertain about what to do next.

Jessie made it easy on him. Intoxicated by the night, she stepped closer, surprised by her desire to feel her body next to his. The old Jessie wouldn't have been so bold. This newer version, at least for right now, had other plans.

He enclosed her hand in his and pulled her against him.

Her pulse quickened. It went completely rogue on her, the damn thing, picking up several beats that, to her finely tuned sense of self, felt as loud as gunshots.

What's happening?

She had no answer for that. Certainly there was no future for their relationship, because she'd soon fly back to the States and leave him here in this fairy land of butterfly blankets and almonds that dropped from the sky. Staying here in Costa Rica wasn't an option.

Rubio guided them in a slow circle.

What if her father had arranged all of this? She wouldn't have been surprised to learn that he'd orchestrated the entire thing, setting his daughter up on the ultimate blind date by way of his own death. After all, he'd hired Rubio *and* he'd taken him fishing. He'd apparently spent a considerable amount of the workday telling stories about her, no doubt making her out to be far more glamorous than she actually was. It sounded just far-fetched enough to be one of Archie's plans.

Rubio was so close that she clearly saw his words: "What are you thinking?"

She lifted herself up to him. "Count me in."

"Count you in? For what?"

"For saving the clinic."

"I'm not sure if I can save anything."

"*We.*"

"All right. I'm not sure if *we* can save anything."

"We'll think of something."

He slid his hand lower down her back. "Any ideas?"

"Sure." She remembered the words on the clinic wall. "A box of rain will ease the pain, and love will see you through."

He seemed to like that. "So…all we need to do is find a box of rain."

"Sounds like as good a place to start as any." She dared to put her head against his shoulder, hoping that the music had no intention of stopping anytime soon.

****

Rubio stepped into the men's room, still smelling her perfume.

It was an American perfume, probably purchased at one of the country's ubiquitous shopping malls, and

227

at that moment it was the most important thing he could imagine. He paused in front of the mirror and didn't immediately recognize the man looking back. He was too out of place. Even the restroom was glitzy, its walls painted red, its urinals made from brushed aluminum. This was as far removed from the marshes of Tortuguero as he could be, so surely that stranger in the mirror was living somebody else's life.

"And I'm not giving it back," he said to himself as he pulled a paper towel from the dispenser and dabbed the sweat from his neck.

Immediately he looked around, afraid that he'd been overheard talking to himself, but he spied no shoes under the two stall doors. He tossed the balled paper at the waste can, scored two points, and was just turning to leave when Gavina walked through the door.

"You're missing the party," she said in Spanish, leaning her back against the door she'd just entered.

By now nothing she did should have surprised him. Letting herself into a guys-only bathroom was not the boldest thing he'd ever seen her do. Yet here he was, still slightly shocked—which was no doubt her intention. "You're in the men's room."

"Must have taken a wrong turn. My head isn't on very straight right now."

"I know you're not drunk."

"Maybe I am. Will that give me an excuse?"

He let out a little sigh. In that revealing cocktail dress with her shoulders and lower legs exposed, Gavina was, perhaps, as pleasing to look at as a woman could possibly be. Leaning back, she had the posture of casual invitation.

"You're not answering me," she observed.

"And you're blocking the only way out."

She let one beat of silence pass. "Come move me."

Somewhere in this world were men crafted from granite. Or men carved from the hearts of oak trees, men who could turn down such an offer when it was so openly given. Rubio had never thought of himself as exceptionally resolute when it came to resisting temptation; he usually lived for the moment and collected good memories along the way. But tonight, for some reason, things were different.

"Are you going to say something," Gavina asked, "or are you going to leave me to whatever Trevor has in mind?"

Rubio made his choice. "I'm looking for a box of rain."

"I'm sorry?"

"Rain. Falls from the sky." He headed toward her.

"Yes, I got that part. Is that some kind of code?"

"Something like that." He reached for the door handle near her arm.

She didn't move away. "Rubio, do you not understand what I'm saying here?"

"Actually, I do. And believe me when I say that I'm very close to shutting my mouth and letting you take me out of here to wherever the hell you want to go. But I think I'd rather find someone willing to hunt down that box of rain."

"I don't even know what that means."

"I know." He pulled open the door, forcing her to step aside, and walked out.

As he left her behind, he wasn't thinking of the look on her face or how his actions might affect his plans to keep the clinic open. The only thing on his mind was what Archie had said to him that afternoon not so long ago: *If you ever laid a finger on her, I'd have to murder you and sink your body in the river.*

"Sorry in advance, doc," he said as he made his way to where Jessie waited at the bar.

Chapter Thirty-One

Jessie rode in the boat with the night wind in her hair.

After leaving the club, they'd quickly parted ways with Trevor and Gavina. Ever alert, Jessie watched for more signs of the relationship that Rubio had once shared with the woman, but Gavina hardly even looked at him. It wasn't as if Gavina had suddenly found an interest in Trevor and his bland stories of middle-management life in Florida. But she'd certainly *lost* her interest in Rubio, or—Jessie suspected—she'd finally tired of being rebuffed.

Jessie looked at Rubio but could see only his silhouette. During the car ride from San Jose to the dock at the gateway of the park, he'd brushed against her more than once and expressed a sincere interest in whatever frivolous thing she happened to be talking about at the time. And that meant something inconceivable had occurred. This handsome, daydreaming bachelor was more interested in her than he was in a thunderbolt like Gavina Herrera.

Could that be true?

Since Jessie couldn't communicate with him in the dark, she didn't feel rude for pulling out her phone and texting Li. *Would you believe me if I told you that I just spent the evening dancing?*

After she hit SEND, she stared at the little screen

until its light faded.

Moments later, from three thousand miles away, Li responded: *With an actual MAN?*

Actual.

Never lie 2 your best friend.

Have I ever?

OMG, 4 real? The studly paramedic? Has he practiced CPR on U yet?

Does holding hands count?

Yes. Not enough hand-holders left in the world.

I agree, Jessie replied.

Where R U now?

On a shaky boat heading back to the village.

Going 2 get nekked?

Jessie put a hand over her mouth to suppress a giggle. Sometimes Li was no different than a teenage girl. And sometimes Jessie liked it. *Will text you tomorrow with details.*

U didn't answer my question.

Goodnight.

Tease!

Jessie put her phone away, and moments later the vibration of the engine lessened, alerting her that they'd arrived. She looked toward the bank to see the sparse lights of Cerro Viejo winking in the trees like fairy candles. When she lifted her face even higher, stars without number spread out around her, as if the village lights were just another constellation in space.

The boat pilot spoke with Rubio, money was exchanged, and ten seconds later Jessie was again on *terra firma*, smelling the scents of human habitation. By now it was so utterly dark that she couldn't understand anything Rubio tried to tell her, and he knew this, so he simply offered his hand.

She accepted, enjoying the warmth of his skin.

They walked into the village.

Jessie had been told that the ocean throbbed audibly here, the closeness of the Caribbean such that—when the breeze came from the east—you could hear the constant rush of water against the shore. Was Rubio hearing it now?

The people had settled down for the night. Even the small curio shops had closed, as the tourists seldom ventured here after midnight. The lights still burning were bare bulbs strung between a few of the houses, more for decoration than anything else. A single dog patrolled the lanes between the buildings, Cerro Viejo's only sentinel. The dog trotted over, and when it got close, Jessie noted it had only one ear but was evidently well fed. Rubio gave it a scratch as they passed, and then the dog was off again, steadfast in its vigil over its sleepy town.

Rubio led her in a direction she hadn't been, not toward the clinic, not toward the small room they'd given her. Moving in the darkness meant that her most important sense was dulled, and she would've been concerned had she been alone. She considered herself slightly above average in the bravery department, having learned a certain courage in following her father into all manners of unsavory places, but all of that went away when she couldn't see. She depended so much on the acuity of her vision that when it was gone, she'd rather be in bed under the covers.

But this was different. This was having a hand in your own. This was being guided through a mystery world with a man who still smelled faintly of the dance club and its flowing warmth.

He stopped just beyond the village's edge. He squeezed her hand, and Jessie sensed that he wanted her to wait her. She nodded.

He slipped away into the night.

Jessie crossed her arms over her chest—a silly, defensive thing to do, but there you had it. Crossed arms would not protect her against snakes, venomous frogs, or the random caiman that ambled too far from the water. She distracted herself by taking account of her surroundings as best she could.

The ground was slightly damp. The nearby leaves hung low with accumulated moisture. The pervading scent was still that of a forest, but if she closed her eyes, she imagined she smelled the scent of salt, and suddenly she wanted to see the sea.

A pair of floodlights bathed her in color. She blinked, and as her eyes compensated, she realized she was looking at Rubio's home.

He climbed down a ladder and smiled at her. "I think on MTV they'd call this my crib."

Jessie didn't know what to say. Two massive mangrove trees provided the house's foundation, holding it about twelve feet off the ground. The twisted trunks and elephantine roots made the trees look prehistoric, not to mention incredibly strong. As such, they easily supported the wooden platform that had been built between their branches, forming the structure's floor.

"A tree house?"

"A little more elaborate than the forts we built as kids," Rubio said, standing under one of the lights, "but yeah, pretty much." He grinned. "You want to come up? Unlike when I was a boy, I now allow girls in the clubhouse."

"You built this yourself?"

"I had a lot of help."

"It's so…big." From her vantage point on the ground, Jessie had only a partial view of it, but it looked to be about the same size of any other home in the village, except that it was cradled off the ground in the arms of its patron mangroves. "It's safe?"

He laughed. "This village is home to some seventh-generation carpenters. It's not going anywhere. And during the rainy season, when we sometimes get flooding, it keeps my socks dry."

"I'm sure it does." She reached uncertainly for the wooden ladder. "This is really strange. You know that, right?"

"Hey, I spent the last several years living in a small apartment in San Jose, crammed in between hundreds of others just like it. I had only two windows. So I'm entitled. Besides, the man who designed it was the only guy in town more eccentric than me, so I can't take all the blame."

"My father." Jessie nodded. "I should have known."

"The skylight was his idea."

"Skylight?"

"Go on up. I'll show you."

It was not an invitation Jessie was going to ignore. The day had already been so unpredictable that she wasn't about to settle for a mundane conclusion. Each hour was more fantastic than the last. Only now, hand on that first rung, did she remember something he'd said shortly after they'd discovered the doll in the ravine. *Let's just say I have a somewhat unusual bachelor pad.*

"I never would have guessed."

She put one hand above the other, and climbed.

****

Rubio followed her up, reminding himself to breathe: one more in, one more out. He thought again of the dance floor, of holding Jessie in his arms, of the feeling of her body against his. What kind of fool was he, to drop through the sky like this for a woman who might turn out to have no parachute to loan him on the way down?

Jessie reached the little balcony at the ladder's summit and looked into the lighted living room beyond. She made a soft sound of surprise.

Rubio fully intended to keep the clinic open, but that was business for the light of day. Right now, with the sea whispering against the sand not far away, he wanted to see how long he could make the nighttime last.

****

A single lamp illuminated a room that might have been from a storybook. A variegated rug covered most of the floor; it had probably been woven by the hands of someone here in the village. The walls had little space for photographs or artwork because windows ringed the room. Glassless, their shutters had been thrown open to the warm night. The coffee table was made of driftwood, rustic and sturdy, but the futon with its matte-black rails had clearly come from one of the trendy furniture shops in the city. The adjacent kitchenette made Jessie wonder how the plumbing worked in a treehouse, which was far too practical a thing to be thinking when you were exploring a place like this.

Rubio said something, but she wasn't looking at him clearly enough to read his lips. "I'm sorry?"

"I said there are only three rooms. It's not a palace, but the books fit."

Stacks of books peeked out from corners and huddled behind the stoneware pots of flowering plants. Jessie glanced at some of the titles and saw everything from travelogues about deep-sea fishing to *El Conde de Monte Cristo*.

"The bathroom is through there, if you need it."

"There's a bathroom?"

"I may live in a tree, but I'm not a total Tarzan."

"That's not what I meant, it's just—"

Smiling, he waved it away. "Don't worry about it. But yes, there's running water, just like in every other house in the village. The pipes just happen to be a little longer."

Jessie investigated. The little room had a toilet, shower, and a sink whose basin was beaten bronze. It smelled like a man in here, which was not altogether bad. Turning a complete circle, she noted that the walls were not like those of her own house, not fattened with insulation and covered in drywall. Rather they were made of simple plywood sheeting painted white, which she supposed was all you needed when you lived in a part of the world where the weather turned neither to fire nor ice.

She looked back at him. "Doesn't the house ever...shake?"

"The winds never get very intense. Sometimes when there's a major storm coming in from the ocean, the branches around me creak a little bit. But I'm very not high up, and did you see the supporting trees? They're like giants. They're not moving."

"So what gave you this idea? To live in a tree house?"

"It's not permanent. I knew I wouldn't work here forever. At first I thought it was just for the summer, and then I'd be back breathing smog in the city. But the place kind of grew on me. And the tourists think it's cool."

"You bring tourists here?"

"As a general rule, no. The guides try and respect the privacy of the locals, and I'm sort of a local by default. But my friend Finn can't help it. He makes up stories about how some kind of witch doctor lives here."

"And people believe that?"

"Finn's customers tend to be a little strange. He doesn't do anything like a normal person. Anyway, the kitchen area has a mini-fridge, microwave—"

"Is that a cappuccino machine?"

"You don't like cappuccino?"

"Well, yeah, I love it, but—"

"But what's it doing in a tree?"

"It's just not something I expected to find twelve feet off the ground."

"There are certain luxuries a civilized human being can't leave behind."

"I agree entirely."

"And right through here"—he motioned toward the only other doorway—"is that skylight I mentioned."

Jessie entered his bedroom.

The room was small, and Jessie's eyes were

immediately drawn to the ceiling, which was comprised of a single sheet of Plexiglas about eight feet on all sides. Beyond it was the universe.

"Wow."

"I have to clean off the bird droppings about once a week," Rubio said, "but other than that, it's worth every dollar I spent to have them haul it out here from San Jose. But I can't take credit for the idea."

"I have the very same person to blame for a lot of my ideas, as well." Directly below this vast porthole to the sky was the bed—except it wasn't really a bed. "Is that a hammock?"

A full-sized mattress was suspended from a metal frame; the headboard and footboard sported springs that connected to grommets in the corners of the hammock on which the mattress lay. Covered in what looked to be a handmade quilt, it appeared comfortable enough, though somewhat unconventional, which matched the rest of the house perfectly.

"I designed it myself," Rubio said, "but one of Finn's friends did the welding."

Jessie put her hand on it and pressed down gently. "Incredible…"

"I'm pretty proud of it myself. That bed and satellite radio are two of my favorite things. And I'm looking at the third."

Jessie held very still, watching him. "I think I must have misread that last part."

"No, you didn't." He slipped his hands into his pockets. "I don't think there's any way I can say this without embarrassing myself, but…I'm really glad you're here. I woke up this morning wondering what you and I were going to do today, how we were going to spend our time, what you were going to wear. I'm as goofy as a teenage boy."

Jessie, hand still on the mattress, didn't move. She was afraid to look away from his face, afraid she might miss a word, afraid that by blinking she might cause the moment to reveal itself as a dream.

"You seem to hear things that other people don't," he said. "You sense things about people—about *me*— without having to hear a word. When I'm with you, I have the feeling that I'm with someone I've known all my life. And now that your father's business affairs are in order, you'll be flying home soon, and I didn't want to let you go without telling you. I've always been someone who makes the most of his chances. You can say something anytime now, please, otherwise I'll just keep on rambling."

Jessie's lips parted, but she made no sound. What could she possibly say?

He leaned against the door jamb. "I think maybe I've had a thing for you ever since I saw that picture on Archie's desk."

Jessie smiled. "A thing?"

"That's probably not the best word for it, but *crush* sounds a little juvenile."

"I don't mind a crush."

"Some women probably think it's childish."

"I'm not some women."

A little color came into his cheeks. "Yeah, well, I just wanted you to know. You're everything he said you were and more. And I can't stop thinking about you."

Suddenly Jessie moved.

She didn't know where it came from, this abrupt force that propelled her the short distance from the bed to where he stood looking casual and awkward at the same time. Maybe it was the need to let her hands experience what her ears could not, or the desire to surrender to what her heart had been telling her for days. Or perhaps it was the simple human yearning to warm herself with another's touch. She didn't analyze it. She didn't let herself get lost in her usual introspection. She just glided. And two steps later she put her arms around him and rested her face against the muscles in his chest. "I don't want to leave."

He lifted her chin gently so she could see him. "Then don't. At least not tonight."

What was the sound of a kiss? Jessie didn't bother to wonder about it. She simply raised up on her toes. By that time Rubio was anticipating her, and he gathered her tightly against him and pressed his mouth against hers.

She let herself go. The last few days had been too full of emotion, and she poured it out, wanting to share it with him and share his in return. She kissed him as she'd kissed no one before.

There was much to savor in that moment, but greatest of all was the feeling of exhilaration. She'd known first kisses before, and each one had been exciting in its own way, but there were layers to this one that frightened her with their depth.

He broke the kiss, searched her eyes, and then kissed her again.

She let it happen, and more than that: she *made* it happen. She spent too much of her life being conservative by circumstance; when you were legally handicapped and missing part of yourself, you had to play it safe for simple self-defense. But there were times when she kicked off the chains and let herself go free. But never like this. Never with such heat.

He took a step, and in response she took one in reverse, then another. The bed was just behind her, that crazy bed that no one else possessed except princes from fairy tales or heroes from other worlds. That's what he was. That's what he *had* to be. How else could she explain the way he'd captured her so effortlessly?

She wanted more than being captured.

She pulled him more tightly against her, letting him know it was okay, telegraphing her willingness to go wherever he wanted to take her. Everything was so easy with him—even reading his lips was easier than it was with others. Or was she simply trying harder with him?

No time for answers now. He guided her down to the bed. The only thing firing through her mind was *It's happening*, but then this last thought dissolved when he lowered his weight on top of her and kissed her neck.

She closed her eyes, her four active senses receiving every sensation as if it were as scalding as a branding iron, making permanent and welcome marks all around her. The hearing world would never know the nuances of these sensations or the full geography found in the dark hollows of a throat. Every part of him was amplified for her: the feeling of his fingertips, the smell of his hair, the taste of his mouth. The bed, suspended in space, move very subtly beneath them. Jessie felt as if she were floating.

Then, abruptly, Rubio lifted himself off of her. He sat on his knees, straddling her legs and looking down at her.

Jessie, short of breath, wondered if she'd done something wrong. "What is it?"

And then Rubio made a sign, pointing at her, then pushing twice with both palms toward her: *You are fabulous.*

Jessie laughed in pure joy. "Someone's been practicing."

He gestured again: *I want you.*

She sat up and balled his shirt in her hands. "Prove it."

Rubio hesitated for only a moment, then skinned the shirt from his body in one fluid motion, revealing what Jessie had seen the first day she'd met him— smooth, dusky skin and a chest like a model in a sculptor's studio. When she saw him that day, sprinting through the village, she never would have imagined herself to be running her hands along his abdominals as she did now...

She quickly removed her own shirt, and this time when he sank down on top of her, she knew the warmth of his stomach against hers.

Things got less specific after that. One moment moved into the next, revealing new pleasures, new touches, new chances for Jessie to forget herself and let go. Her inhibitions burned up, leaving only reckless desire, so that she didn't even stop to worry if she'd worn a suitably sexy pair of panties this evening. It didn't matter. She was out of them in seconds.

And then, with nothing else impeding them, she hooked her hands around his shoulders and pulled him into her.

What sounds they made she would never know. If he cried out with each lunge forward, she didn't hear him. If the frame of this homemade bed jangled to their endless rhythm, it was lost on her. But replacing this was a feeling of exquisite physical pleasure, amplified by beautiful silence.

She rode the waves as long as she could, and when she called out his name, she imagined she could hear the word carrying through the window above her and out into the stars.

Chapter Thirty-Two

Something landed on the skylight.

Jessie's eyes had been half-opened when it happened, the morning sun pink beyond the window. For the last twenty minutes she'd been semi-awake, nestled against the bare warm body of a man who made her feel like no one ever had. She'd slept profoundly, like a woman happily trapped at the bottom of a well. The water in this wonderful well was just hot enough to let her drift peacefully from one dream to the next. The first coherent thought she had upon waking up was *Am I falling in love?*

Then something fell from the sky. It was the size of a baseball, bouncing from the window before Jessie's weary eyes could make sense of it. Could this be another of the almonds that dropped from the trees? Or was she still dreaming?

Rubio's phone had buzzed at some point in the night.

She'd almost forgotten. But now the memory returned. Rubio's phone had awakened him, and his movements had roused Jessie from sleep. At that hour they'd both assumed it was bad news, an emergency from the village. But it wasn't. A woman named Pilar was simply calling to say that they'd taken her sister Hanna to the hospital in San Jose and had arrived safely. They expected a baby to soon be born into the world, and since Rubio was their shepherd now that their first shepherd was gone, the family wanted him to know.

Another object struck the pane overhead. This time Jessie was ready, and her finely tuned sense of sight noted the roughly spherical shape and the pale red hue. Was that a fruit of some kind? With a bite taken out of it?

It rolled out of sight.

She put her lips near his skin and breathed his name rather than spoke it: "Rubio."

He moved almost imperceptivity.

Jessie inhaled their mingled scent. Once again she replayed the events of hours earlier, the way she'd rolled on top of him, the feeling of her hair knotted in his fist. In the aftermath, her body had tingled, and she craved a return to that perfect state. "Rubio."

Maybe he made a sound in response or maybe he didn't. But he shifted a little to let her know he was aware of her but not quite ready to return to the surface for air.

Another red projectile bounced from the window.

She nudged him gently. "Rubio?"

She felt the vibration in his chest that she knew indicated a wordless "Mmmm?"

"I think the sky is falling."

He rolled onto his back, blinking against the light of the new morning.

Jessie wiggled onto his chest and looked at him from inches away. "*Buenos días*."

He smiled. "I'm in trouble, you know."

"Well, you were certainly into *something* last night, but I wouldn't call it trouble."

"Trouble with the man upstairs."

"With God?"

"The *other* man upstairs. Dr. Alomar is glaring down at me right now."

"Don't sweat it. If he's giving either of us the evil eye, it's definitely me. He and I had the birds and bees talk a long time ago, but that didn't keep him from frowning every time I went out with a boy."

"This is a little bit more than going out."

"And you're not a boy." She kissed his chest. "You have a strange bed, by the way, but surprisingly comfortable."

"Is that what you woke me up to tell me?"

"What? Oh, I already forgot." She glanced at the ceiling. "I swear I've seen multiple pieces of fruit falling on the roof."

"Water apples."

Jessie thought she'd misread him. "What apples?"

"Water. They're a bit smaller, shaped sort of like a bell. Some people call them wax apples."

"And it rains wax apples here in Costa Rica?"

He grinned, his eyes lighting up with mischief. "Not exactly. Do you want me to show you how it happens?"

"Do we have to get out of bed?"

"We don't have to do anything."

Jessie heard the truth in that. They were free, tied to no one and nothing. Like castaways on an uncharted island, they could wile away the hours in each other's arms without regret. "I don't suppose you have an extra toothbrush."

"I wasn't expecting company. Especially not *your* company. But I have plenty of mouthwash, and I make a mean omelet."

"What more could a girl ask for?"

Yet Rubio made no move to free himself from the soft quilt. "What would he say, do you think?"

"If he saw me lying naked with someone? I don't think that's something a dad is ever going to enjoy thinking about, no matter who he is."

"I mean about us together, not necessarily us undressed."

"Together?" It wasn't a word she'd considered. When you were *together* with someone, it generally wasn't a good idea if one of you was living in Central America and the other one in the Flagstaff suburbs. "They say I'm an expert at reading lips."

"I believe it. You'd have to be, right?"

"No, I mean even better than the average deaf person off the street."

"Your father raised an overachiever."

"It's not just that. I anticipate what's being said. Even when I can't exactly make out the word, like when you just said 'undressed,' I'm able to make a good guess."

"And what you're guessing now is…"

"What I'm guessing now is that things have changed."

"What things?"

"You. Me. Everything."

"Changed for the good?"

"As for *that*, my luscious lover"—she kissed his chin—"nobody knows for sure."

****

After breakfast, Rubio led her outside to investigate the apples.

He felt like one of the immortals. Like he would never die. Like something had happened inside him last night and made him just a little bit indestructible. As soon as they reached the bottom of the ladder, he took Jessie's hand and walked around the side of the house.

"There." He pointed into the trees.

A troupe of spider monkeys cavorted in the highest branches. Small and agile, they plucked apples from the trees, took a bite or two, and then hurled the remains—perhaps just for fun. On the ground nearby were nearly a dozen partially eaten water apples, glistening in the dew.

Jessie shook her head. "I don't even know what to say to this. Costa Rica is an unpredictable place."

"In more ways than one."

"Are they here every morning?"

"They show up every few days. I think they make a circuit through the trees. I'm glad they chose today to make an appearance."

"Me, too. I have another question for you."

"Sure."

"Are we going to locate Beatriz today? She's the last link we have to what my father might have been doing at the ravine."

"We'll call the information center from the landline at the clinic. We'll find her."

"Deal."

They left the house in the care of the monkeys and walked across the village, talking of nothing in particular along the way, just enjoying the thrill of togetherness. When they reached the clinic, Rubio swung open the door and stepped inside, still holding Jessie's hand.

Greta looked up from her desk, then at the clock, then at him. "Usually you here already and not later like this," she said in Spanish, her eyes full of disapproval.

He replied in English: "We're not shutting down. We're going to save the clinic."

After that—silence. Since Rubio had met Greta nearly a year ago, this was the first and only time he'd ever seen her speechless.

Chapter Thirty-Three

They called the information center at the wharf and left a message for the elusive Beatriz, who was out of the office again but supposedly working the afternoon shift. Jessie made a point not to express her agitation, redirecting her energy to the clinic, though her motives were not altogether humanitarian. Her motives were, in fact, quite selfish. She simply enjoyed being close to Rubio, flirting with him, looking up and catching him staring at her. She imagined what the night would bring. Her anticipation increased every time she thought about it.

Greta caught on by ten o'clock. She didn't comment on what she sensed between them, only cast Jessie a single look that Jessie interpreted as, *If you break this man's heart, I will haunt you forever.*

Jessie took that very seriously. She knew the value of holding a heart in your hands.

In between patients, Rubio sat down and continued his list of possible financial donors. When Jessie realized what he was doing, she thought about her plane ticket. Her return flight was scheduled for two days from now, and that was something she didn't want to consider at the moment. But in the meantime, she saw an opportunity to put her skills to use.

She crouched beside Rubio's desk. "I can help with this."

"I'm open to suggestions."

"I'm not much use as a nurse," she said, "so I don't know how much good I'm doing here today—"

"You're doing fine."

"—but I *do* know something about *this*." She tapped his notepad. "I'm a grant writer. I get money from people. That's what I do."

He leaned back, tapping his chin with his pen.

"I don't speak the language," she continued, "so you'll have to do the work on the phone, but I can show you where to go, how it's done, whom to call. I don't know if this country works the same as mine, but I'm betting there are sources of funding out there, government and private, and it's just a matter of asking them formally, in writing."

After a moment of consideration, Rubio said, "I could have fallen for a truck driver or a trapeze artist. Sounds like I got lucky with a grant writer."

"I also bake."

"Sounding better all the time."

"I'm serious about the writing. Let me do this."

"Doesn't it take a long time? To get money like that, I mean."

"Do you want to keep this place open or not?"

He leaned overand kissed her. "I'm beginning to agree with those people who say that all things happen for a reason."

Jessie wasn't quite ready to accept that—she hadn't yet found a reason her father had to die—but she agreed that sometimes things worked out. "It all starts with research. Just get me a chair and translate the web pages for me. I'll do the rest."

"I've seen that look before," Rubio said.

"Have you? Then you know it means business."

"Yes, ma'am." He quickly found a second chair.

That night, hours after Greta had left the clinic for the day, Jessie was absorbed in her new found work when Rubio took a phone call. He spoke for several minutes, then hung up and said, "Beatriz finally called back."

Jessie immediately forgot about the paperwork in front of her. "And?"

"She seemed...nervous."

"Nervous about what? Did she know my father?"

"That's why she was nervous. As soon as I mentioned him, she acted as if she wanted to get off the phone as soon as possible."

"Why? Did she...sound like Dad was in some kind of trouble before he died?"

"I don't know. It was strange. But she gave me a name."

Jessie never looked away from him, but positioned her pen over the page in front of her, preparing to write.

"Cordelia Opaz." He spelled it for her.

"Is that someone you know?"

"Never heard of her. But Beatriz told me where she lives."

"And what is it that this Cordelia person is supposed to know about Dad?"

"Beatriz didn't say, and I can't begin to guess. I have half a mind to take a boat over there right now, but it's the middle of the night and I'm afraid we might scare her off."

"So we just wait until the morning?"

"As patiently as possible."

"I think mine is running out." She drummed her

fingers on the desk, wondering.

****

There came a point that night when Jessie hit the wall. After nine hours of camping at the keyboard, taking volumes of notes, and setting up an organizational flowchart, exhaustion brought her to a mental standstill. She stared blankly at the monitor for three minutes before realizing that her thoughts were no longer on the subject of funding procurement. Instead, she was thinking of the woman in her father's drawing.

"I think I have to call it a day," she said. "Aspirin and caffeine can take a woman only so far."

"Here. Greta brought us some sun tea before she went home."

"How long ago was that?"

"Hours."

"Really?" She yawned. "What happened to the day?"

"*You* happened, mostly. I've never seen one person produce so much paperwork in a single work day. Sorry I had to be back and forth so often. It seems we're having a run on summer colds. I must have seen a third of the village today."

"And Hanna?"

"No bouncing baby yet. I'm sure someone will call the moment there's any news." He turned his chair backward and straddled it. "How about we do the Manatus for dinner again?"

"I have to find her."

For a moment Rubio said nothing. Then he nodded. "Tomorrow. We'll find Cordelia Opaz and settle this, one way or the other."

"Scout's honor?"

"Would you settle for paramedic's honor?"

"Are paramedics generally trustworthy?"

"For the most part."

"I suppose I'll have to take my chances."

He kissed her lightly. "Now, I hate to suggest this, because I would really love to spend the night otherwise occupied, but do you think…" He gestured to the carefully ordered stack of papers that Jessie had compiled.

Jessie wanted nothing else but to spend the evening in his arms. Her time here was nearly at an end. Every second with him mattered. But he was right; there were forms to be completed and essays to write. Heaven knew that this wouldn't be the first time she'd written grants at two in the morning. But now she happened to have a much better way to use her after-midnight hours. "Are we taking our work home with us?"

"Believe me, that's not my first choice, but…"

"I know. We don't have much time to get these documents submitted. My flight home leaves—"

He kissed her before she could say it.

Chapter Thirty-Four

As they sat on Rubio's floor, wine bottle and mostly empty glasses within reach, Jessie found the money.

She blinked, looked up. Had Rubio just said something? For the last two hours they'd worked virtually without speaking, Rubio touching her leg only when he wanted to get her attention. He sat with his back against a wicker chair, bathed in the light of a laptop, his cheeks in need of a shave, his shirt unbuttoned halfway down his chest.

Reluctantly, Jessie looked away from him and returned her attention to the printout in her lap. Okay, so maybe she was being optimistic. The funds available through this particular grant were certainly sufficient to cover at least half of Rubio's projected operating costs, but on second glance, the criteria seemed more focused on supporting research than daily medicine. Other than this, though, the clinic matched the grant perfectly. So...was there a way? Could she somehow convince them that Cerro Viejo was a research site?

An answer teased her, promising a solution, but between the wine and her craving for the man next to her, she couldn't pin it down.

She pushed the papers away and leaned into him, nudging the laptop aside. Rubio closed the computer, and Jessie wiggled up against him. He put his arms around her. With her head resting on his chest, she felt the vibration when he spoke.

"I can't hear a word you're saying," she confessed, "but I'm sure it's eloquent."

He pinched her playfully.

"Watch it," she warned. "Never start something that you can't finish."

He said something else, and this time she looked up. "Hey, I was comfortable."

"Sorry. Looks like we could both use a break."

"Agreed. And that's not all I could use." She kissed his pectoral through the open gap in his shirt.

He waited until she glanced up again before saying, "Tempting, but I have something else in mind."

"Something else?" She couldn't conceive of anything more gratifying than letting him remove her clothing one article at a time right here on the floor. "Whatever it is, it's not as good as what I'm thinking about."

He smiled like a man privy to a great and wonderful secret. "What if it *was* as good? What if I told you that you've never seen anything like it in your life?"

"Then it better be one hell of a surprise."

The smile lingered, deeper now. "If you trust me, Jessie Alomar, I'll lead you out of here, walk you through the night air to the ocean, and show you something that will make you live forever."

Such an offer was more tempting than any woman could resist. She took his hand. "Show me."

****

Hand in hand, they walked through the darkness.

Jessie could see little around her, only layered

shadows, black against black. The sky, however, was radiant with stars and the dusty smear of the Milky Way. Rubio had picked up a flashlight before they left, but so far he'd yet to turn it on. Jessie wanted to ask him yet again where they were going, but without the light, she wouldn't be able to see his response.

She depended on her other senses. The farther they walked along the wide path through the trees, the more she smelled the sea. That was one of the things that was hardest for those people not blessed with an acute sense of smell to understand—that water had an odor, especially the ocean. Jessie couldn't hear any movement against the shore, but she could certainly smell it. And then they stepped out of the trees and into a long clearing. The ground changed beneath her feet.

She stopped. This wasn't normal dirt.

Asphalt? Out here?

Rubio finally turned on the light, illuminating his face and squinting. "It's okay. It's a runway."

"A what?"

"A runway. For the one plane that makes the circuit here every day, a little twin-engine thing that drops off tourists. Check it out." He swept the light to the ground.

It looked just like a street—a street out here in the middle of the wilderness. A giant number 5 was painted in the middle of it. The strip of pavement extended well beyond the range of the light.

Apparently planes had been landing and taking off every day since she'd arrived, a mere stone's throw from the village, but Jessie had been unaware of it.

"Story of my life," she said too quietly for Rubio to hear.

He tugged her hand and got them moving again.

Half a minute later, a red light appeared in the gloom. Someone approached.

Rubio's light fell on the man's face as the three of them converged. He was middle-aged, his skin darker than Rubio's, his body adorned with bracelets and necklaces. He wore an earring and rubber boots.

He must have understood that reading lips was difficult under such circumstances, so he used the light as best he could and kept things short, "Jess, this is Finn Vargas. Don't leave him at home with the family silver."

"Hello," she said.

Pointing a red-beamed flashlight at his own face, Vargas replied, "What it's like being deaf?"

At one point in her life, Jessie might have been taken aback by such a spontaneous question from a stranger, but recently she'd learned to be ready for anything. "It sucks."

Vargas shook his head and laughed. And then he did something even more incredible. He made the sign for *You're cool*.

Before Jessie had the chance to express her surprise, Vargas turned and led them from the runway along a track through the weeds, and then—

The ocean appeared. Revealed under the starlight, the Caribbean rocked mostly gently against the shore, the water pushing its way up the sand. The breeze off the water stirred Jessie's hair and snatched her breath, and for a moment she didn't breathe, captivated by the sensation. The beach rolled out to her right and left, and all along its length, the sea concealed it only to reveal it again, a rhythmic in-and-out that Jessie could have stood and watched forever.

Rubio had by now turned off his light, leaving only the red beam Vargas used to guide them across the damp sand. Holding Rubio's hand even more tightly, Jessie followed, unable to take her eyes from the endless, restless ocean only a few feet away. It seemed almost to be reaching for her, as if it wanted to take her away with the tide.

Vargas stopped, and Jessie became aware of another presence on the beach. The three of them were not alone.

The red light revealed it.

Resting in the sand beside them was an immense sea turtle. She was huge and prehistoric and beautiful, straddling a deep hole she'd dug in the sand. Now, exhausted from the effort, she waited, barely moving, her great flippered limbs folded back.

Jessie's lips parted, but she made no sound.

The turtle's shell was slick with moisture and lined with sand. She had a scent like that of the sea itself, but more vital, as if this beach on this night was the only thing that defined her. Though only a yard away from where Jessie stood frozen in awe, the turtle seemed unaware she was being observed. This was her mission, and she had swum a thousand miles to complete it.

Vargas silently sank to his knees. Rubio followed suit, guiding Jessie to the ground.

The red light moved slightly, focusing on the back half of the turtle and the moist pit she'd excavated beneath her. It must have been tiring work, digging like that with limbs made for swimming rather than moving heavy sand. Jessie could not have looked away had her life been at stake. At that point in time, she cared for nothing else but what was happening here, just like the turtle herself.

A white sphere appeared.

The egg was glistening white, the size of a golf ball and perfectly round. It stuck for only a moment to its mama, and then it released, dropping into the hole. Another appeared, its pure whiteness defying the red light, the only bright thing in an otherwise dark world.

Jessie, on her knees, leaned even closer, and had she extended her hand, she could have caught that wonderful jewel as it fell into the nest to join its sibling.

It happened again. The sea turtle, completely devoted to her labor, didn't move, didn't shift, didn't interrupt the repetition of eggs.

Jessie took the lightest of breaths, her hands trembling. She was no longer aware of the damp sand beneath her knees, the wind in her hair, or the universe overhead.

Even thoughts of Rubio had faded. The only movement she made was to wipe tears from both eyes.

How long they held there, watching, she couldn't say. The timelessness of the event held them captive, and one after the other, the turtle deposited the eggs she would never see again.

She buried them.

Jessie gasped when the creature moved, her inelegant flippers turning suddenly powerful. Sand fanned out with each determined stroke, the walls of the hole collapsing and providing a haven for her unborn young. Jessie didn't move, letting the sand strike her. Like the birthing itself, this task took time. What the turtle lacked in precision she made up for with dedication, and after several stops and starts, she filled the hole completely.

Then she turned.

Rotating her ponderous body, she aimed herself at the sea. At least a hundred feet of rock and wet sand lay between the nest and the water, but now that her life's mission was complete, she had only to save herself. Jessie rose to her feet, eyes never leaving the red light that Vargas trained on the mother now bound for home. Each step the turtle took was an obvious struggle. Her shortened, inflexible limbs had not been made for this. But standing there behind her, Jessie realized with goose bumps rising on her arms the reason for the turtle's immense size: nothing else would have been large enough to contain so much heart.

Methodically the four of them moved toward the water's edge—Jessie, Rubio, Vargas, and their spirit guide, who led them to places they could barely begin to understand.

Every five feet or so the turtle paused, regathering her strength, and then she shoved herself forward again, not looking back at the treasure she'd buried behind her. Twenty minutes later they reached the fingers of the tide, the water nudging toward Jessie's sand-caked shoes. She had escorted the turtle on this final leg of the journey, and now she held her breath in anticipation.

The next time the sea swept in, it embraced the turtle, and the mother who had come so far and worked so hard was awarded the gift of grace. All at once she become agile, propelling herself into the water with a swiftness that belied her form.

In a moment the red light lost her, and all that remained were her three human ushers, looking lost under the watchful sky.

Jessie threw her arms around Rubio's neck and—crying—whispered in his ear: "Thank you."

This had been the best day of her life.

Chapter Thirty-Five

A single bird alighted on the morning water. Its wings were the color of the sun that rose, only an hour old, behind the eastern trees. Nothing moved. The bird floated, placid and at ease, as if this serene causeway had never known the growl of a motorboat or the dipped paddle of man's canoe.

Crouched on the grassy shore, Rubio Mora made friends with the silence.

When he and Jessie had returned from watching the turtle lay her eggs, they'd said nothing. Neither of them had any words worth speaking after that. Their bodies had spoken for them. On the floor of his tiny living room and then again in the shower, they had tried to express the kind of urgent passion they'd witnessed on the beach that night. When it was over and Rubio lay beneath her, exhausted and glorified, he knew he still hadn't captured whatever the turtle had known, but he was close. Perhaps together he and Jessie would one day obtain it…assuming she didn't board that plane tomorrow and be lost to him forever.

He turned when he heard her moving through the trees. She stopped behind him but still said nothing, only held out her hand.

Rubio took it and stood up, finally understanding that this was her world, a world without sound, a world that depended on touch and intuition. He kissed her but didn't speak.

A minute later, the boat appeared.

Its noise seemed an affront to the stillness, but considering its purpose, Rubio didn't mind. It was taking them to the end of the riddle that Dr. Alomar had left behind.

Rubio nodded to the boat pilot and helped Jessie aboard. Having arranged this taxi ride yesterday, he had no need to give directions. He sat down beside Jessie, and she held his hand in her lap.

I am in love with you, he thought but didn't say.

The boat increased its speed, and as the light flashed between the trees, Rubio found himself wishing for his sunglasses. But that was not his greatest wish. In fact, if he counted his wishes, they numbered exactly three. One—to help Jessie find contentment in her father's death. Two—to secure the funds to keep the clinic operational. And three—to stop that damn plane from taking off to Arizona.

What were the odds of all three being fulfilled?

The only sound for the next forty-five minutes was the drone of the outboard motor. They passed other boats, some bearing tourists who waved, others carrying local fishermen intent only on the water. Rubio never let go of Jessie's hand. Whenever he looked at her, she smiled.

Do you love me, too?

He sensed the answer to this and tried to trust his instincts. Jessie had already showed him the magic of believing in hunches, of siding with your gut when your gut seemed to know what it was talking about. Rubio was in the process of working all of this through the channels of his heart when the engine slowed and the boat bumped a narrow pier decorated with silver tinsel several months out of season. They had arrived.

Rubio tipped the pilot and climbed out, and then he and Jessie made their way down the uneven planks of the pier. At the end stood a single cottage, its shutters painted the alternating blue, white, and red of the Costa Rican flag. Flowers of varieties Rubio had never seen grew in brilliant clusters, turning the yard into a patchwork quilt. According to Beatriz, with whom he'd finally spoken early this morning, this was the home of Cordelia Opaz, the woman in the doctor's drawing. What did she know about his death?

Stop.

Rubio paused a few feet from the front door.

Jessie looked up at him, and their wordless connection was strong: *What's wrong?*

Finally, after hours of silence, Rubio spoke. "I don't want to hear what she has to say, because that gives you a reason to go home."

He should have known by now that Jessie wouldn't respond in any predictable way. She did not assure him that she would remain in his country, nor did she vow to depart when her work was finished. Instead, she touched his face, and then put her hands over both of his ears, completely covering them. She said softly, "Can you hear me?"

Though her voice was muffled, Rubio could make out the words. "Yes."

"No. Can you really *hear* me?"

He realized then that she meant more than simply listening with his ears. She was asking if he understood her, if he felt what she was feeling, if he was able to listen to all those parts of her that made no sound.

He took her hands and gently removed them, then gave her the only other word in sign language he knew, the universal one that needed no translation. He nodded.

"Good," she said. "Then let's go knock on that door and see what happens next."

****

No one answered.

Jessie knocked again, feeling the vibration travel from her knuckles across the back of her hand. She pictured the sound carrying in concentric waves through the room beyond. She'd read that sound didn't travel in a straight line, but moved in all directions, seeking ears to make it real. But that made little difference when she was standing here on the stranger's doorstep and growing more impatient by the second.

"Don't make me kick in the door," she said, mostly to herself, and then raised her fist to give the thing a more solid whack—

Rubio caught her wrist. "Someone's inside. She said she's coming."

"Oh. Sorry."

"No harm done."

"Yet."

"What's that mean?"

"The way I'm feeling at the moment, I can't be held responsible for my actions."

"I'll keep that in mind."

The door opened.

Cordelia's black hair was interrupted by strands of silver, the way the night sky is accented by stars. Her face was lined, but not in an unpleasant way. The beauty of her youth was no longer radiant, but neither had it entirely dimmed. A necklace of turquoise and beaten copper lay at her throat, and she wore a familiar caduceus pin on the strap of her homespun dress. Her eyes were dark and deep, and she looked at her visitors with curiosity but not with surprise.

"He told me you would come," she said at last.

Jessie thought she'd misread the woman, despite the fact that the words were spoken in English and well-enunciated. "Excuse me?"

Cordelia smiled, and everything about her changed. She expressed herself completely in that smile, her confidence, her decades of wisdom. "I know who you are, child. Legend has it you're the greatest human being on the planet." She stepped to the side. "You two better come in. Stand there too long with your mouths open like that and something's bound to fly inside."

Feeling as if she were dreaming, Jessie stepped across the threshold, and Rubio followed.

****

They drank tea from wooden cups. The small living space around them was a reflection of the woman who inhabited it. Nearly everything appeared to have been made by hand, from the woven rugs to the stained-glass mobiles hanging in the sunlight at the open windows. But Jessie saw little of the décor, as her eyes were fixed on the photo of her father.

He wasn't smiling. He observed the person who wielded the camera, looking both thoughtful and inquisitive, as if he were just about to ask a question he desperately wanted answered. He wore his old Diamondbacks ball cap, his gray curls trying to escape from the edges of it. Jessie knew that face better than she knew her own, as she'd seen him far more often than she'd looked in any mirror. She'd never seen this picture before. Just looking at him made her chest tighten.

Rubio got her attention and nodded toward Cordelia, who evidently had spoken.

"I asked how you found me," she said.

"A woman named Beatriz," Jessie replied.

"Ah. I think my friend talks too much."

"Can I ask you…well, I have a *lot* I'd like to ask you but I'm not sure where to start."

Cordelia examined her tea, as if consulting it, then looked up. "Ask me what you came here to ask, Jessica Raye Alomar. Life is too precious to waste even a few moments of it in indecision. He showed me that."

Jessie had to hand it to her dear old dad. He was managing to keep several steps ahead of her, even after he was gone. What business did he have tossing out her full name to total strangers like this?

On second thought, Cordelia was no stranger. And that's why Jessie was here. "I came because my father died not far from here. I came to settle his accounts and to find out what happened. I came and all I found was this." She slipped the doll from where it had been riding in the pocket of the light jacket she'd donned this morning. "I came because no one knows how this doll got out there, but all the signs are pointing to you."

Cordelia's eyes had settled on the doll.

"Ma'am, were you out there the day my father had his accident?"

Finally Cordelia looked at her, the sadness evident on her face. "I have never been loved like that before."

Jessie looked at Rubio for translation, thinking she'd missed something, but he only shrugged. He said to Cordelia, "Did Dr. Alomar…I mean, were you and he…?"

"Lovers? Young people are called lovers. At our age, it's more…intricate."

Jessie didn't know what to say. Her father had been involved romantically? How had he kept that a secret from her? *Why?*

"Yes," Cordelia said softly, "much more intricate than that."

If Jessie hadn't already noticed the woman's sorrow, she couldn't have missed it now. Though she played the role of the perfect hostess, Cordelia held herself together from the inside. How many tears had she cried? Enough to match Jessie's own?

"Was my father…in love with you?" Even asking felt like a trespass, as if she were intruding on something she wouldn't understand. "He never said anything. He never told me."

"I'm sure he would have, with time. But for now we were enjoying our secret. Somehow it made us feel giddy, you know, keeping it from the world like that. Besides, it wasn't the kind of flaming affair we might have had thirty years ago, back before the weather started making our joints ache. It was an old-fashioned courtship, slow and courteous and secure. They don't make those anymore."

Of all the revelations that Jessie had been hoping to discover here, this wasn't anywhere on the list. Her father had been in love. It wasn't just the clinic that had kept him down here. It was this woman, this woman who clearly longed to have him back. Jessie wasn't so sure she wanted to share the right to grieve over him. After all, Cordelia had known him only a matter of months, while Jessie had—

She cut herself off in mid-thought. How could she ever begrudge someone the chance for love? If there was any man in the galaxy who deserved it, it was her dad.

Cordelia wiped away an errant tear, and that made the moisture return to Jessie's eyes. Before she broke down like a total mess here in this cozy living room, she focused herself on the plantain doll. "I really would like to know about all of that, what you and he shared. I'm...I'm stunned by the whole thing but I swear it's true when I say I'm so happy for you I can't describe it. And for him. But right now, if you could maybe tell me about this..."

"I'm a seamstress, among other things," Cordelia said, patting the corners of her eyes with a gingham handkerchief. "I used to own a shop in San Jose, before I retired out here. That little dolly you have there had lost an arm. It belongs to one of the girls my friend watches after while her parents are at work. Beatriz gave it to me to fix. I had it with me the day that...the day that it happened."

Jessie nudged forward on her seat. "You were there? When he...?"

Cordelia nodded.

"You saw it?"

She swallowed. "I did."

Jessie looked at Rubio, whose expression mirrored her own. Turning her attention back to Cordelia, she said, "What did you tell the police?"

"Nothing."

"They didn't require that you give a statement? That's how it works in the States so I assume it's pretty universal but I could be...wait a minute." A new thought occurred to her. "You never talked to the police, did you? You left before they arrived. No one knows you were ever there."

Cordelia folded her hands in her lap and looked at Jessie with affection. "You have more than his eyes, child. You also have his intuition." She sighed. "Your father died to save me."

Chapter Thirty-Six

Walking along the edge of the gorge, Archie Alomar remembers telling his daughter the bedtime story about the jars full of scents.

"You should have seen her little face," he says. "She was far too damn thoughtful for her age, that's for sure. Still is!" He laughs, because laughter is his rod and staff.

"One day I will like to meet her," Cordelia says.

"Oh, she doesn't have time for beaten-down old Cadillacs like us."

"Why do I think that you're lying?"

"You're right. Jess would fly down here in half a heartbeat if I rang her up, as the British say. When is this beautiful but medieval country of yours ever going to improve its cell service?"

"Probably long after you and I are gone, darling."

"Bah! Haven't you heard? I'm never going to die. And by virtue of association, neither are you."

"And our bodies? We'll just keep accumulating wrinkles and liver spots?"

"Hmmm. I see your point. Immortality's overrated, I suppose, if you have to take your arthritis with you. I'll need to talk to God about that one."

"I have no doubt that if He were going to bargain with anyone, it would be you."

Archie laughs again. "Come here, woman." He

kisses her rapid-fire on the lips, and then they come to a steep grade in the side of the gorge.

"You have brought me to a ditch," Cordelia observes.

"Indeed I have, my dove, indeed I have. But one man's ditch is another man's…" He scratches his beard. "Well, can't really think of a fitting way to end that little idiom. At any rate, what you see before you is actually the Valley of Gold."

Cordelia searches the gully, lush with flowers and green vegetation.

"You're not seeing any gold?" Archie asks.

"I can only assume this is another of your magic tricks."

Archie's eyes twinkle like those of Father Christmas. "One of my best." Holding her hand, he walks the rim, careful to place each step along the precipice. "Here, this should be just about the right spot."

"The right spot?"

"Did I ever tell you the story of how the Hindu god Indra made the rain?"

"More than once."

"Oh. Well…perhaps I'm running out of stories."

"I doubt that will ever happen. And even if it does, you can simply recite the old ones to me over and over again."

"Careful, woman, you're starting to make this sound like a permanent union."

"I'm afraid it was permanent the first moment I saw you." This time she is the one who initiates the kiss, and she does it at a woman's pace, as if all her love is encapsulated in it.

With a hand at her waist, Archie feels something in the pocket of Cordelia's sweater, the red one with the lightweight weave and the buttons made of wood. Sensing his curiosity, she extracts a little girl's doll. "Recently mended," she says. "I promised Beatriz I'd have it back to her today."

Archie examines the doll. "You know what would make an excellent anthropology paper? The comparison and contrasting of little girls' dolls from different cultures. I was never much of an anthropologist myself, and I haven't published in ages, but…" He looks at the doll like a man trying to read his fortune there.

"Darling?"

"Sorry," he says, shaking it off. "For a second there I was thinking about Noxy."

"Who?"

"My daughter used to have a stuffed elephant named Noxy."

"You think about her often."

"More than I think about myself."

"As a father should."

"And then there's you. Between these two demanding women in my life, how will I ever get in a decent thought about myself?"

"I've never met her," Cordelia says, "but I have a feeling that she would agree that we are the luckiest—"

She falls.

The soft ground on the edge of the gulch crumbles. Cordelia's foot goes straight down, her balance evaporating in an instant, gravity ripping her away from him.

Archie enjoys making fun of his old bones and rusted reflexes, but there is evidence of neither as he whips out a hand and grabs Cordelia's wrist. He makes a startled sound that sends birds flying.

The doll tumbles and disappears below.

"Hold on!" Archie shouts. He slings himself over the side and plants his boots in the soft soil of the sharply angled wall.

It isn't enough. In a moment he'll lose his grip on her, and she'll follow the doll. Archie puts both arms around her and heaves.

Cordelia grabs for weeds, roots, anything to grasp. With Archie shoving from below, she's able to gain a bit of ground. The air rushes in and out of her lungs. She scrambles upward, pushing with her legs for leverage.

This sudden thrust is more than Archie can support. As Cordelia climbs up, he lets go and madly pinwheels his arms.

And then he's gone.

He rolls violently down the slope, his full body weight driving his head against the ground at an unnatural angle. Cordelia fights to her feet at the summit a moment later, and when she turns around, chest heaving, Archie lies unmoving at the bottom.

She calls his name just as the sun slips through the trees and turns the valley to gold.

****

Jessie opened her eyes.

She'd kept them closed for the last few minutes because she didn't want any more words. Whatever commiseration Rubio or Cordelia had to offer would be insufficient. And so she retreated to her oldest friend, silence, until she was sure she could look at them without breaking.

"Why didn't you say anything?" she asked.

Cordelia wasn't crying. Jessie suspected that this woman's tears were like her love affair, a private thing. Yet she held very still, as if she too were only one word away from losing control. She wet her lips. "I was ashamed."

"Ashamed? Of what?"

"That such a man gave his life for mine."

"You can't honestly think that."

"Can't I? Am I not entitled to that? Had the world lost me, child, what would it be without? A retired dressmaker who spends her days reading Agatha Christie and pruning her plants. But instead it lost one of its heroes. I can certainly be ashamed for that."

Jessie concentrated on each breath; the tightness in her throat warned her of imminent tears. "The fact that my father…" She swallowed.

Rubio held her hand tightly.

She tried again. "The fact that my father died while saving someone, while saving *you*, that's all he would have wanted. That's everything. Growing old was never his style."

Now it was Cordelia's turn to close her eyes. "I'm sorry. I didn't want to say anything. I didn't want to be responsible. I couldn't visit the village. I couldn't see anyone without thinking of what I'd taken from them." She clutched her hands so fiercely in her lap that her fingers had lost their color. "I wish I could have been the one who fell that day. *I'm so sorry.*"

"Look at me."

Cordelia didn't move.

"*Look at me.*"

Slowly the woman opened her eyes.

"I could not love him more than I do now," Jessie said. "You may not understand that, but it's true. He had purpose, even at the end, and it was probably the greatest purpose it could be. He died for love."

"He died for a used-up old woman."

"Yes. A used-up old woman who he loved more than his own life."

Cordelia looked away, gathered herself, and then met Jessie's stare. "You are indeed your father's daughter."

"So they tell me," Jessie said, and then she lost her fight against the tears.

Chapter Thirty-Seven

Rubio held open the clinic door. "You okay?"

"If you ask me that again," Jessie said, "I'm going to kick you in the left knee."

Realizing that she wasn't entirely joking, Rubio followed her inside. They'd spoken little on the trip back from Cordelia's bungalow. What was there to say that love of one kind or another hadn't already said?

Greta greeted them as they entered, switching between Spanish and English as it suited her, but Rubio heard little of what she said. For the last few days his emotions had been like the tide, covering him one moment and exposing him the next. He wanted everything at once—to take Jessie in his arms and hold her here, to fly away with her to America or anywhere she wanted to go, to kiss the dark hollow of her ear and know that she could feel his lips there, speaking with touch, the only language she could hear.

At the same time, he felt inadequate. Dr. Alomar had died for a woman. What could his protégé ever hope to accomplish in comparison? It was one thing for Rubio to keep his hand on the wheel of the man's medical practice, steering it steadily along, but to live like that, full force? To *die* like that?

He bumped into Jessie when she froze in the middle of the floor. Greta noticed and stopped talking.

"It's over, isn't it?" Jessie said, perhaps to herself.

Greta clasped a clipboard to her chest and watched.

Rubio knew that Jessie couldn't hear him when he was behind her. Had that been her intention? He waited for whatever came next.

"I came here," she continued, slowly, "and I found his world, and I met all these people whose lives he made better, and now it's over." She turned and faced Rubio. "But it's not, is it? Not everything."

"Well…" He wasn't sure what to say. "I guess we need to submit those grant applications, but there's no hurry. After what you just went through—"

"No, I'm ready. I'm okay now, more or less. But I have one more idea. I know how we can make it work, how we can get the money, how we can keep the clinic open. At least I hope so."

Rubio didn't know if she was about to laugh or cry. It could have gone either way. "What else is left? I don't have any more tricks up my sleeve. We've done everything we can. Haven't we?"

"Maybe not. I thought of something when Cordelia was telling her story." She gave him a partial grin, tinged with sadness. "Actually Dad reminded me."

"He did? How?"

She turned to Greta. "May I use your land line? I get really lousy reception, and I need to call Texas."

"Texas? As in the Alamo?"

"One and the same. And I'm going to need one of you to do the talking because I won't be able to hear what the professor's saying."

"Professor?"

"You better just do as she asks," Rubio said, sensing the change in Jessie's voice. It was almost as if old Archie was back again, filling up the lobby with his unpredictable dreams.

****

As Greta held the phone to her ear, Jessie didn't waste time wondering again what a human voice sounded like when channeled through the airwaves. Instead, she glanced down at the business card in her hand and read it one more time.

PERCY J. RAMSHEN, Ph. D.

PROFESSOR EMERITUS, ANTHROPOLOGY

UNIVERSITY OF TEXAS AT DALLAS

Cordelia had described the last few words she'd shared with Jessie's father before the accident. There had been talk of the doll, of publishing an academic paper, of anthropology. And that had reminded Jessie of the man she'd encountered during her flight from Phoenix, noteworthy not only for his profession, but also for the fact that he hadn't once shown any signs of giving a damn about her deafness. He'd treated her not just like an equal, but like a woman, and everyone could go to hell if they said that gentlemanly behavior was dead.

"Hello?" Greta said into the phone. "Hello? I'm calling for"—she glanced at the card—"for Professor Ramshen. My name is Greta Steiner. I'm phoning from Costa Rica on behalf of my friend, Miss Alomar, who I believe you met recently on a plane…"

Epilogue

Jessie stood in the sun outside the airport terminal, listening.

The jets lifting into the faultless sky made a noise like that of a train, only bigger. And the dozens of people gathered here with their signs and expectant smiles, well, she knew they sounded excited, shot through with life and the eagerness to greet a lover or an uncle or a son. Those were the noises of a place like this, at least according to the stories. For a solid minute, Jessie pretended she could hear them, pretended she was surrounded by them, pretended she was—

She frowned. Didn't all of that noise get a little annoying from time to time? Maybe she'd been misguided all these years. Hearing was for suckers.

That made her laugh.

Someone touched her arm.

She knew that someone. Knew him in a way that mattered as much as the ground under her feet. But instead of explaining herself, she simply leaned back until she felt his chest against her. Having someone stand behind you was the *safest* sensation she'd experienced. Even when everything was crumbling, just put a person like this at your back, and you'd end up okay.

Or *more* than okay.

"Rubio Mora," she said, her eyes still on the glass

terminal doors.

She felt the brief vibration when he said, "Yes?"

"My house plants are going to die."

This time he had no choice but to lean around where she could see him. There was his face, more handsome than she deserved. Had her father felt this way about Cordelia? She knew the answer to that.

Rubio raised his eyebrows. "Plants?"

"They need water. I should text Li, tell her to get her skinny butt over there and keep my peace lilies from shriveling up."

The practical thing would have been to fly home and take care of these matters. And maybe in a week or so she would—or not. Her father had given himself up for love, and as she always did, Jessie followed his advice as best she could.

"I look forward to meeting her," Rubio said.

"Li? Oh, now *that* will be interesting…"

The crowd shifted. A new energy swept through those gathered at the automatic doors.

Jessie waited.

She'd been doing that all her life: waiting. She realized that now, here in this foreign city. She waited for grants to come through and she waited at traffic lights and she waited on the popcorn bag to swell in the microwave on Saturday night. But now there were several things for which she was no longer waiting. In fact, she suspected that waiting time was over and *doing* time was here.

A gray-haired man stepped through the terminal doors, wearing a suit fifteen years out of date but wearing it well.

She pulled Rubio through the crowd. "That's him."

Her plan involved anthropology. The largest of the grants she'd found required the site in question to be a place of active scientific research. She'd explained all of this to Dr. Percy Ramshen over a series of phone calls in which Greta and Rubio had acted as intermediaries. The aging professor—though semi-retired—had not only warmed to the idea but taken the reins and driven it onward. He'd tossed out several ideas about possible research subjects and quickly decided that he couldn't formalize anything without seeing Cerro Viejo in person. He'd told her, "This is just the kind of quest that an old windmill-tilter needs. My other option is playing dominos with blue-haired ladies at the senior-citizens center. I assure you, my dear, this is the better choice."

Jessie knew that her father would have gotten along with this man beautifully.

"Dr. Ramshen!"

He saw her, waved, and when they converged, Jessie hugged him, even though she barely knew him. "It's good to see you again."

"Not as good as seeing *you*, I promise. And none of that 'doctor' stuff. My Christian name is Percy, which isn't the most manly name, I admit, but it's how I'm known among saints and sinners alike."

Jessie couldn't stop smiling, which she understood was strange, as not so very long ago, she wondered if her smiles would ever be real again. "Percy, this is Rubio."

"Ah, the gallant voice on the other end of the phone."

"It's a pleasure," Rubio said.

"You haven't forgotten what I told you?" Percy

asked.

Jessie looked at Rubio. "What did he tell you?"

Rubio tried and failed to hide his smile.

Jessie pinched him. "What?"

"I told him," Percy said, putting an arm around Rubio, "that if he let you get away, I'm having him committed to the first insane asylum I find in Costa Rica."

Jessie kept her eyes on Rubio. "I'm not going anywhere."

From the corner of her eye, she saw a man in glasses tap Percy on the arm. "Uh, Professor?"

Percy turned. "Oh, gods, I apologize. My manners aren't where they used to be." He gestured to two people who had apparently accompanied him from Texas. "These are my ever-eager assistants, the post-docs Andy and Rachel."

They shook hands.

"You didn't have to come down in person," Jessie told him. "We could have handled a lot of this through email or videoconferencing."

"Young lady," Percy replied, "my particular ivory tower is still fixed quite firmly in 1967, back in a time when my collars were much wider and my correspondence traveled in trucks rather than fiber-optic cables. And now that I'm in my dotage, I prefer not to change. Besides, when a damsel calls, it is my duty to present myself in person." He winked.

"And he got free airfare," Andy interjected. "We flew on the university's tab."

"Quite true," Percy confirmed. "I wouldn't have it any other way."

Jessie led them to the driver they'd commissioned

for the ride to Tortuguero. She was aware of the talk that continued around her as Rubio and Percy conversed, but she had no desire to join them. It was enough to feel the warmth on her cheeks and to wonder why some things work out while others are left to drift away. Had her father not given himself up for love, she never would have come here and found love in return.

Just as they reached the taxi, Rubio's phone apparently rang, because he slipped it from his pocket and glanced at the face looking up at him from the screen. "It's Finn. That's usually not a good sign. He only calls when he's trying to recruit me for his next get-rich scheme." He put the phone to his head. "*Hola, amigo.*"

Andy and Rachel assisted the driver with their bags. Percy, his chin clipped between his fingers, gave Jessie a shrewd stare. "Why do I get the feeling that I may be in for a true adventure down here in the land of pineapples and rum?"

"I guess adventure is sort of the Alomar family motto."

"A hereditary trait, is it?"

"My only inheritance."

Rubio slipped the phone back into his pocket and shook his head, clearly amused.

"What is it?" Jessie asked. "What did Finn say?"

"The great baby lottery is finally settled. Hanna gave birth a little over an hour ago."

"That's great! A boy or a girl?"

"A girl. As healthy as the day."

"And who won? Who picked the winning time?"

"Well, I'm not giving her the pleasure of naming any names, but let's just say we're going to be greeted by one self-satisfied Spanish-speaking German receptionist when we get back."

Jessie laughed. "Go, Greta!" She knew her own laughter didn't sound like everyone else's, not as loud, not as clear. It was one thing she *hadn't* gotten from her father. And because it was her own, that made it all the sweeter. She caught Rubio's hand just as he was about to open the taxi's back door. "Kissing me now would be okay, if you wanted."

Percy said, "Dammit, son, if I were half a century younger, I'd race your ass to accept an invitation like that."

Rubio never took his eyes from Jessie. "You wouldn't win, Professor." When he pulled Jessie toward him, she kissed him through her laughter.

A word about the author...

Lance Hawvermale published his first books under the female pseudonym of Erin O'Rourke. Since then, his poetry and fiction have garnered numerous awards. In 2016, St. Martin's Press released Hawvermale's fifth novel, *FACE BLIND*, a thriller set in Chile's Atacama desert.

Hawvermale is an alumnus of AmeriCorps and continues to believe in the power of giving. He has worked as a college professor, an editor, and a youth counselor. He lives in Texas with his family and their honey bees.

Visit his website at:
www.lancehawvermale.com

www.ingramcontent.com/pod-product-compliance
Lightning Source LLC
Chambersburg PA
CBHW051526260626
47170CB00003B/796